# Luke sat at his desk, staring at Marnie McLaughlan's reservation

It was made out to a Mr. and Mrs. Scott McLaughlan, and yet she'd shown up here alone…and without a wedding ring. Where was Mr. McLaughlan? Amanda at the front desk said he'd been very friendly on the phone and so disappointed when they didn't have a vacancy that she'd offered him the room on the top floor. But why hadn't he arrived with Marnie if he was so anxious to come here?

Luke tapped the desk, his mind running over the possibilities.

His concerns aside, he'd been surprised to find his son, Ethan, hanging off the woman's leg when he got to the front of the house, but she seemed to take it in stride. What could have been an embarrassing situation had turned into a pleasant interlude with a beautiful woman. And with her heart-shaped face framed by dark curls and her well-toned body, Marnie McLaughlan was gorgeous and sexy….

Her husband probably planned to arrive later, a simple enough explanation, and Luke hadn't given her much opportunity to explain why they hadn't arrived together. He would simply come up with a diplomatic way to find out when her husband was going to join her. It was essential that there be no disruptions during the inn's Christmas event for couples, and a woman as beautiful as Marnie McLaughlan could prove to be a *serious* disruption…

Dear Reader,

Christmas is my favorite time of year. I love nothing better than to root around in my dozens of boxes of Christmas decorations, digging out all the ornaments, lights, wreaths and mantel decorations needed for every room. Each year my husband and I decorate two fir trees in our home, simply to be able to breathe in the scent unique to evergreens. Christmas for me is both a happy time with my family and also a sad time, as I recall one very lonely Christmas during which I spent hours caring for my sister Elizabeth as she made her graceful exit from this world.

This book is also based on my experience as a mystery guest for a hotel chain near my hometown. Being a mystery guest is a lot like living in a parallel universe, as you will see in *A Christmas Inn*.

But most of all, this story is about a man who's surrounded by a self-made wall of loneliness and the inability to forgive, and a woman who has to overcome her fear of rejection to find that common ground called love.

I believe that inside each of us is a Luke or a Marnie waiting to be rescued from our insecurities and fears to find the one person who makes life truly worthwhile.

Please enjoy *A Christmas Inn,* and stay in touch by visiting my website, www.stellamaclean.com.

Thank you, and may your Christmas season be filled with love, hope and the spirit of giving.

Sincerely,

Stella MacLean

# The Christmas Inn

## STELLA MacLEAN

HARLEQUIN®
entertain, enrich, inspire™

Recycling programs
for this product may
not exist in your area.

ISBN-13: 978-0-373-71817-7

THE CHRISTMAS INN

Copyright © 2012 by Ruth MacLean

This book is dedicated to all those people who serve the public as members of the hospitality industry. Thank you for being there and making the lives of people like me more enjoyable.

And thank you to Sharon Allaby, friend, reader and fabulous cook.

# CHAPTER ONE

ELEVEN DAYS UNTIL CHRISTMAS and Marnie McLaughlan hadn't finished her shopping, but that was the least of her worries. She eased open the back door of the salon. The only sounds were the comforting hum of the refrigerator in the staff room and the clacking of a keyboard in the office to her right. She waited for the familiar click telling her the door had locked behind her before she headed for the office.

This was the day she'd wished for and worried over.

She was about to sell her half interest in Total Elegance, the hair-and-aesthetics salon she and her partner, Shane Walker, had co-owned for the past ten years. Her brothers, the superachiever foursome, would jump out of their jock straps if they knew she was in the process of selling her part of the business without their input. She had come in today to get her copy of the agreement to go over with her lawyer before signing. She was quite proud of the fact that her brothers wouldn't be involved. Their best-before date as inquisitive overseers had long since passed.

At the door of the office she had shared with Shane through all the growing pains of their business she hesitated. This was it. She would read the agreement one more time, then take it to her lawyer. She took a deep breath and tapped lightly. He glanced up, his spiked mullet bobbing like a rooster's comb as he stood to greet her. "Hey, great to see you," he said, all brightness and light. Marnie had only one wish where her soon-to-be-ex-partner was concerned. She'd like him to change his hairstyle. When she first met him he'd styled his dark hair to frame his face, softening his angular features, and now the vertical spike of hair only made his nose appear longer, his chin more pointed. Worst of all, his haircut made him look dated.

It was a word that everyone who was anyone in the beauty industry hated to hear, and Marnie didn't have the heart to tell him. Then again, maybe he knew and just didn't care. But why should she worry about it, anyway? In mere weeks, she'd be able to put Shane's hair, and all the other issues that came with running a salon, out of her mind. "Freedom thirty-five," she'd dubbed her decision.

"It's great to see you, too," she said, crossing the narrow space and sitting down in what passed for the guest chair—a warped, plastic lawn chair she'd pilfered from her parents' garage.

"So, are we ready to sign?" he inquired, his eyebrows doing an odd dance over his forehead, a rather peculiar move for a man, and one that had left questions in the minds of some of their patrons as to his sexual orientation. But those in doubt didn't know Shane's history where women were concerned. He was a consummate professional at work and a regular tomcat at night—that is until a particularly clever feline had put an end to his roaming ways.

Her name was Gina, and Shane planned to marry her, which was why he'd offered to buy Marnie's half of the business. Gina, it turned out, was also a hairdresser and she and Shane were working on more than marriage plans.

"Slow down, Shane. Like I told you yesterday, I want my lawyer to read it before I sign." She reached for the document, intending to pop it into her oversized bag.

"Sorry. It's just that I'm so anxious, you know. God!" He sandwiched his head between his hands. "I've never felt like this before! We'll be celebrating our three-month anniversary in a week, can you believe that?" he asked, giving her the same wide-eyed look she'd seen at least a dozen times a day for the past few months.

If he launched into yet another of his long-winded sagas about the wonders of love at first sight, about his plans for marriage and a future with the soon-to-be Gina Walker, she was going to have to slap him. She'd never slapped anyone except her brother Scott for telling Andy Capson she wanted to go out with him. But if Shane didn't stop talking about how great love felt, how happy he was… As far as Marnie was concerned, love was nothing more than a word in the dictionary somewhere between *lovat*—a tweed of muted green—and *low*—inferior or depressed.

All the boyfriends she'd had to date could be slotted into one of two categories: they either had issues around commitment, or they bordered on being illiterate. And if that wasn't bad enough, they'd all turned out to be liars. Every man with whom she'd had a relationship had been dishonest in one way or another.

"Your three-month anniversary?" she repeated idly, as she skimmed the opening paragraphs of the sales agreement, glad to see the main terms of the agreement in writing, especially the financial ones. There was a non-competition clause, restricting her from opening a salon in the city, which was fine with her.

Shane put his hand on her shoulder. "Look, take your

time and read through carefully, but I would like to have it all settled before Christmas. Is that possible?"

She looked up from the document as she considered what he'd said. As much as she loved the business, she'd often wished for something more. She was a good manager, and she wanted a bigger challenge in her life, but he hadn't considered acting on her discontent until Gina had started at the salon. The unfortunate truth was that she couldn't work with the woman. She was bossy and overbearing.

Marnie hadn't busted her butt for ten years to end up taking orders from a woman whose only qualification, other than that of hairdresser, was that she had snagged the other owner. And with the cash from the buyout Marnie would be able to start a different business. She didn't know what yet, but she'd figure it out. All she needed was a little time.

"Before Christmas? I don't see why that should be a problem," she said.

"Great. I'll go out and put the coffee on so we can have a cup to celebrate. I brought a bag of these special beans Gina loves. They're from Costa Rica. I'll go grind them and be right back. Do you want a cappuccino? Or just regular?"

"Why don't we splurge and have a cappuccino?"

He winked at her and smiled the goofy smile he'd recently acquired. "You got it."

After he left, Marnie skipped through the legalese to the important parts of the agreement, and made sure they said what Shane had promised.

She sat back and let her gaze move around the office, remembering the long hours she'd spent there, the worries she and Shane had had over the finances, whether they'd be able to grow their client list and hire the best hairdressers. But most of all she remembered the sense of accomplishment she'd felt when she and Shane had been written up in one of the local magazines, commended for their successful partnership. And now, as she faced the fact that this would all be over in a few weeks, she felt a sudden pang of longing.

For ten years she'd lived and breathed Total Elegance. She'd borrowed her share of the start-up money, and then prayed that the salon would be enough of a success to pay off her loan. It was and she had. She'd proven to her family that she could succeed on her own terms, and it felt so good.

Marnie swallowed against the hard lump in her throat. This was not the time for tears. She and Shane had had a good ride, but it would be fun to spend a few weeks considering her next venture, sleeping in until noon, shopping when she felt like it.

Shane reappeared with two mugs in his hands, and with what had become his signature wide-body smile, only to come to a dead halt. "Hey, Marnie, is something wrong?"

His words startled her. "No. Nothing. Why?"

He passed her a cup with her usual two teaspoons of sugar and went to sit behind the desk, placing his mug on a coaster Marnie's mother had crocheted for the office—to give it a homey touch, as she'd put it. "For a minute, I thought I'd left something out of the agreement," he said, hefting his size-twelve shoes up onto the corner of the desk.

"Not at all." She took a sip of her coffee, letting the aroma infiltrate her nostrils while the caffeine hot-wired her mind.

"Well, what do you think? Is it all right?"

"I'm sure it is.… I'll miss this place."

"I know you will, honey. If you'd like to work in the salon until you decide on a new career, that's fine by me," he offered, his words holding the nuance of a man who just realized that he should run the idea past his woman.

"Thanks. I appreciate it," she said. "But I think I'm going to concentrate on what I want to do next."

"Have you considered going back to university?"

Having flunked her first year, she didn't intend on repeating the experience. Besides, she didn't want to waste her hard-earned cash on learning things she'd never use. She was far too practical. Of course, not having made up her mind about her future would mean she'd have to sit through the next dozen or so family dinners, and be subjected to all sorts of unwanted advice.

"School isn't for me, at least not right—" A loud banging sound interrupted her.

"Someone's at the back door at this hour of the morning?" Shane asked, a frown on his face.

"I'll go and see," Marnie said, hopping up from her chair and heading out back. Deliveries didn't start until 9:00 a.m., and there was little chance that any of the staff would appear ahead of their shift. She peeked through the little hole in the middle of the door.

"No!" she moaned. Turning, she braced her back against the hard surface. She would unlock the door and let her nuisance of a brother into the salon when pigs wore roller skates. Scott couldn't be certain she was there, and besides, even if he persisted in banging on the door, she wasn't going to answer.

"Marnie. I know you're in there, and we need to talk."

LUKE HARRISON HAD ZERO interest in Christmas. As far as he was concerned it was everyone's excuse to run up bills they couldn't pay, but that didn't mean he wasn't excited for other people and for all the planning that came with the season.

As of today, The Mirabel Inn was fully booked for what he and his staff had named the Christmas Getaway Event. The event had been designed for married couples who didn't have family plans or who had finally decided to skip the Christmas madness, and simply have a quiet, elegant holiday by themselves. He'd done it on a smaller scale last Christmas but had run into problems when other guests booked into the inn who weren't part of the program—one of the single women had flirted with one of the married men, resulting in the wife packing up and leaving. A messy, uncomfortable situation he didn't want to have repeated this year.

This year the event included five days—three before Christmas, plus Christmas Day and the twenty-sixth. It had taken months to put together a good marketing campaign, but it had paid off. The only room left in the inn was a small one, with a double bed, that was earmarked for renovation, making it into an office for the housekeeper Mary Cunningham.

He'd been up since six that morning, thanks to his four-year-old son, Ethan, who'd been promised a chance to help decorate the huge balsam fir that was presently being strung with lights in preparation for a tree-trimming party. The staff and their families had been invited to a luncheon due to start at noon, after the tree trimming, a party to show appreciation for the staff of the inn. Luke, as the manager, had to be there to kick off the celebration. It was important to hold this party before the getaway event began as many of the staff would be working throughout the holidays.

Despite his aversion to Christmas, Luke enjoyed this

event because he got a chance to give back to the staff and their families whose support was important to the success of the inn. The lunch buffet would be set up in the glassed-in patio along the south side of the two-hundred-year-old inn. The chef, Max Anderson, was making lobster quiche, this year's special dish, along with the usual turkey, ham and all the vegetables, rolls and condiments people enjoyed as part of the Christmas festivities. Family members of the staff, who liked to bake, provided the desserts, showcasing the recipes of some of the best bakers in the region.

Tidying the cost projections report he'd been reading at his desk, he placed it on top the pile, intending to work on it later. When Luke had first come to work at The Mirabel Inn, he'd gotten rid of the stark furnishings in the office and added his own touches along with state-of-the-art computers to assist in managing the inn. But his favorite piece in the office was an antique oak desk with hidden drawers, pigeonholes and a roll-up top, a special gift from his grandfather. Grant Harrison had left the desk to him in his will, and now it was a part of his life. A daily reminder of his grandfather, who had owned one of the largest inns in Connecticut years before.

He was closing his computer when someone knocked on the door. Before he could answer, Mary Cunningham opened the door and Ethan rushed in behind her.

"Well, hello there, big guy," Luke said, getting up from his desk in time to catch Ethan in his arms.

"Daddy!" the little boy yelled, a red-and-green cap balanced precariously on his head.

"Where did you get the elf hat?" Luke asked. Scooping Ethan up and holding him close, he breathed in his scent—usually a mixture of dirt from playing with his dump trucks in the garden plot next to the back patio, and sweat from racing around the property. But today there was just a hint of cinnamon, enhanced by frosting smudges on his cheeks, which meant Ethan had been in the kitchen driving the pastry cook crazy with his questions and his pleas for more sweets.

"Mary gave it to me," Ethan said, triumphantly.

Luke had planned to spend the day with his son, but an urgent call from the owners of the inn had meant he'd been forced to work on cost figures this morning. He was proud of his management of the inn, which was located only a few miles from some of the best skiing in the eastern United States.

Digging a tissue from his pocket, he wiped the frosting off Ethan's cheeks. "Hope he hasn't been too much trouble."

Mary smiled, a warm smile that had been so welcome in those early months after Anna's death in a car accident. She'd been the mother figure to a one-year-old toddler who had no comprehension of why his mommy had left, only that she was gone from his life. Mary had helped both his son and him through the proceeding months of agony and loss, and her generous support and advice had held Luke's life together during a very difficult time.

"Evelyn and Ethan made a batch of sugar cookies with Santa faces on them for the children who are coming."

"How many cookies did you eat, Ethan?" he asked.

The boy grinned and held up five fingers.

"You didn't! Did you share them with anyone?"

Mary laughed. "Henry probably has a tummy ache. I put him in his crate in your apartment. It seemed safer that way."

Henry was a stray part-terrier, part-spaniel that had arrived at the inn on one of the coldest nights in January last year. Henry and Ethan had been constant companions since that frozen evening. "Great. We don't need a four-footed tree trimmer joining the excitement."

"Daddy, I patted the branches of the tree."

"You patted them?" He glanced at Mary.

"Yep. He patted the tree and helped open the boxes of ornaments."

"I found a red bulb this big," Ethan said, opening his arms wide and grinning at his father.

"Wow! You've been busy," he said, reveling in the joy of his son's face. The past three years since his wife's death had been the hardest of his life. Each morning he woke to the fact that Anna wouldn't be there to share the day, to see their son grow into a young man, to face each moment with her inexhaustible enthusiasm. In those early weeks after her death, he sleepwalked through each meaningless day. His only connection to the world around him was Ethan. All those lonely months had been made bearable by the presence of his little boy.

But there was a part of him that couldn't forgive his wife's reckless behavior. She'd insisted on driving to Boston to do some last-minute Christmas shopping and hadn't heeded his warning to stay there until the ice storm had passed and the roads had been cleared. As much as he tried, it had been hard for him to understand how she could have acted the way she did, knowing the risks involved. The kind statements from their friends about how Anna did what she thought best were drowned out by the heartbreak of life without her.

"Are we ready to start trimming the tree?" Mary asked, reaching for Ethan.

Luke hugged his son before putting him down. "Don't

know about you, but it will be the bright spot in my morning."

Ethan nodded so vigorously his elf hat fell off, and he raced from the room.

"Where does he get the energy?" Luke asked.

"Kid power is what I call it." Mary chuckled as she rescued the hat. "And I should know."

"By the way, how's Troy doing at college?"

"Not bad for his first term. Better than his sister and brother did. Peter and I were figuring out the amount of free cash we'll have once Troy is out of school. We'll be living well, let me tell you," she said, a smile spreading across her round face.

Luke had never thought that far ahead: he'd been too busy keeping his life on an even keel and working long hours at the inn. Because of the good friends he'd made since he'd come to work at the inn, he wanted to stay on there for the long term, and maybe someday own an inn like his grandfather had. Owning an inn was not the career his parents had dreamed of for their only child. His father had wanted him to get a law degree and become a partner in his law firm—a profession Luke had no interest in, despite his father's love for it.

"I'm sorry your parents can't come for Christmas this year. Ethan is growing up so fast, and Christmas is all about children."

"I am, too, but it seems they have a prior commitment to spend Christmas with friends in Australia."

It hurt to say those words, words that only increased the disconnect he felt where his parents were concerned. He'd tried to get them to be more involved in Ethan's life, and they'd made promises they hadn't kept. And now with it being Christmas…

"The FedEx truck will be here tomorrow," Mary said,

as if she were reading his thoughts. But in all honesty, it would shock him if his parents had the foresight to send a Christmas gift to their only grandchild.

"We'd better get out there before Ethan hangs all the ornaments on one branch," he said, remembering last Christmas when he'd let his son decorate a small tree for their apartment, and Ethan had hooked every ornament on a branch near the bottom of the tree. Luke had left it that way and had emailed several photos of Ethan's efforts to his parents in Hong Kong.

They walked together to the front hall, where a throng of inn guests and local residents had already gathered around the tree. A group of carolers from Wakesfield had arrived to provide the entertainment, filling the large entry hall with familiar Christmas songs. Luke made his way through the crowd to the tree where Ethan was attempting to string a garland of colored popcorn onto a branch. "Hey! Don't pull the tree over," Luke warned, kneeling to help him.

"Daddy, I love popcorn," he whispered, bringing the strand to his mouth. "Want some?"

"You can't eat that. It's a decoration for the tree."

Ethan's lips formed a pout. "I'm hungry."

"You can't be."

Ethan ignored him as he pulled on the strand of popcorn.

"Here, let me help," Luke said, following the string down past Ethan's feet to a spot under the bottom of the tree where it had become entangled. Reaching in, he freed it, and then lifted Ethan so he could place the garland on the outer tips of the branches.

The people standing around the tree clapped, and Ethan smiled as he hugged his father's neck. Balancing his son in his arms, Luke finished stringing the popcorn on the tree.

The group gathered closer as they all joined in decorating the tree. Several of the men took turns hoisting Ethan up so he could reach the higher branches. Everyone was intent on decorating the huge tree, reminding Luke once again how lucky he was to have this extended family as part of his life for the past eight years.

The sense of family and being together for the holiday season caused a lump to form in Luke's throat. It wasn't that he disliked Christmas as much as the idea that his son would never remember a Christmas that included his mother.

But he couldn't focus on the past, especially with so much riding on the next few weeks. He'd heard rumors from other managers of hotels and inns owned by Advantage Corporation that the CEO, Angus McAndrew, and his management team were looking at all their resort holdings with an eye to selling some of their properties. He hoped the rumor wasn't true, but he knew better than to think that they'd be concerned with what he believed or how he felt.

Still, it was worrisome because he'd worked for Advantage for years, starting at a smaller inn and then being promoted to manager of The Mirabel. Right now, with Ethan finally happy and content once again, he didn't look forward to any change that would affect his son's life, not to mention his own. If Advantage chose to sell this inn, they would probably offer him a job somewhere, but if they decided that his performance wasn't up to their standards or they didn't have a position to offer him, he could end up looking for a job with another organization. In either case it would mean a different location and a new place to live. For now, he didn't want to consider the impact it would have on them. He just wanted to watch his son enjoy the festivities that would kick off the Christmas season.

"Up, Daddy," Ethan demanded, a large angel dangling from his fingers as he held his arms up to his father.

"An angel wants to put an angel on the tree," Mary said over the din created by the crowd.

And Ethan was an angel—the baby he and Anna had dreamed of and waited years for. "Okay, Ethan, let's see you hang this ornament," he said, holding his son aloft as he leaned into the branches to hang the angel near the center of the tree. The staff had already placed a huge lighted star on top. Luke stepped back with Ethan still held high in his arms.

"This is probably the nicest tree we've ever had at the inn," Mary mused, as they all gazed up into the tree.

STILL KEEPING THE DOOR CLOSED against her brother, Marnie considered her options. How had he known she was in here? Knowing him, he would've driven by her house, then over here and found her car in the parking lot. Had he discovered her plan to sell?

Scott was the last person she wanted to see right now. He'd rant on and on about how she was making a huge decision without seeking the family's advice first. The unspoken issue was that Marnie McLaughlan, the youngest member of the McLaughlan clan, wasn't allowed to make any changes in her life without their involvement.

"Go away, Scott," she yelled through the door. "I'm not doing anything that concerns you."

"Marnie, listen to me. Mom is all worked up over

Christmas and worried about you. You know what she's like," he said.

Her mother loved the holidays; she relied on Marnie's support for whatever scheme she had in the works. This year she planned to have Santa arrive complete with sleigh and elves, which meant that Marnie had to be there to act as Mrs. Claus, a role she'd flat-out refused, much to her mother's chagrin. The problem with Eleanor's party schemes was that they always seemed to involve an unattached male—usually the temporarily single son of one of her mother's bridge-playing friends—with whom she'd be forced to socialize. "I'm well aware of our mother's ability to be a drama queen."

"Not fair, Marnie. Mom has always had your best interests at heart."

*Right. Good old Mom, not to mention good old Dad and my four good old brothers.*

How she'd like to snap her fingers and have Scott disappear. But Scott's Velcro tendencies were legendary once he decided to become involved in something. He beat a tattoo on the door, making her clap her hands to her ears.

If, just once, her family could see her for what she was rather than what she wasn't, her life would be so much easier. Reluctantly she turned the lock, opened the door and forced a smile. "What brought you here so early this morning?"

"I heard that you were selling your half of the business."

"Who told you?"

"Dad heard about it through some friend at the Elks Club—a friend of a friend of a woman named Gina something or other. Is it true?"

"I'm not going to change my mind."

Dressed in his uniform of an immaculately tailored dark suit, silk tie chosen to match the tiny thread of magenta woven into the suit fabric, Scott gave her a persuasive smile—the one he usually saved for his marketing clients—as he stepped past her into the tiny office.

"Hello, Shane, it's great to see you, and I hear that congratulations are in order." Scott was about to plunk himself down in the lawn chair, took a closer look and reconsidered.

As Shane launched into the story about how he met his new love, and soon-to-be new partner, Marnie leaned back against the wall and enjoyed the look on Scott's face. Her brother had problems with any conversation he didn't control. Scott wasn't mean. He was constantly thinking ahead to the next step in his plans, and thus he didn't have much patience for small talk. Not surprisingly, it didn't take him long to interrupt Shane and ask a couple of pointed questions concerning the contract.

"Shane, you don't have to answer," she said hurriedly, wanting to block Scott's interrogation of her friend.

Shane closed his mouth and sank his neck into his turtleneck. "That's right, I don't," he confirmed, his eyebrows rising to meet his hairline.

"Shane, would you excuse my sister and me for a couple of minutes?"

With an expression of resignation Shane rose from the chair. "I'll be in the salon going over the renovation plans," he said, giving Marnie his "chin up, kid" smile as he walked past her out the door.

"You have yet to sign, and he's already going over plans?" Scott asked, disbelief evident in his tone.

"They're old blueprints Shane and I had considered a couple of years ago. He and Gina are going to revisit them and see if they're feasible for the expansion they want to make."

"This Gina person is certainly moving fast."

"That's their business, not mine. What's the family's problem with me selling to Shane?"

Scott scooped up the agreement Marnie had carelessly left lying on the desk and took his time reading it before he answered. "We want to be sure you're being paid fair market value for the business and this building. And that Shane hasn't slipped in a noncompetition clause that would stop you from working as a hairdresser once you leave here," he muttered. "What's this?" he asked, pointing at the page.

"What?" she asked, refusing to glance at the page.

"You can't work in Boston as a hairdresser?"

"We agreed it was only fair. My client list and the goodwill I've built up in the city are part of what he's buying beyond the physical assets," she said, exasperated with Scott's attitude.

"Marnie, I'm your brother, and I don't want—"

"Scott, will you leave it alone?" she said, struggling to remain calm. After all, her brother did have his good qualities; the problem was she couldn't remember any of them at the moment.

Still clutching the agreement, Scott leaned against the ancient file cabinet in the corner. "Okay, you take this to your lawyer, and you sign it. What happens the day after you sign? What are you going to do with your life?"

"Run away to the south seas? Go on safari for a few weeks?"

"Get serious. You must have a plan."

"I'm working on that. Please tell Mom not to worry," she said, thankful that he was still concentrating on the agreement and couldn't see the uncertainty in her eyes.

Her family always looked for reasons to freak out over what she was doing and how she was doing it. She understood their concern in the beginning. Two major surgeries she'd had to undergo, one when she was eight to fix a heart defect and one when she had a serious car accident fifteen years ago, had given her family reason to worry. But not anymore.

Scott placed the document on the desk before turning his intense gaze on her. "Tell you what. Angus McAndrew, the CEO of Advantage, you remember him, don't you?"

Scott once worked for Advantage Corporation in their PR department. "He's the guy who got me in to see that superrenowned orthopedic surgeon in New York after my car accident."

"Our family owes Angus a lot. I'm convinced that without his help, you wouldn't have had such a complete recovery." He smiled down at her, warmth showing in his eyes. "Even though I left his company to start my own business, he and I have stayed in touch. He has a property in the Berkshires, The Mirabel Inn, and he's going to put it up for sale. But before he does, he needs a business survey of the region, which one of my staff is working on, and he wants to know that the inn has no operational issues that could derail the sale. He's asked me to hire a mystery guest right away as he has a potential buyer for the inn and he wants to make the kind of pitch the purchaser can't resist. You'll work the three days prior to Christmas, all expenses paid. All you have to do is fill out a bunch of forms. Shouldn't be too stressful," he said.

Ever since her car accident fifteen years ago and her difficulties with her rehabilitation, her family had kept a close eye on her. In those first months after the accident, she had desperately needed their help and support. Now, years later, it felt more like they simply wanted to run her life. "Why do it right before Christmas? A mystery guest? What does that mean?"

"Angus is a perfectionist, and he leaves nothing to chance. He's also very driven, and when he wants something, he goes after it. If he wants to sell this property he'll do it Christmas Day if he has to. As for being a mystery guest, it means you behave like a regular guest, and the management doesn't know who you are or what you're doing there. Meanwhile, you collect information for me on how the inn functions, based on questionnaires the company will provide. Before you leave here, I'll give you the questionnaires so you can read them over to know what aspects of the inn to evaluate. Once you've completed an area, such as the spa or the bar, for instance, you enter your responses online, and then email them to me on a daily basis. I'll take care of the rest. I'll be in touch with you each day to see how you're making out with the survey, and we'll take it from there."

"I don't like sneaking around, trying to get proof that someone isn't doing something right. Besides, why would I want to go north where it's cold and I don't know anyone?"

"Because you need time to think before you sign this agreement."

"I can sign my agreement without going off alone to someplace cold first," she said, feeling she'd got him on this one. "I don't need to go away to think about my future."

"Well, I need you to think about my future and the future success of my company. Angus McAndrew is offering my firm a chance to do work for him, based on how well I handle this project, and how quickly. I need your help."

She blinked. "*My* help? Why me? You must have dozens of people you could order to go to the Berkshires."

He peered at his hands for a couple of minutes. "Peanut, you're the one person I know who has the expertise to evaluate the inn's hotel operations and its spa on such short notice."

Scott must really need her help if he was using the old nickname he'd given her when she was a kid with a leaky heart valve. He'd been so sweet to her back then. She had to admit that with his drive and encouragement her recovery had actually been kind of pleasant. He'd been so good to her, so full of fun ideas to help her forget that she'd just been through major surgery. She owed it to Scott to help him.

"Okay," she said "But there are conditions."

"Name them." He eyed his cell phone.

If she stayed at this inn, she'd be free of all the family pressures involved in getting ready for Christmas. That alone would be fantastic. But there was another equally attractive reason to do it. Despite what she'd said to Scott, she did need to escape for a little while. She'd put so much effort into proving that she could run a successful business that she'd neglected herself in the process. Thanks to her brother she was being handed an opportunity to relax and evaluate her life.

"I want you to tell Mom and the rest of the family that you've sent me on an urgent assignment, and I won't be back until Christmas."

"What? Mom won't believe that."

"Why? It's the truth."

With an exaggerated sigh, he said, "Yeah, but I was hoping you'd do the explaining."

"I'm working for you—you can deliver the news. All I want is a few days of peace and quiet away from the McLaughlan family, and that includes Mom. Agreed?"

He squinted at her. "You're sure that's all?"

"If you can pull it off."

"Of course I can."

"You're going to keep Mom, Dad, Liam, Gordon and Alex off my case for the entire four days that I'm away doing this job for you?" she asked.

"I will, but you'd better turn off your cell phone or I can't be held responsible."

"I'll manage my cell phone if you promise me that Mom won't follow me to the inn."

"Nothing would drag Mom away from her kitchen this close to Christmas." He patted her on the head. "I promise to keep everyone out of your life for four full days."

"Which four days?"

"Okay, you'll arrive there on December 21st, and do your survey work December 22nd, 23rd and 24th, getting back here as early as you can on the 24th."

"That close to Christmas?"

Scott shrugged. "Afraid so."

"Angus McAndrew doesn't celebrate Christmas?"

"He does, but it seems that this deal is very important to him, and he hopes to have it to bed by the New Year. That means he needs the results Christmas week."

"If you say so."

"I do, and I wouldn't be asking you to do this, but I need someone I can trust completely."

He brother trusted her and needed her, and she really owed him a lot. "Okay, I'll go to your precious inn."

"And you have to keep everything confidential. You can't tell anyone at the inn that you're doing this, and under no circumstances are you to tell anyone that the inn is about to be sold. Understood?"

She gave him a snappy salute. "Aye, Captain."

He wrapped her in a bear hug. "Thanks, Peanut."

"And there's something else."

He looked at her as if she were a flawed business proposal. "Let's hear it."

"Stop calling me Peanut."

His jaw worked, he frowned and rubbed his cheek. "Won't happen again."

## CHAPTER TWO

A WEEK LATER JULIE CRAWFORD, Marnie's best friend and Lady Gaga look-alike, sat on the foot of the bed while Marnie packed her bag for the trip to Wakesfield. "What do I tell your mother when she calls? I really like her, and this doesn't seem fair."

Marnie rubbed her forehead in consternation. "Probably not, but I don't know what else to do. It's like this every Christmas. I've joked about running away from home at Christmas so many times, only this time it's going to be true."

"Can you talk to her about how you feel?"

"I've tried, but each time, I end up giving in, mostly because I don't have a reason not to go along with her plans. This year I have, and I need to get away for a bit. This whole negotiation thing has been a lot more stressful that I expected."

"Still…"

"Tell her that you can't reach me, which will be true since I'm turning off my cell, letting my calls go to voice mail, and only turning it on when I need it."

"You're really not going to talk to her?" Julie gaped.

Marnie sighed. "Don't worry. I'll call her eventually."

"So while you're off for a restful few days in the mountains, I'm left to deal with Gina. If she tells me one more time about her matching wedding band to go with her square cut diamond—" Julie pulled a thick blond curl from behind her ear and examined it for split ends. "She's already acting like she owns the place and you haven't even signed the agreement yet."

Hearing the despair in her friend's voice, Marnie sat down next to Julie. "I know how hard it is for you to watch what's going on with Shane."

"I know you do." She gave Marnie a huge hug. "Why did I have to fall for a man who is making a total fool of himself over a woman who—" Julie grimaced. "You know, when I first came to Total Elegance, the first time I saw him, I really believed I'd met the one person for me. And look at me now, sitting here with you feeling like I've lost everything." She tucked her chin into her neck, hiding her face.

"You haven't lost everything," Marnie said, wishing she could ease her friend's heartache.

"I have! Meeting Shane made me believe in love at first sight. I felt so alive, so thrilled to be around him…and now I feel like a walking cliché. What's even worse, he's about to marry a woman who is so completely wrong for him," she wailed.

"Love at first sight went out with the dinosaurs."

"Like you'd know." Julie snorted.

"I've seen firsthand what it does to people."

"You mean Shane?"

She sighed. "Julie, Shane is getting married, and you and I may be upset with him, but there's nothing either of us can do about it. You're going to have to get used to working with Gina, or you're going to have to leave the salon."

"If she keeps pissing people off and the staff and clientele make tracks, Shane won't have anything left of what you and he built together. Won't you feel bad if that happens?"

"Of course I will, but I can't change how Shane lives his life. Neither can you."

"Promise me you won't sign until you come back? Please?"

She and Julie had spent many late nights over bottles of wine discussing Gina and Shane. Julie had wanted to intervene, but Marnie had managed to convince her to stay out of her partner's personal life.

"I can't make that promise. I've agreed to sell, but he's allowed me a few days to reconsider should I need it. I don't think I will, but it never hurts to be cautious. Meanwhile, you have to face the fact that nothing will change Shane's mind about Gina," she said gently.

Tears shimmered in Julie's eyes. "He can't marry her, Marnie."

"Julie, we've been over this."

Julie gave a disgusted sniff, checked her manicure and tilted her chin toward the mirror on the dresser beside the bed. She got up, smoothing her fiery-red top over her narrow hips. "On a whole other topic, our landlord called before you got home, and he has agreed to the estimates for cleaning up the flood damage in the basement."

Marnie and Julie had clothes and personal belongings destroyed by water damage a couple of weeks ago when a pipe broke in the basement of the house they rented. "That's great. We can shop for new shoes and purses now."

"Guess so." Julie tucked one booted leg under her as she settled back on the bed.

Marnie pulled her one black dress out of the closet. "Darn! That reminds me. I don't have a decent pair of heels to take with me."

"You're telling me you don't have one pair of high heels you could wear with a black dress?"

"None. Remember, I'd been reorganizing the closets when the flood happened—all my shoes were on the floor in the basement, along with boxes of my winter clothes." She stuck her head into the bottom of the closet and reappeared with a pair of three-inch heels. "All I have is this pair of canary-yellow ones, and I don't have time to shop for a new pair."

"Not given your inability to make a decision where clothes are concerned. Now, if it were me, I could buy ten pairs in an afternoon. Guess you'll have to make a fashion statement with your yellow ones. I wonder if you'll have to dress up for dinner?"

"I went on the internet to see how formal this place is. There was no mention of a dress code, but the photos of the dining room are pretty classy," she said, worrying that she might not have the right clothes. So much of her wardrobe involved casual pants and tops for work, or jeans.

"You'll be fine."

"I want to look good, but not draw attention to myself. It would make my job a whole lot more difficult if people began to notice me. If they started paying attention to me they might wonder why I was checking things out."

"You wouldn't be that obvious." Julie got up again and sauntered over to the chair next to the window. "So, how does this mystery-guest thing work?"

"Scott made the reservation for me and guaranteed it with his credit card. All I have to do is show up, enjoy every service the inn has to offer and fill out a bunch of questionnaires. That's it."

"Sounds simple enough. Hope it doesn't snow too

much while you're there. You might not make it home for Christmas."

"Christmas is the last thing on my mind." Marnie bundled her curling iron, makeup and hair products into a bag and packed them in her suitcase. She gave the room a quick once-over. "Well, I guess that pretty well does it."

Julie peered over the edge of the suitcase. "Underwear?"

"Oh, yeah." Marnie scooped her undergarments out of her dresser drawers, dropping her pink bustier onto the floor in her haste.

"Wow! Are you up to something on the man front without telling me? Planning on meeting a hunky skier, perhaps?"

"You never know. I'm going to pamper myself, and if there's an available male, you just never know what might happen. I haven't had a decent date in months, and now that I won't be logging tons of time at the salon, a decent date just went to number one on my list of priorities." She stuffed the bustier and the rest of her underwear in her suitcase and closed the zipper.

"Well, here's hoping that none of the guys you meet up there in the Berkshires bear the faintest resemblance to Mario." Julie arched her eyebrows in warning.

"So I'm lousy at picking men."

"No, you've got to stop letting them pick you. There's a difference. As I've said before you've got to be assertive and pick the best apple from the dating tree, not the duds."

Marnie smiled out of the corner of her mouth and reached her arms out to her friend. "Wish me luck on all fronts."

"Absolutely." Julie jumped up, towering over Marnie as she hugged her. "Call me as soon as you have a free minute and let me know what the man situation is like. I might take a couple of days off from the delightful repartee with Gina the Hun and join you so I can look for a mountain man of my own."

LONG HOURS LATER AND NEARLY out of gas, Marnie crested a hill, following the road as it trailed along a stream that wound through the countryside like a velvet scarf. To the right, in the middle of a sweep of land framed by pine trees, she spotted a sign in navy blue edged with gold announcing The Mirabel Inn. Beyond the sign, a long driveway led up a gentle slope to the inn.

Marnie had never seen anything quite so beautiful and majestic in her whole life. She pulled to a stop on the side of the road, captivated by the sight. Two large wings extended back from either side of the inn's front entranceway and peaked roofs accented the elegant structure sparkling in the afternoon sun. The Mirabel Inn looked like something out of a fairy tale. Its generous expanse of windows glittered in the light and the wide verandas wrapped around two sides. The eaves adorned with intricately carved wood emphasized the inn's Victorian feel.

Her research revealed that The Mirabel Inn had once been the private residence of a lumber baron who owned most of the land in this part of the valley. It stood as a magnificent testimonial to his wealth and position in the community during the early years of development in this area of the state.

When Marnie was a child, she'd dreamed of living in just such a place, a dream that was immediately tempered by the reality that only the very rich could afford a house like this. But she could still dream, and she now had days to experience what living in a house like this would be like.

She started along the winding drive leading to the entrance with its tall white columns framing a beautiful front door, festooned with the largest Christmas wreath she'd ever seen, and set off by inlaid glass panes on either side of the door. She passed a towering fir tree, whose brightly colored Christmas lights added to the ambience, before entering a section of the driveway flanked by sprawling rock gardens. She could only imagine the types of flowering plants and shrubs that the gardens would hold in the summer. At the moment they were mulched and ready for winter, the bark chips peeking through a light blanket of snow.

Why would Scott's client want a mystery guest to assess this inn? There wasn't a shingle missing off the roof, or a bit of peeling paint anywhere to be seen.

But Marnie's only concern was getting a few questionnaires filled out while she relaxed by the fireplace in her room with a hot toddy. Add to that a soaker tub where she could soothe her sore muscles after a nice hike along some of the trails she'd read about in the brochure. Absolute heaven.

She parked in front of the door and got out. Clutching Scott's emailed directions along with her confirmation number, she slung her purse over her shoulder, and crossed the stone driveway toward the entrance. Her hand was on the huge brass doorknob when a little boy raced around the corner of the inn toward her, screaming in excitement as he grabbed the back of her jacket. A small dog that resembled a barrel with legs circled her, its fervent bark adding to the pandemonium.

"Ethan, come back here!" a man, following in pursuit of the child, yelled.

Marnie looked down into the bluest, roundest eyes she'd ever seen, and couldn't help smiling. The child had what looked like tomato sauce on his cheeks and a grin that made him impossible to resist. "Well, hello there," she said, kneeling down.

"Sorry," the man said, coming to a stop in front of her. "My son believes this inn is his private play area, and he's a little too young to get the message that not everyone who arrives here wants to play with him." He gathered the boy in his arms.

"And I take it the dog has the same idea," she said, still kneeling as she patted the animal, which immediately lay down, rolled over and offered his belly for a rub. "What's his name?"

"Henry. He adopted us a year ago." The man's smile reached into an untapped part of her heart, creating a sense of longing so unfamiliar it stole her breath, followed by the sensation that they'd met before. But they hadn't. She would have remembered a man who looked this good.

Trying to regain her composure, she focused her attention on the little boy. "He's so cute," she said, groaning inwardly at her use of such a cliché, but surely she could be forgiven for being so predictable. The man was beyond handsome. Sure, there were lots of movie stars who looked good—thanks to special lighting and camera work—but this man was every woman's dream personified. He was tall, taller than any of her brothers, and he appeared very at ease with himself. His jet-black hair and sea-green eyes—haunted eyes—completed the package.

*Get a grip! He's got a son. And he's probably married.*

But Marnie couldn't help marveling at her luck. First,

the most beautiful place she'd ever seen was to be her home for the next few days, and now this…

"Can I help you?" the man asked, giving her the full benefit of his sexy smile as he hoisted his son onto his shoulders, much to the delight of the child, who promptly clutched his father's forehead and grinned down at Marnie.

"I'm expected. I have a reservation."

His eyes darkened, and the smile faded from his face as he glanced at her car and back at her. "You have a reservation here?"

"Yes." She held out her brother's email, with her confirmation number scribbled along the bottom. "I have a reservation for The Mirabel Inn, starting tonight and checking out on the twenty-fourth."

"Is your…husband, I mean your spouse…partner… here?" Consternation knit his brows together.

Marnie didn't know how to respond to such an outrageous question. All she wanted was to check in and relax before dinner. "Do you have to have a husband to stay here?" she asked in her you've-got-to-be-kidding tone.

Hesitating, he gently tugged on his son's legs. "No. No, of course not. At least most of the time you don't. But as of tomorrow night, the inn will be filled with couples. It's our Christmas Getaway event and it's meant for couples wanting to enjoy the romantic holiday away from all the stress of Christmas preparations. I'm sure the person doing the reservation would've told you that."

She couldn't stay here because she was single? Was this covered in the Constitution? It had to be. She had a valid reservation because her brother wouldn't make that kind of mistake. But why was she wasting time talking to someone who was clearly a lot more handsome than he was gracious?

"Look, I drove all the way up here. I have a reservation and I'm going to check in." With that, she opened the door and strode into the lobby. Immediately, Henry jumped up and ambled in behind her, his nails clicking on the hardwood flooring.

Under different circumstances she would've stopped to admire the fabulous Christmas tree filling the main hall with the scent of balsam and outdoors, but she had to determine if her brother had made a mistake. If there'd been some mistake with the reservation, she'd be forced to return to Boston. If that was the case, surely they could help her find a place to stay somewhere in the vicinity as she was too tired to drive any farther. She walked to the desk off along one wall and rang the antique bell resting on the gleaming mahogany.

A woman appeared, dressed in a classy black dress, a smile warming her angular features. "How may I help you?" she asked.

"I'm here to check in. My name is Marnie McLaughlan, and I have a reservation."

A frown knitted the woman's perfectly tweezed eyebrows as she scanned a printout. "Could you wait just a minute?" she asked before disappearing into an office down the hall.

The man she'd met outside came in with his son, his expression neutral as he edged past her and went into the same office. Henry promptly settled in behind the reception desk, his chocolate-brown eyes pensive.

Was everyone in this place either frowning or looking far too serious for such a lovely day? What was the problem with them? She was here, and all she wanted was a pleasant room with a soft bed and a deep tub.

She'd gone over the questionnaires before she left Boston, and there was a section covering the reception desk. She'd be sure to give them a failing grade on how they received guests. Only the little boy and the dog had shown her any true courteousness so far.

She resisted the urge to tap her foot as she gazed up at the vaulted ceiling with its dark wood and hanging brass light fixtures. No wonder Advantage Corporation wanted this place checked out. No hotel employee should be this unpleasant with a paying guest, regardless of what plans had been made for activities at the inn.

She was left to twiddle her thumbs for a few minutes longer, and then the man reappeared without the child, the woman trailing behind him. His smile was back on his face.

"I'm Luke Harrison, manager of The Mirabel Inn." He held out his hand, a welcoming smile on his face.

*Now, that's more like it.*

The warmth and the firmness of his touch drew her in despite his recent behavior. So this was the manager of The Mirabel Inn. His penetrating gaze could prove dangerous should he have reason to believe that she was anything other than a paying guest. The last thing she needed was for him to suspect that she was doing a private assessment of his operations. It would probably be a good idea not to press him over his preoccupation about her traveling alone. The less involvement she had with the man over the next few days, the better.

"It seems we've made a mistake. You're right, you do have a reservation, but I'm afraid the only room available is on the third floor. Unfortunately, it's very small and the bathroom doesn't have a Jacuzzi tub. It is not up to the standards of the other rooms here and is seldom used."

"Does it have internet access?" she asked.

"It does, but only because it's about to be converted to an office."

"Well, as long as it has a bathroom—"

"We're sorry about this situation. We don't normally rent that room. If you'd like, we can call another inn just a couple of miles down the road. The Chancellor is very intimate and offers the best of everything, including a four-star dining room. They have a vacancy, and we'd be more than happy to compensate you for our mistake."

Obviously she preferred a full-size room to what sounded like a broom closet with a bathroom. But she didn't have a choice. She had to stay at The Mirabel Inn. Still, she could indulge her curiosity. "Does the Chancellor have a spa?"

"No, it doesn't. Was our spa part of your reason for choosing The Mirabel Inn?" he asked, pleasure lighting his handsome features.

He was clearly proud of his spa. "Yes, it was."

"That's really too bad. But this is a very popular season of the year, and we'd like you to have the best experience possible during your stay at our inn. We could, of course, offer you a certificate toward booking another time. We would be pleased to provide the Ambassador Suite, should you decide you prefer the accommodations of the Chancellor Inn for this visit, and then return for another visit here." His eyebrows lifted, his parted lips showing off his perfectly straight teeth.

She wished she could agree to his offer—the chance to see him a second time adding to the appeal—but there was her brother to consider. "No, I prefer to stay here. I've read so much about your inn."

He nodded slowly. "Then welcome to The Mirabel Inn. I do hope you have a pleasant experience here with us," he said, giving her a forced smile before turning on his heel and marching out of the lobby. Henry issued a mammoth dog sigh as he followed the man down the hallway.

The woman in the black dress stepped forward. "I'm sorry about this. You are travelling alone, correct?"

Marnie stared at the woman in disbelief as she yanked her cell phone out of her purse. The minute she got to her room she would get Scott on the line and have him deal with these people. With the way they were acting toward her, she'd happily get back in the car, find a gas station and get out of here. "What is the big deal?" she muttered.

The woman started to say something, then thought better of it.

Marnie leaned closer to read the woman's name badge. "Amanda Buckland, is that correct?"

"Yes…"

"Mr. Harrison didn't seem very pleased when I refused his offer to switch inns."

The woman passed Marnie a form for her signature. "Mr. Harrison is anxious that each guest have the best possible experience while staying at The Mirabel. He's simply concerned for you. Starting tomorrow, the only guests here will be couples."

An inn full of romantic couples—just her rotten luck. But there was the spa, and hiking and good food, and a timeout for her. "Not to worry. I understand. I'll be as quiet and discreet as possible. I won't interfere with your special Christmas event."

"We have a large clientele who come here for pampering and socializing with other guests. Our manager simply wants each guest to enjoy his or her experience with us." Amanda pursed her flawlessly painted lips.

"I understand." In truth, as gorgeous as Mr. Harrison

might be, what the manager of this inn wanted came in last on her list of priorities.

"Mr. Harrison is a lovely man and a great manager. Everyone here at The Mirabel likes him, and of course Ethan is such an adorable little boy. We're like a family."

The whole family thing didn't live up to its billing as far as she was concerned. Yet, she had a job to do and she would do it.

Amanda passed her an antique key embossed with a coat of arms. "I hope you have a wonderful stay with us, and if there's anything any member of the staff can do for you, please don't hesitate to ask. I'll show you to your room."

"That's not necessary. I'll get my suitcase and go up by myself. Room number 311, right?"

"Yes. If you'd like someone to park your car for you…"

"That would be nice." Oh, she could get used to this sort of luxury very quickly. She imagined the spa and what treats awaited her there. She intended to indulge in all of them.

Amanda pulled the long velvet pull cord hanging at the back of the desk area and a bell tolled somewhere deep inside the building. "Again, please enjoy your stay, and let one of the staff know if you need anything."

Marnie got her bag from her car, gave her keys to a young man who was waiting outside for her and then headed up the stairs to the third floor. The wide-angled staircase, carpeted in heavy paisley-patterned carpet, led to a much narrower stairway leading to the third floor. Reaching the top of the stairs, she faced a narrow corridor with a tall window at the far end. Her key clutched in her hand, she huffed along down the hall, dragging her suitcase until she found her room. Unlocking the door, she discovered a narrow room made even narrower by the slope of the roof.

Although the room was small, it was a decorator's dream. The double bed, bracketed by two brass lamps, was covered with a heavy brocade bedspread in shades of cream and gold. The walls were covered in antique fleur-de-lis wallpaper, and the carpet beneath her feet was a rich shade of blue, and so thick she nearly stumbled on it.

She put her suitcase down on the luggage rack at the foot of the bed, catching a glimpse of the tiny bathroom as she did so. But neither the size of the room nor the bathroom mattered as she kicked off her boots, pulled back the bedspread and sank onto the mattress, her head coming to rest on a pillow that felt like a cloud. Somewhere in the back of her mind, she remembered that one of the questionnaire sections related to the comfort of the bed, and she'd be sure to give the inn a perfect rating on that feature.

But it had been a long drive and she needed a short nap before dinner....

LUKE SAT AT his desk, staring at Marnie McLaughlan's reservation. It was made out to a Mr. and Mrs. Scott McLaughlan, and yet she'd shown up here alone...and no wedding ring. Where was Mr. McLaughlan? Amanda said he'd been very friendly and so disappointed when she didn't have a vacancy that she'd felt sorry for him, and offered him the room on the top floor. But why hadn't he arrived with her if he was so anxious to come here? His wife hadn't made any mention of him or when he'd be joining her.

It didn't make sense. He tapped the desk, his mind running over the possibilities.

His concerns aside, he'd been surprised to find Ethan hanging off the woman's leg when he got to the front of the house, but she seemed to take it in stride. What could have been an embarrassing situation had turned into a pleasant interlude with a beautiful woman. And with her heart-shaped face framed by short, dark curls and her well-toned body, Marnie McLaughlan was gorgeous *and* sexy....

Her husband probably planned to arrive later, a simple enough explanation, and he hadn't offered her much opportunity to explain why they hadn't arrived together. He'd simply find a diplomatic way to learn when her husband was going to join her, because otherwise, a woman alone meant problems from seating arrangements in the dining room to any activities planned for the next few days. Married couples, especially the wives, came to this event because they wanted to escape and spend time with their husbands. It was essential that there be no disruptions this year—and a woman as beautiful as Marnie McLaughlan could prove to be a serious disruption.

He was still distracted by the problem of Marnie when Jack Fowler, the bartender, appeared at the door. "You look awful, my friend. What's up?"

"We've got a single female guest for the next three days, unless her husband decides to join her." He picked up the reservation, and noted down Scott McLaughlan's number. "And we have thirty couples who've registered for the Christmas Getaway event, most of them arriving tomorrow. I wanted this thing to go off without a hitch. I'd like to really promote it next year and maybe build a little momentum around our programming for the winter months. The last thing I need is a beautiful woman making the wives feel on edge or jealous."

"I hope she's not one of those women who likes to hang out at the bar. The last one of those just left yesterday and I'm exhausted," Jack grumbled.

Luke knew what he meant. Although the bar was popular with the guests because of Jack's charm, in addition to the quality and variety of the liquor offerings, no one appreciated a guest wanting to spend the night getting drunk. In Jack's case, he had another reason for wanting to see his guests leave the bar at a reasonable hour. His wife, Lindsay, was expecting their first child and was anxious about the delivery, especially with respect to getting to the hospital on time. Jack didn't like leaving her alone and had worked mostly day shifts until this week.

"I don't know anything about her except that the reservation was for two, and here she is, all checked in and ready to enjoy her stay…alone. Her husband insisted that the small room was fine for them. I can't shake the feeling that something else is going on here." Restless, he picked up a steel pen, one his parents had given him years ago.

"I assume she's beautiful."

"That, too."

"I take it you tried to convince her to reconsider?"

"I suggested the Chancellor but she refused. It seems she's very interested in our spa."

"Well, then I wouldn't worry. Her husband will probably show up," Jack said, rubbing his hands through his short-cropped brown hair. "Maybe she and her husband had a fight, and she decided to come on her own, hoping he'd follow her and they could have great makeup sex."

Luke groaned. "I don't need that—her deciding to cry on one of the other husbands' shoulders when hers doesn't show, and we end up with an argument, or worse still, the couple leaves. Not the image I want to portray."

"You know there is something you could do if you're worried about the other guests."

"What's that?"

"Until the other guests arrive, I don't see a problem. But if her husband isn't here by tomorrow night for the dinner that launches the Christmas Getaway event, you could invite her to be your guest. That way you'll be able to keep an eye on her."

"And if she doesn't want to be my guest?"

Jack shrugged. "She won't object. Half the women I serve at the bar ask me about you. Married or not. They're all interested."

He hadn't dated anyone since Anna died. There was simply too much to deal with between raising Ethan and running the inn. And if he were to be perfectly honest, a new relationship with a woman would mean he'd have to face his feelings around Anna's death, feelings of anger over her unwillingness to listen to his warning about the road conditions, all the emptiness of having been left alone.

Yet, meeting Marnie had sparked something. He was attracted to her, and he didn't want to be. First, she was married, and second, he didn't want to care for someone when caring could lead to so much hurt. "That might work for tomorrow," he conceded.

"Her husband will probably arrive tomorrow, anyway."

"Then why didn't she say so?"

Jack shook his head. "Did you ask?"

"No." He sighed. "I should have."

"My advice? Leave it for tonight, and deal with it tomorrow."

MARNIE WOKE WITH A START—nothing seemed familiar, and the only sound was someone outside the door talking about a room number. Then she remembered where she was. How long had she slept? She checked her watch. Six o'clock! She'd planned to go for a hike, but now all she'd have time for was a walk around the grounds. She jumped up, hitting her head on the sloped ceiling. "Ow!" she muttered, rubbing the spot just above her hairline.

"That's what you get for agreeing to stay in this room," she said to the empty space as she bent over, searching for her hiking boots. Pulling them on, she noted how dark it was outside, only the sliver of moon peeking through the blind. She hurried downstairs and out the front door. Taking a quick look around, she spotted a stone path leading to the side of the inn. She took it, past a cluster of spreading juniper toward the back. The path led to a stone patio where someone had removed all the snow.

Near the edge on the other side of the patio, Ethan was on his hands and knees digging in the soft loam of a flowerbed, while making loud dump-truck sounds. Squinting around the poorly lit patio space she realized the little boy was out here alone. Except for Henry, who had settled in near the patio door, his chin on his paws, one ear flopped rakishly over one eye. He observed her carefully, his ears doing a flip-flop before settling back.

She went over and knelt down beside the boy. "Ethan, what are you doing?"

"I drive the truck," he announced proudly, his blue eyes taking her in, a smile dawning on his face. "I need help. You push," he ordered, getting behind the toy dump truck loaded with dirt and giving it a shove.

She laughed. "You want me to drive your dump truck?"

He nodded, then stepped back and nodded his head again.

"Okay, here goes," she said, pushing the truck along the edge of the flowerbed toward a spot where he'd clearly dumped other loads.

He toddled along beside her, and when she stopped he pulled the lever that raised the box on the dump truck, spilling his load onto the ground.

He promptly got behind the truck and with a cacophony of enginelike noises he drove the truck back to the spot where she'd found him. She hugged herself against the chill of the night air. "Aren't you cold?" she asked, noting his fleece jacket partially zippered.

"No!" he howled, looking up at her and scrunching his tiny face. "I'm not cold."

"Okay. Do you want to load the dump truck again?"

"Yes." He began shoveling dirt into the truck with his plastic shovel, and again she wondered if anyone in the inn knew this child was out here on his own.

"Where's your daddy?"

He pointed to the tall windows overlooking the patio. Inside, she could see a cluster of tables covered with white tablecloths and candles, and staff moving around the room. The room looked so inviting with its twinkling chandeliers, the golden walls and dark trim. She went to the window for a closer look, only to attract the curious attention of one of the young female servers. Embarrassed, she wiggled her fingers at her, then turned away and went back to where Ethan was busily filling the dump truck.

"Push," he ordered, pointing at the truck.

Dutifully, she knelt down and pushed the truck toward the dump spot to the tune of Ethan's squeals of delight. They dumped the dirt out together, and then Ethan turned to her, a bright smile on his face. Wrapping his arms around her neck, he hugged her.

Startled, at first she didn't know what to do, but feeling his arms tighten, she hugged him back. What a wonderful feeling! How she missed this now that all her nieces and nephews were older. Feeling the warmth of the little boy's body and breathing in his little-boy scent, she felt a strong sense of missing out on life....

He sprang out of her arms. "You help me some more?"

"Sure. But why don't we go inside for a bit first?" she asked, the evening air cooling rapidly.

"No!" He pushed his lips out in a pout. "I don't want to."

She had begun to shiver and tucked her chin into the top of her jacket. "But it must be time for you to eat," she offered, hoping to encourage him to go in with her. She got up, stretched her legs and moved toward the patio doors. "Why don't you come with me?" she asked, glancing over at the sound of the door opening. Henry barked and ambled toward the door, slipping past the man back-lit by the light of the room behind him.

Luke Harrison stood there, his face in partial shadow. "Oh, it's you."

"Yes, I went out for a walk around the property and discovered Ethan playing with his dump truck." Why did she feel nervous? Was it the detached tone of the man's voice? Did he think she was trying to kidnap his son?

"One of the serving staff told me a strange woman was out here, so I came to check."

"I've been called a lot of things, but until now 'strange' hasn't been one of them," she said, making an attempt at humor. After her previous encounter she wanted to make a better impression this time around, if only to ease his concerns over her being here alone.

Moving toward her, he chuckled, a deep, sexy sound that made her body tingle. "I didn't mean to imply that you're strange."

"That's a relief."

"Thanks for being here with Ethan. I got called to the phone and meant to return sooner than this."

Ethan had moved to stand between them, his head tilted back, staring up at them. "He's going to be an engineer when he grows up," Marnie said.

"Or a dump-truck driver." Luke glanced down at his son, then back at her. "I want to apologize for the way I behaved when we first met, but I was concerned about whether you'd enjoy your stay here with us. I don't normally rent that room, and certainly not on such a special occasion. How is it, by the way?"

She remembered the bump on her head, but didn't mention it in case he tried again to convince her to move to the Chancellor Inn. "It's…cozy."

"That's one way of describing it," he said, picking Ethan up in his arms and nuzzling his rosy cheek. "You're cold, little buddy."

"I'm hungry," Ethan said.

"Maybe it's time to go inside. Want to come?" he asked her, making her feel included, part of his world.

"Sure." She followed them inside, and was surprised to find the lobby bustling with activity. The first seating for dinner would begin momentarily, and the bar across from the dining room was filled with guests, most of them older than she was, all of them laughing and talking together.

Luke carried Ethan to the office and stepped back,

inviting her to enter the room first. "Have you met our housekeeper, Mary?" he asked, nodding to a woman seated at a tiny desk near the back of the room.

"Nice to meet you," Mary said, extending her hand in welcome.

Marnie shook hands with her. "Nice to meet you, too," she said, taking in this woman's open, direct smile. She liked her immediately. "I'm looking forward to my stay here. And my room is—" she let her gaze drift to Luke—and only one word came to mind "—gorgeous. Though a little small," she added, eliciting a smile from him as he lowered Ethan to the floor.

"I'll take Ethan for his dinner and maybe I'll see you later," Mary said, giving Luke a long sideways glance before taking Ethan by the hand and leading him out.

"I'm hungry," Ethan announced again on his way out the door.

"How does mac and cheese sound?" Mary asked.

"Yes!" Ethan could be heard racing down the hall despite Mary's warning to slow down and wait for her.

"He's a sweet little boy. He and I had a great time outside."

"Thanks again for watching him. I don't usually leave him alone like that, especially at this time of the evening."

"Not a problem. You and your wife must be so proud of him."

Luke's eyes swept her face, and his expression faltered. "My wife died three years ago, around this time, actually."

"Oh, I'm so sorry! I didn't know."

"There's no reason you should."

Her heart went out to him. How hard it must be to lose the one person you loved, especially at Christmas, and be left to raise a child alone. She searched for something appropriate to say, but realized that he was past being helped by words of sympathy. No wonder his eyes looked so haunted.

He smoothed his hand over his hair. "Would you—" He stopped as if he remembered something. "Would you like to have dinner with me this evening?"

He smiled his son's smile, and Marnie was captivated. "I would."

"Then why don't I meet you in the bar around nine? We could have a drink and talk—" He shrugged. "Talk about anything you want."

He seemed uneasy. Why? Surely he had his pick of women who would happily go to dinner with him. "I would love to have dinner with you." She waited to see if he'd say anything more, and when he didn't she headed for the door, sucking her stomach in, hoping to appear thin and beautiful in spite of the fact that she was still wearing the same pair of jeans she'd been napping in only a short time ago. "See you soon," she said.

Marnie was nearly bursting out of her skin. She had a date with the most gorgeous man she'd ever met, and that was the truth, pure and simple.

A real live date. Wonders never ceased.

She literally skipped up the first flight of stairs. Belatedly, she realized that she had exactly one dress with her that would be suitable for a date—a little black dress that was still in the bottom of her suitcase. And one pair of canary-yellow heels to wear with it.

## CHAPTER THREE

A HALF HOUR LATER MARNIE stood at the entrance to the bar, trying not to look at her feet. She had bigger problems, she noted, as she held her head high to keep the V of her dress from puckering. The few times she'd donned this dress she'd worn her Victoria's Secret push-up bra to take up the slack created by her less than impressive "front bumpers," as her brothers used to call them. But the bra in question was resting peacefully back in her underwear drawer at home.

As for what was on her feet, there was nothing she could do about that particular issue, either. She'd packed her only pair of high heels, prepared to look different and sexy.

She had different covered, all right.

When she entered the bar, some of the men stopped talking and watched her walk past them. Sliding up onto a bar stool, she quietly assessed the bartender. He was a man around her age, she guessed, and the hairdresser in her wanted the opportunity to restyle his hair, shorten the top, maybe....

He came over to her immediately, and with a welcoming smile planted his hands on the bar. "What can I get you this evening?"

He had a pleasant voice, and his manner put her immediately at ease. "Chardonnay?" she asked, feeling good about herself, all because she was about to have a glass of wine while waiting for her date. So maybe it wasn't a regular date, and maybe there'd only be one, but one was better than none.

"Coming right up," the bartender said, snapping open a bar fridge under the counter behind him. She peered up at the ornate carving on the wood framing the bar. It looked like a stag and a dove.

A woman dressed in a bright red top and black pants sat down on the stool next to her. "Do you mind?" the woman asked, her blond hair—a good color job, Marnie noted—swaying around her high cheek bones and sparkling blue eyes.

"Not at all. I'm Marnie." She smiled, happy to have someone to chat with while she waited for Luke.

"I'm Cindy. So nice to meet you."

"You, too. Are you staying at the inn?"

"Yes. It's our fifth wedding anniversary. My husband and I were married here in Wakesfield just before Christmas five years ago. The minister from the local Episcopalian church married us. I wanted a church wedding so much, and my husband was willing to go along." She adjusted the neckline of her red top. "You know how men are about weddings. They'd just as soon go to a justice of the peace, but I wanted a big wedding."

"I did, too, once," Marnie said, drawn to this woman's openness.

"Are you married? Are you taking part in the Christmas Getaway event?"

Marnie tucked her naked ring finger out of sight. "No, but the getaway sounds like fun."

"When we heard about it, my husband and I were thrilled. He doesn't usually take this much time off so close to Christmas, but I talked him into it. One of the couples we met this afternoon is also here celebrating an anniversary." She glanced toward the door. "I don't know what can be keeping my husband. Even though we're on holiday, he's calling his office, but it shouldn't be taking this long."

Glad to be off the hook on the marriage thing, Marnie leaned forward wondering where her drink was. She noticed that her dress was gaping open, and she pushed her shoulders back. "Where does your husband work?"

"He owns a business in Boston. And he's always so busy, I worry about him."

"It takes a lot to start a business these days, but it's even harder to make a success of it."

"Don't I know it! I'd like to start a family, but my sweetie feels we're not ready. He says after he hires one more salesperson, we'll be able to concentrate on starting a family." She smiled wistfully at Marnie. "Do you have children—"

"One California Chardonnay." The bartender interrupted their conversation, his gaze sharp as he placed the wineglass on a Christmas napkin in front of Marnie. "Are you staying at the inn?" he asked.

Sweet relief! Saved by a drink. "Yes, as a matter of fact, I am. Nice spot. I've never been here before, but it's really lovely," she said, happy to chat with him rather than answer questions that would raise the issue of her being here alone. She'd have to be careful to keep a low profile while she worked on the questionnaires.

"You'll love it here, trust me. Isn't that the truth, Cindy?" he asked, taking the drink order of the woman sitting next to her—a dry martini.

"It is. We've come back here on our anniversary the past two years. And Jack's the best martini maker in the state. I had my first martini right here at this bar on my wedding night."

"I remember that night. The entire inn was booked for your wedding," Jack said, taking down a bottle of gin from the shelf at the back of the bar.

As he moved down the bar to prepare the martini, Marnie watched him, searching her memory for some of the questions she'd need answered in order to complete the bar section of the survey.

Cindy gave him a grateful smile when he returned. "Thank you," she said, reaching for the glass.

He placed the napkin in front of her as she took the glass. "Enjoy."

Jack turned to another customer, leaving Marnie to observe the efficient way he moved, mixing drinks while keeping up a flow of conversation with the patrons. He certainly knew his job, she mused, watching him as he loaded a blender with ingredients from the fridge and the counter in front of him.

"Is this bar always this busy?" she asked Cindy.

"Yes. And I'm sure Jack has a lot to do with it," she said, her voice trailing off. Again her gaze moved to the door. "What could be keeping my husband? I'd like you to meet him."

"I'm sure he'll be along soon," she offered to ease the woman's obvious anxiety. "Do you live in Boston?"

With a huge smile, Cindy answered. "We live in Boston. I'm a kindergarten teacher, and I love it. The four-and five-year-olds are so cute."

"Like Ethan?"

"Oh, you've met him already? Isn't he the sweetest little boy? And so sad that he lost his mommy."

"Yeah. It must have been hard for his dad, too." Marnie checked her watch, wondering where Luke could be.

"I see we're in the same boat." Cindy nodded at Marnie's watch. "We're both waiting for the men in our lives." Cindy smiled at someone behind Marnie. "And here's mine now."

Marnie turned on her stool and nearly fell off. Coming toward them was Brad Parker, the man she'd nearly married eleven years ago. The man who told her he couldn't marry her because he didn't want a wife who put her career first. What he really meant was he couldn't give up the playmate he'd stashed away in an apartment in downtown Boston.

For about ten seconds Marnie considered walking out of the bar to avoid him. But she hadn't done anything wrong, unless you counted falling in love with a loser. A love that died the evening she'd grown suspicious of his frequent business demands and followed him across town to his girlfriend's place. She'd nearly turned her brothers loose on him, but she decided that he wasn't worth it.

She watched, waiting for his phony smile to come her way, as she knew it would. Brad could never resist sizing up the women in any room he entered. And sure enough, after a smile tossed his wife's way his eyes swerved to her. The muted light of the bar was still bright enough to expose the sudden blanching of his skin and the rigor mortis smile claiming his handsome features.

"Marnie, this is my husband, Brad Parker. Brad, this is Marnie." Cindy looked from Marnie to her husband, her face beaming.

Feeling nothing for the man standing in front of her, Marnie waited for Brad to say something to smooth over the awkward moment, something Brad was very good at when he wanted to be. If he used his usual technique, he'd make some remark about where they might have met, and she'd take her cue from him.

He hesitated. Then he moved in between them, his

arm going around his wife's shoulders as he stared at
Marnie. "Do I know you?" he asked.

"You look familiar," she said, her smile easy, despite
her shock at seeing him and his refusal to at least acknowledge her.

"I'm often mistaken for other people. Don't know
why," Brad said, his cautionary gaze fixed on Marnie.

Leave it to Brad to take the coward's way out, but
Cindy clearly loved her husband, and Marnie wouldn't
do anything to hurt her. She forced a smile. "Probably
that's it."

There was a long pause during which Brad waved the
bartender over. "I'll have a double bourbon."

Cindy finished her drink in one long swallow, and
placed the empty glass on the bar. "Honey, I'm going
to the ladies' room, but I'll be back, and then the three
of us can have a drink together."

"I'll be right here, waiting for you," Brad said, pulling her hard against him and kissing her on the mouth.

Marnie waited until Cindy left the bar. "Brad, I—"

"What are you doing here?" Brad asked, as he looked
her up and down.

For years she'd dreamed of meeting Brad somewhere
and calling him out on his scandalous behavior, but not
tonight. Tonight she intended to rise above all the pain
that he'd caused her.

But as she gazed into his eyes and saw not a hint of
remorse for what he'd done the words spilled out. "I'm
here to enjoy myself, and that means staying away from
you. Remember me? I'm the woman you almost married. Let me see, it was just a couple of weeks before
our wedding day as I remember it, and you and…what
was her name?" She frowned to cover the hurt she was
feeling inside. "You had an urgent meeting in her bed-

room. I believe she was a lawyer from the law firm your company dealt with—Mary Ellen something or other."

He downed his drink. "Marnie, I'd really appreciate it if you'd not mention this in front of my wife."

"Give me a little credit," she snorted.

He glanced past her, frowning as he twirled his empty glass. "We're here for the Christmas getaway, or whatever the hell they call it."

"Trying for a few brownie points? Is she catching on to your story? The one where you pretend to be so busy at work that you can't be at home with her?"

"Your bitchiness is showing," he muttered.

She caught the bartender watching her, bringing her back to her senses. "Brad, I want you to know that as angry as I was back then, I now realize that marrying you would have been the biggest mistake of my life."

"Okay, so can we leave it there?" he asked, anxiously glancing around.

"Is everything okay?" Cindy asked, appearing around the corner of the bar and startling them both.

"Everything's just fine, darling." He put his arm around Cindy, towering over her. "I've got a surprise for you. I was saving it for tonight."

"What's that?" Cindy asked, her face turned up to his.

"We're going back to our room and ordering champagne, followed by room service, followed by a little rug time in front of the fireplace." He winked at Marnie behind his wife's back.

Cindy blushed and smiled sheepishly at Marnie. "I'm sorry, but can we have a rain check on the drinks? I'm sure we'll see each other again during our stay. Maybe you and your boyfriend can have dinner with us some evening."

"Sounds lovely," Marnie said, dredging up as much sincerity as she could muster.

"Then it's settled. Maybe you and I could go into Wakesfield to shop tomorrow?"

"Maybe," Marnie said, making a mental note to steer clear of both of them.

"Let's go," Brad said urgently.

Cindy giggled and linked her arm through his as they moved off toward the door, and Marnie immediately started planning how to stay clear of Brad and Cindy for the remainder of her stay. Since they were here on their anniversary they wouldn't come down early for breakfast, she figured. As for lunch, she'd be sure to arrive early and sit at a table for two, and for dinner she could always order room service—whatever it took to avoid them.

She was still mulling over her plan when she saw the bartender approaching her.

"Are you okay?" he asked.

"Yes, why?"

"You looked…anxious, a little upset." His squint was quizzical. "Are you friends with the Parkers?"

"No. No, I… We were just talking," she mumbled, struggling to remember if either she or Brad had raised their voices.

She didn't want any reports going back to Luke about her behavior at the bar. He was already far too paranoid about her being here alone. Learning that she'd had some sort of interaction with one of his precious getaway couples could wreak a whole lot of havoc. And she was definitely not into havoc.

Jack hesitated. "Can I get you anything?"

"No, I'm waiting for Luke. He must have been delayed."

Upset and out of sorts over her altercation with Brad, she took a good big sip from her glass of wine and gave the drink menu the once-over as she planted a pleasant expression on her face and offered up a prayer that Luke Harrison would make an appearance soon.

LUKE SIGHED AS HE LISTENED to Jack describing a woman at the bar, a description that fit Marnie McLaughlan perfectly. Why had he agreed to meet her there of all places? Why had he agreed to have dinner with her? "Yeah, that's her."

"Still no indication as to when the husband's arriving?" Jack asked, over the din of the bar.

"None, and I talked to her not that long ago."

"And what did she say?"

"Not much. It's a long story. I wish her husband would show up."

"Might be a good idea. She just had a pretty heated discussion with the Parkers before they left for dinner. I can't be sure what it was about, but she and Brad definitely knew each other."

Luke groaned inwardly. He couldn't have Marnie involved in anything having to do with the guests until her husband arrived. He had a lot riding on the next few days.

He glanced at his watch. He'd agreed to meet her at the bar and he was already late. "I'll be there in a couple of minutes."

"You don't have to do that. I'll keep an eye on her."

"I invited her to dinner."

"You did what?"

"You were the one who encouraged me to have her as my guest for dinner, remember?"

"True. And maybe that's the answer…until the husband shows up. I'll see you when you get here."

Luke got up from his desk, leaving behind his operating-cost projections for the first quarter of next year, and adjusted his tie. When he entered the bar, Marnie was sitting by herself, reading the drink menu, her slim legs creating a smooth, enticing line from the hem of her short skirt to…bright yellow three-inch high heels. Who wore yellow shoes with a black dress? Who looked *that* good in yellow shoes and a black dress?

Jack was polishing glasses, his gaze locked on Marnie. A quick survey of the room showed him that all the men were watching her. The success or failure of the Christmas Getaway event appeared to rest on one sexy woman who didn't seem to notice any of the attention directed at her.

Steeling himself for any questions she might have around his earlier behavior and her earlier argument over why she needed a husband here with her, he strode toward the bar. She caught sight of him, a smile lighting her face and warmth shining in her clear gray-green eyes. All he could think about was how attractive she was, how the dress fit her body like a glove.

A beautiful, sexy woman was waiting for him—Luke Harrison. It had been three years since anyone had waited for him. He sucked in a breath as he struggled to remember why he'd been so annoyed with her. "Sorry I'm late," he mumbled as he slid onto the bar stool beside her.

"That's okay. I'm glad you're here." She took a sip of her wine.

"Why? Did something happen?" he asked, hoping she'd give him her side of the story around the Parkers.

"No. It's nothing. I'm just not used to being stared at."

She gave him an apologetic smile as her fingers pleated the napkin under her half-finished glass of wine.

With this beautiful woman's eyes focused solely on him, he couldn't think of an intelligent word to say. And if that wasn't enough, he suddenly felt awkward, out of his depth. "Why don't we go to my office before we go to dinner? I need to talk to you about something."

She wrinkled her perfectly smooth brow. "If you'd like." She slid off the stool and waved to Jack who waved back, and then winked at Luke. "But if your concern is over my room, I'm quite happy with it, and I'm really looking forward to having a spa treatment tomorrow."

His thoughts rattling around his mind like marbles in a tin can, he followed her from the bar, mesmerized by her walk, and the curl of hair snaking down the nape of her long neck.

*You need to get out more, date a few women.*

When they reached his office, he closed the door and moved quickly to sit behind his desk. He needed to be behind his desk, otherwise he'd be tempted to touch her, and touching her was out of the question.

"Ah, we have a problem," he said, forcing himself to get straight to the point.

"A problem? With what?" she asked, looking completely perplexed and totally endearing.

For a few minutes he considered backing out of his decision to find out what was going on with this woman and her reservation. But tomorrow was the first day of an event that was critical to the success of the inn's winter season, a season he'd spent thousands of dollars of his advertising budget on, and he couldn't let it be jeopardized.

His conversation with Jack made it even more urgent that he find out what was going on with her. "You're aware that this Christmas Getaway event is starting tomorrow, and those couples signed up because they want to have a stress-free Christmas vacation, right?"

"Yes, you explained all that."

"Your reservation is for two people." He cleared his throat to ease his nervousness. "Will your husband be joining you tomorrow?"

"My husband?" she asked, her expression one of complete disbelief.

"Your reservation is made out in the name of Mr. and Mrs. Scott McLaughlan."

She choked. "What?"

Why the surprise? Had she planned all along to come without her husband and now she'd been found out? Was she meeting one of the other guests? Surely not Brad Parker. He and his wife seemed so happy when he met them at the reception desk earlier. But if there was something going on between Brad and Marnie, it might explain why she insisted on staying here.

He pulled the reservation from the pile of papers on the corner of his desk. "See, there it is." He pointed to the names on the reservation. "We've been heavily promoting this package. Your husband would have been informed when making the booking that it was a couples event."

She read it slowly, her lips pursed into a stubborn arch. "You wouldn't have accepted the reservation unless I was coming here with…my husband."

"Not for the next few days. The package officially starts tomorrow, the 22nd, and runs until the 26th of December. We have a dinner party as the final event."

"So, what do you want me to do?" she asked.

She hadn't made any comment about her husband's name being on the reservation, and she hadn't offered any explanation for his absence. "It would be helpful to know when your husband is going to join you."

She started to speak, then lowered her head and peered at her hands resting in her lap. "I don't know."

"Is he delayed?"

"He's... I'm calling him this evening...."

He rubbed his face, a deep sigh escaping his lips. "In the meantime, we have to come to some sort of... arrangement."

"An arrangement." Her voice dropped twenty degrees, but two bright red spots appeared on her cheeks.

What in the hell was he doing? What arrangement would work that wouldn't get him into more trouble? "Please try to understand my predicament. If you're to stay here alone until your husband arrives you'll have to keep a low profile. It might work best for you to be my...assistant."

*An assistant? Any other brilliant ideas?*

She gave him an incredulous look. "You need a date that bad? None of the local girls want to go out with you?"

"No, I don't need a date. You're just too...too much of a distraction. The men here are supposed to be concentrating on their wives."

"And if they don't, it's *my* fault?" she said, her voice rising.

"No, it's just that..." He managed to come up with a smile. "I'm just digging the hole deeper, aren't I?"

As ANGRY AND EMBARRASSED as she was by the predicament Scott had put her in, she found Luke's earnest tone reassuring. He wasn't trying to offend her; he just wasn't good at dealing with this sort of situation. He was obviously not good at talking to women, which made him more appealing in a way.

*So, why don't you tell him Scott's not your husband, that he's your brother? If you're going to do it, now would be the time.*

But if she told Luke the truth, how did she explain her brother's strange behavior? And what sort of person had a brother that would claim his sister was his wife? And what would Luke think of her when he learned the truth?

She could suggest that the inn must have made a mistake, but she knew they hadn't. Scott would have been told about the event, and in his single-minded way, he got around it by putting his name on the reservation, without thinking that there might be repercussions for her.

She could have said that Scott was going to come with his wife, and couldn't at the last minute, but that wouldn't work because Scott had been told that it was a special Christmas package for couples. So for Scott to send her alone made even less sense. So what sort of explanation could she offer to Luke that would explain her presence here this week of all weeks?

No, offering up another lie was out of the question. She hadn't told Luke the truth originally and now the opportunity to do so was rapidly slipping away.

*Face it. You're stalling for time. As angry as you are at Scott, you don't want to leave, and the reason is sitting across from you.*

"You're digging a huge hole, but it's not necessarily your fault," she said, barely able to contain her embarrassment. Scott hadn't said one word about the couples program when he'd given her the confirmation number, and he'd left her to face this man knowing she was supposed to have a husband.

"If we could come up with some sort of explanation for you being here alone… I mean, did you come to think…or to resolve some issue?"

His expression was a mix of uncertainty and determination, and she felt sorry for him. After all, despite his poor handling of the situation, he was trying to run a business, and she wasn't being much help.

She cleared her throat and tried for an encouraging smile. She'd deal with her sneaky, underhanded brother tonight. "I had planned to have a nice break for a few days." That was the truth, and another reason she planned to do something really nasty to Scott when she got home. "But I didn't realize that my being here would cause such a problem for you. I'm really sorry for causing so much trouble."

Luke fidgeted for a few seconds, breathing life into her fantasy that if she could stay for a couple of days, and if she could somehow get out of the lie Scott had told, she might have a chance to get to know Luke. "I gather the inn will be busy for the next few days, and I used to run a beauty shop and spa. If I could help you out somehow, make up for any difficulties I may have caused," she said, seeing his expression turn hopeful.

"It would certainly be much easier for everyone if you were inconspicuous…that's why I suggested you be my assistant."

"What will the other members of your staff say about this?"

"Nothing. To be honest with you, we all want the Christmas Getaway event to be a success."

"I'm really that much of a concern?" she asked in disbelief.

He nodded sheepishly. "A lone single woman during this sort of event can't help but stand out." He shrugged.

"This must sound silly to you, but appearances count when it comes to creating a romantic experience such as the one we have planned for this week."

The heated exchange between herself and Brad came back to her, and she suddenly had a flash of realization. "The bartender called you, didn't he? To report on me?"

He nodded. "Jack has a lot going on this week, as well. His wife is expecting their first child and she's due any day. But I've gotten way off topic."

So Jack told on her. If she had simply walked away from Brad, surely Luke wouldn't be so anxious to keep her hidden. "That's okay, and a new baby is always exciting," she said.

"Would you be willing to pretend to be my assistant until your husband arrives? During our Christmas Getaway event, many of the staff will work longer hours than usual. With you here, I'll be able to offer them at least a few hours off, which means you'll be too busy to attract any of the guests' attention." He gave her the cutest look, nearly making her forget that she was here under false pretenses.

She had no idea why he was so anxious for her to stay, but clearly he was, and she wanted to stay, especially with the added bonus of working with him. Whatever else she did, she'd make sure she didn't go anywhere near Brad or his wife, which would ease Luke's concerns.

By helping out around the inn, she could also do her questionnaire work without being noticed. "Let me sleep on it, and I'll give you my answer tomorrow. How's that?"

"Great. In the meantime, what about dinner? The getaway event doesn't officially start until tomorrow."

Dinner was out of the question tonight. She was only

hungry for the chance to ream Scott out. Food could wait. Besides, if she got really hungry, she had trail mix in her backpack. "If you don't mind, I'm a little tired. I think I'll just go to my room."

She'd been so determined not to feel anything while Luke talked, not the surprise, the hurt or the embarrassment, brought on by the actions of her brother. And to add insult to injury, there had been the run-in with Brad. She swallowed hard and clenched her hands to steady herself.

"I'm sorry. I didn't mean to upset you. You don't have to eat with me if you'd rather eat in your room. Why don't I get the chef to send up some dinner?" Luke said.

Why not? She'd probably be ravenous when she got done yelling at Scott. "That would be wonderful."

"Despite what I've said here this evening, I would've been more than pleased to have dinner with you." His smile touched her heart, making her wish that she could tell him the truth about her, about why she was there in his beautiful inn.

"Thank you." Before she succumbed to his brilliant smile and the promise of what the evening might have offered her—if not for her brother's behavior—she got up and left the office, not stopping until she was in her room with the door locked behind her.

FINALLY FREE TO EXPRESS her frustration, Marnie pounded her fists into the bed, and felt the hot sting of tears. To think that her brother had done this to her, embarrassed her this way, was too much for her to handle. Scott had to have known what was going on at the inn, and he'd let her come up here anyway to deal with the consequences.

And humiliate herself in front of the one man she'd met in years who truly seemed like a decent guy.

Her fingers fairly danced over the keys of her cell phone in her rush to reach Scott. He answered on the first ring.

"How could you do this to me?"

"Hello, Marnie, and what did I do to you?"

"You registered me as one half of a couple, using your name, and I just spent a humiliating hour being grilled by the staff and the manager over the fact that I'm here alone."

"I'm sorry, Marnie. I had no choice. They'd only take the booking if I made the reservation under both our names. Is that a problem?"

She nearly choked on her anger. "No, not at all, if you don't mind being told by the manager that you can't stay unless you pretend to be his assistant so no one will see a single person here during the Christmas Getaway event for couples—only couples. But the most fun of all is that I have to lie to people about who I am," Marnie yelled.

Someone knocked at the door. "Is everything all right?" a man's voice inquired.

Damn! All she needed was for someone to go down to the desk and complain about a crazy woman screaming on the third floor. "I'm fine," she called through the door, summoning the voice she used to calm unhappy clients.

"Who are you talking to?" Scott asked.

"You. I'm talking to you. I'm not spending the next three days here under these circumstances."

"Point taken. But calm down a little while I think."

"There's nothing to think about! I'm coming back tomorrow. You and your questionnaire are history. Don't ever ask me to do anything for you ever again."

There was a long silence, giving Marnie time to catch

her breath and settle onto the bed, being careful not to hit her head this time. "Did you hear me?"

"I did. I did. But look, I really need this survey done, and you're the only person I can call on at such short notice to do it."

"But why do you need it if they're simply going to sell the inn anyway?"

"I told you. They have this buyer who's interested, but he doesn't want any problems on the operational front. He's looking for a turnkey operation, and Angus McAndrew is determined to sell him one. That's where you come in."

"And if I find a problem?"

"Just get the forms filled out and get them off to me. Angus is calling daily to hear if there are any problems, and I need to know the minute you find anything, understood?"

Scott never allowed anything to get in the way of what he wanted. He'd been like that since the day he found out he stood to qualify for the Olympic swimming team. He'd not only practiced with the best coach available, he'd driven himself and the rest of his family nearly crazy in his quest to achieve his goal, and he had succeeded. He was a champion athlete—the pride of the McLaughlan clan. "I'm not sure if this will work."

"I'm depending on you, Marnie. Don't let me down."

She didn't know what to say. She was here, and she'd promised to do this for him. She owed him a lot, and this was the first time he'd ever asked her for a favor. "I wish I hadn't agreed to this."

"Look, I know you can do it, and I've kept my side of the bargain. Mom thinks you're away with no cellphone access, so we've both had to tell little white lies."

"And your little white lie will also get me in trouble

with Mom if she finds out the truth. She'll never blame you. She'll blame me for putting you up to it."

"No, Marnie. If it ever comes out, I'll take full responsibility. I promise."

"Then take responsibility now. Call the inn and tell them the truth."

"What? That you're there under false pretenses? That not only are you not married, but that you're there to check up on the inn's operations? What would that accomplish?"

"I don't know.... You can't tell them why I'm here, but you could tell them we're not married, that you made a mistake. With the way my life is going at the moment, they'd probably ask me to leave."

"Why? You're a paying guest."

But how could she have any relationship with Luke that wasn't based on honesty? As long as Luke believed she was married, and she didn't tell him the truth, there would be no chance for anything with him beyond the occasional cup of coffee.

"The manager has offered me to pose as his assistant for the duration of my stay, and as nutty as that sounds, it might work at least until you tell the truth."

"Then do it. You go along with the idea of being the manager's assistant. That will make your mystery-guest job easier, and you can be out of there by the latest the day after tomorrow."

"Have you forgotten that I came here partly to rethink my life?"

"Okay, then what about this? You get your survey questions done ASAP. And once Christmas is over, I'll buy you a ticket to any vacation spot you choose."

She had to hand it to her brother; he had a gift when it came to persuasion.

"Listen, Marnie. I'm really sorry about all this, and I'll fix it, I promise."

Her brother had all the answers. And if she went home now, her mother would want her to be Mrs. Claus.

"I want to go to Hawaii the first week of January. And I want a second ticket so I can take someone with me."

"Are you hiding something, Marnie?"

"No, I'm not hiding anything. I just don't want to go to Hawaii by myself." She had no idea who she'd invite, but she figured Scott didn't have to know that.

"Agreed. Now I've got to go to bed, get my handsome rest," he said.

"Sleep will not make you handsome. A few spa treatments, maybe."

"Don't have time for such pampering, but I do need to get some rest with the holiday season in full swing here. Talk later," he said.

"When you have my tickets ready," she reminded him.

"Don't worry, Marnie. I realize that you're off to a bad start, but things will get better."

"And you know that because...?"

"Because you're my baby sister and I love you."

"You have a strange way of showing it," she said, before snapping her phone shut, ignoring the warm feelings his words provoked. Regardless of how angry Scott could make her, she still wanted his approval. It had always been that way between them, mostly because he'd been the one brother of the four who had always been there for her.

She gazed around the room, at the mess she'd made of her clothes in her rush to find her black dress. In her haste, she'd forgotten she'd packed a black lace bra and panties and the hot-pink bustier, just in case she met someone.

That was before she discovered that the only available male at the inn wanted her to disappear. She couldn't tell him she wasn't married, and she certainly couldn't tell him about the questionnaires she was working on. If he discovered that she was spying on his inn, it would be the end of everything.

That left her with one option. She would enjoy tonight's dinner while she prepared her explanation to Luke. She would tell him what her brother did, and what he'd asked her to do. That she couldn't lie to him regardless of what perks her brother offered. If Luke was still interested in her after that, then they might have a chance. If not, it was better for her to learn that now before her heart got involved.

She was about to put the bustier back into her suitcase when someone tapped on the door. It had to be room service with her dinner. "I'll be right there," she called out, tucking the bustier behind her back and opening the door.

Before her stood Luke dressed in a dark suit and a tie that matched the green of his eyes. "I decided to deliver your dinner myself."

# CHAPTER FOUR

"THANK YOU SO MUCH, I really appreciate this," she said, dropping the bustier on the floor behind her, and kicking it behind the door with her foot as she reached for the cart.

He pushed the serving table into the tiny room, wedging it between the bed and the door to the bathroom.

"Do you mind if I stay a minute so we can talk?" Luke asked.

"Talk? S-sure," she said, reluctantly closing the door and praying he wouldn't notice the bustier among the rest of the clothing strewn across the floor. "Sorry for the mess."

He chuckled and shook his head. "Don't worry about it." Then his face took on a more serious expression. "Scott called me just a few minutes ago, and said how sorry he was for making a mistake involving the booking."

"He what?" Had her brother found an easy way out of the whole Mr. and Mrs. debacle?

"He wanted me to understand that he was the one who made the mistake."

"Exactly! Yes," she said. Heat rose in her cheeks as she envisioned the possibilities that were now tantalizingly within her reach. She could only hope that Mary was babysitting Ethan tonight.

"I wish I'd known earlier, I wouldn't have been so

blunt with you. Your husband said he made the booking as a special vacation for the two of you, and then he suddenly got called away on business."

"Called away on business?" she croaked. While she'd been trying to come to terms with how she'd manage to work for this man, and do the questionnaire, *and* find a way to explain things, Scott had gone behind her back again and told another one of his ridiculous lies.

It all had to stop now because when the truth came out—and it would—she would lose all her credibility with Luke. Besides, she refused to spend the next few days before Christmas lying to this man who had been nothing but honest with her.

LUKE SAW THE WAY Marnie McLaughlan's eyes glistened, and he admired her control. He didn't know how he'd feel if faced with having to stay alone at an inn when it was supposed to be a romantic vacation. "Scott said he wasn't sure when he'd be able to join you here, but in the meantime I want you to know that you can still be my assistant if you'd like." He shrugged.

"Thanks," she said. "But I'm not sure I can stay."

He could identify with loneliness, with being the one single person in a sea of couples. "You've been a good sport about this. And Ethan likes you. When I was putting him to bed tonight, he explained to me that you're his new friend."

Her expression brightened. "He is so sweet."

"So what do you say? Why not enjoy your dinner, and we'll talk tomorrow morning. I usually have breakfast with Ethan around six-thirty. Would you like to have a hot date with the only two unattached males in the building?"

"I would love that. I've never had a date with two men before in my life."

"Then I hope we live up to your expectations."

"I'm sure you will," she said, the look of happiness on her face, making him want to hug her. He liked this woman with the short haircut and the yellow high heels. It had been a long time since he'd felt the way he was feeling this minute.

He opened the door, before turning toward her one last time. "Wait until you see what Ethan eats for breakfast."

"I'm looking forward to it," she said and waved.

THE NEXT MORNING, LUKE'S feelings regarding Marnie had changed again. The trouble was he couldn't imagine why any woman who loved her husband would want to stay by herself at an inn filled with married couples. It was such a lonely way to spend the days leading up to Christmas. Surely she had friends or family she could visit instead of coming to an inn on her own.

There was something about the situation that didn't sit right with him.

*Gullible, that's what you are. Or starved for female company.*

He hadn't told Marnie the whole conversation he'd had with Scott McLaughlan. Scott was less than convincing when he explained that he'd been called away on business, and his eagerness to have Marnie stay at the inn made it sound as if he wanted his wife out of his way. The guy was probably having an affair.

And Marnie's behavior at the bar last night raised further questions in his mind. He'd spoken with Jack again last evening after he left Marnie's room, and Jack was convinced that Brad Parker and Marnie McLaughlan knew one another. The other odd thing Jack said was that after the Parkers left the bar, Marnie had asked all kinds of questions about how the bar operated.

Luke glanced impatiently toward the entrance of the dining room. There was still no sign of Marnie, and there were two couples already seated in the dining room. Adele and Thomas Lewis, and Mae and Walter Pearson, both great couples and repeat guests. They were also avid hikers and were leaving shortly on a two-mile trek that they'd arranged with the guide the night before.

Last evening Marnie had seemed interested in staying at the inn and helping out. So where was she?

"Daddy, more syrup," Ethan demanded, pointing to his half-finished plate of French toast.

"You've had enough," he said absent-mindedly.

"Hi!" Ethan yelled, wiggling in his seat and smiling at someone.

"Hi, yourself." Marnie slid into the chair next to Ethan and across from Luke. "Sorry I'm late, but I couldn't sleep last night. I went out for a walk this morning to clear my head and left my watch in my room." She picked up her napkin and spread it on her lap, watching the female server who was pouring coffee for her.

It was still dark outside. *A walk in the dark?* he wanted to ask, but left it. It was none of his business.

"We need to get organized for the day ahead. It's going to be a busy one," he said, hearing the stiffness in his tone. Once again, he was drawn to her, to her bright smile, her easy manner. No wonder Ethan liked her. Hell, despite all his misgivings, he still liked her.

"Finished!" Ethan stated in his outdoor voice as he spotted Mary coming toward the table.

Mary took Ethan's hand. "Come with me, and we'll get you ready for day care."

Ethan leaned toward his father. "Miss you."

Luke pulled his son into his arms, his heart pressing against his throat. How he loved these words spoken every morning by his son, words that kept him centered. "Miss you, too, buddy. Have a good day, and I'll see you when you get home."

He watched his son leave the dining room before turning his attention to the woman sitting across from him.

"This is so beautiful," she said, nodding at the large space with its tall windows, gleaming wood floors and linen-draped tables.

"The inn belonged to a lumber baron during the years when lumber was the main export in this part of the country. It was a lavish home, complete with its own water system located on the roof of the house. There used to be horse stables with carriages, but they were lost in a fire sixty years ago."

"Imagine living in so much luxury. It must have been a magical life." Her eyes shone with wonder, and he could see how easily people would like her, how easily she would make friends.

But they weren't friends, and he needed a few more answers from her. "We have a problem."

MARNIE FIXED HER GAZE on the single rose in the center of the table. She had no idea what was coming next, but after a restless night she knew one thing for certain. She wanted a chance to get to know Luke Harrison. It had been so long since she'd met a man she genuinely liked. It was no secret that she was lousy at picking men, and maybe her interest in Luke was a lost cause, but she had a right to find out one way or the other. "What sort of problem?"

"I don't understand why you'd want to stay at the inn when your husband isn't here."

She squeezed her napkin, trying to soothe the apprehension gnawing at her gut. Scott's stupid lie had gotten her in a ton of trouble, and now she was faced with a choice. She could perpetuate the lie, or she could tell Luke the truth. She desperately wanted a chance with him, but she couldn't spend another night wrestling with her conscience. "I have to explain something to you." She took a deep breath and looked into his gorgeous, trusting eyes. Oh, God… "Scott is not my husband. He's my brother."

Luke's expression froze. "Would you care to explain that?" he asked, his voice tight.

Marnie wanted to crawl under the table, slink out of the room and make a run for her car. Instead she studied the huge silver Christmas tree near the window while she collected her scattered thoughts. Luke was angry and she couldn't blame him. "My brother wanted me to be able to stay here at your inn. I needed a break away from my… I'm selling my hair-and-aesthetics salon, and I needed a little time to think about the future."

"You could have done that at any number of resorts. I offered you the Chancellor. Why this one?" he demanded, his words harsh.

What could she say? If she told him about the questionnaire, there was no way he'd ever speak to her again. Clutching her napkin tight in her fingers, she wished she could tell him the whole truth, that there wouldn't be any secrets between them. "I'd read about your inn, and it was so picturesque, so perfect."

"And you wanted to stay here." His eyes were hard.

She was certain she'd just lost any chance she had with him. "Yes, but then when I got here and realized that it was just couples…"

"You wondered how you ever got a booking here."

She nodded slowly. "When I found out that Scott had told the story of us being husband and wife in order to make the reservation, I was upset, and I…" She rubbed her forehead in desperation. This wasn't going well at all. "I should have told you the truth last night. I'm sorry."

"And you had no idea that your brother had said you were husband and wife in order to make the reservation?"

"I had no idea," she said, with a sigh of relief. Keeping the truth from him even for a few hours had been so difficult.

Her shoulders ached from the tension, her eyes hurt from lack of sleep. It was over now. Whether she wanted to or not, she couldn't stay here, especially now that Luke knew what outrageous lengths her brother had gone to in order to get her a reservation.

There was nothing she could say that would change what Luke thought of her and her crazy brother. Scott could find someone else to be his mystery guest. She didn't want the job.

"Now that you know the truth, there's no reason for me to stay." She pushed her chair back from the table, her appetite gone. "I'll pack my bags. This was a serious mistake, and I want you to know how sorry I am. I didn't mean to deceive you."

His scowl eased, and a smile edged the corners of his mouth. "Wait a minute. Are you saying you don't want to be my assistant for a few days?"

"I…I don't understand."

"Does it really matter why you came here? You're here. I'm facing the busiest season of the year, and I need help. If you own a beauty salon you know how to manage people and clients. I could use your expertise for a few days."

She couldn't believe her ears. "You mean it?"

"I do. You said you came here for the spa facility, and I could use your input on the spa. Anything you see that might be done differently or make the spa experience for our clients more enjoyable, I'd like to hear about it. I'm not into that sort of thing, but it's an important guest service. I'd be willing to pay your for your time and expertise. What do you say?"

She wanted to help him more than anything in the world. To have a chance to spend time with him without Scott's stupid marriage lie coming between them.

And after all, she'd come here uncertain of her future plans, and she'd been handed an opportunity to learn about a new type of business that involved the public.

Oh, yes, and she'd promised her lying brother that she'd do his damned survey, even though at the moment, it was her last priority. While she had her hair and nails done, and enjoyed a nice massage, she'd decide what to do about Scott.

She sighed in relief. "Sure, I'd love to stay, but you don't have to pay me."

"I want to."

"No, you don't have to pay me. You've given me an opportunity to stay here and give you input on your spa. But, what if somebody's wife gets upset...."

"Stay close, keep a low profile and let me worry about the rest."

Sticking close to this man wouldn't be a problem. "You sound so sure."

He nodded. "I'm interested in your input. By the way, what does your brother do for a living?"

Not her brother again. "Mostly he makes my life miserable," she grumbled.

The sound of Luke's laughter filled the room. "Wish I had a brother to drive me nuts."

"I have four, take your pick. I'll trade you one brother for a month of R & R at your inn." She took a sip of her coffee, her mind luxuriating in the fact that she would get to spend some time with Luke after all.

"Well, that's settled. Welcome to the staff of The Mirabel," he said, his disarming smile doing strange and awesome things to her.

"I'd better eat my breakfast. I see you've already finished." She wasn't the least bit hungry, but a piece of toast might be a good idea.

He waved his hand, and a server appeared. "My assistant would like…" He arched his eyebrows at her.

"Toast. Whole wheat toast."

After the server left, Marnie smoothed her napkin over her lap while all sorts of thoughts swam through her head. "Running a place like this must have its challenges," she said. They made small talk as she sipped her coffee, and the pretty, young server returned with her toast.

Once she'd finished it, she wiped her lips on her napkin and placed it beside her plate. "So, I have to get to my manicure appointment, only I don't know where the spa is."

He pointed toward an archway leading from the dining room to a back corridor. "Straight through there, and to the right. Can't miss it."

"Thank you."

"See you in my office when you're finished."

THE DOOR TO THE SPA was a deep mahogany-red with gold letters announcing Spa Delights. Marnie eased the door open and a woman with a mass of long red hair and a welcoming smile greeted her. "I'm Francine, and you must be Marnie McLaughlan. Love your name, by the way. Not a common name in these parts."

"Probably not anywhere else, either," Marnie responded, instantly liking this woman.

"You're booked for hair and nails first, so I'm going to take you to Lucy, who'll do your nails, and then to Eileen for your hair. Your massage will be with me. How does that sound?"

"Wonderful." She followed Francine to where Lucy waited at the manicure table.

"Enjoy yourself. I'll see you later."

Marnie studied her half-chewed nails and torn cuticles before holding them out to Lucy. She'd been so preoccupied with selling her salon that she hadn't bothered to have her nails done. Not a great advertisement for someone in the business...well, not in the business much longer. "Looks like you've got your work cut out for you," she said.

Lucy grinned and put a bowl of warm, soapy water in front of her. "Let's start with your cuticles."

The woman worked away on Marnie's nails, and although she was friendly, her technique was lacking. She didn't get out a new emery board for the nail filing, and she smeared the polish remover over Marnie's fingers instead of just on the nail beds. Because this spa would have few repeat clients, it ought to be using disposable tools or putting those nondisposable tools through a thorough cleaning process. Fungal infections were easily spread by lack of proper clean technique and hard to get rid of once a nail was infected. As for the nail polish remover, the drying effects of the solution would dry the cuticles even more.

She made a mental note of deficiencies she'd experienced with the manicurist. The selection of hair products Eileen used on her was professional with lots of client choice. She didn't have her hair cut or trimmed, so she'd have to leave those questions unanswered. Once Eileen had finished blow-drying her hair, Francine appeared and led Marnie to a room where muted light and soft music created a restful space.

Once she had positioned herself on the state-of-the-art massage table, Francine began her massage, putting Marnie instantly at ease. "So, you're going to be Luke's new assistant."

"Wow! News travels fast."

"This is a very close-knit group of people, and we all care about Luke. He's been through so much."

Marnie couldn't resist the subject of Luke. "I was told his wife died."

"In a car accident just before Christmas three years ago. You can't imagine what a sad place the inn was that year. He wanted to cancel all the reservations, but everyone pitched in and took over for him. He was incapable of anything other than tending to Ethan. We were all afraid he might have a nervous breakdown."

"He loved his wife a lot," Marnie said, wishing that someone might love her that much some day.

"He did. And she loved him, but Anna was headstrong and determined about everything. If she'd listened to him when he told her to stay in Boston that night, maybe she'd still be alive today. And that's the part Luke struggled with for months after she died, and still does."

"She probably just wanted to get home to her husband and child."

"That's true, but I don't know if Luke saw it that way. And how could he when what she did destroyed his life, and left his son without a mother?"

"But surely he can't believe his life is over. A man like Luke shouldn't have any trouble finding someone to love."

Francine sighed. "He's shut himself off. It's as if he can't bring himself to care for another woman. His whole life is Ethan and this inn."

"How different his life must be now."

"Luke's been lucky to have Mary Cunningham. She's been like a grandmother to Ethan, and Luke couldn't have managed without her. We all take turns babysitting Ethan when we're needed."

"It does sound like one big family."

"Even more so since Anna died. Luke passed up a promotion five years ago because he wanted to stay here. With Ethan in his life now, he's even more determined to stay put."

Angus McAndrew and his management team probably wouldn't understand a man who wouldn't take a promotion because of his attachment to a community. They'd want to know if the manager was operating the inn with the intention of supporting his staff, rather than supporting their profit goals. "What if the manager's job here wasn't available?"

"He'd look for a job in the area," Francine said with certainty.

"You have to admire someone who knows what he wants."

"Well, you'll find out soon enough, Luke can be a very demanding boss."

Francine finished the massage, and Marnie regretted that she couldn't simply stay and have a nap. "That felt so good."

"I'm pleased, and I hope you like your job here at The Mirabel Inn. I don't know if anyone told you this, but Anna was Luke's assistant before he proposed to her. He hasn't had an assistant since they were married, so you must be pretty good at what you do."

It was so weird to feel flattered over something that wasn't really true. Luke hadn't picked her to be his assistant because she was good at it. He picked her because he felt sorry for her. "Thank you for the massage."

"You're welcome, and I'm sure we'll see you around."

Marnie signed the bill to her room and left. Her cell phone was buzzing where she'd left it on the top of the dresser when she unlocked the door. She checked the call display.

"Scott, what do you want now?"

"Is that any way to greet your dear brother?"

"Skip the chitchat. What do you want?"

A moment of silence was followed by an exaggerated sigh from Scott. "I guess I want to know why you're in such a bad mood."

"You told Luke Harrison that you'd arranged a trip to this inn as a surprise for me, your beloved wife, and then you said that business had called you away."

"Whoa! You and this Luke guy must be getting pretty friendly for him to have shared that information with you."

"Friendly or not, you had no business lying…again."

"I'm sorry, Marnie. I wanted to fix things, to make your stay there as easy for you as possible. I had no idea that you and he were close enough to discuss such things."

Did her brother have no scruples? "What do you want?"

"Mom is calling me wanting to know when you'll be back. I told her three days, but now she wants to talk to you. It seems your Mrs. Claus suit arrived today."

Because she was the only one in the family who was single it was assumed she would be available for whatever anyone in the family needed, and she was sick of it. She wanted to enjoy her time here with Luke, she didn't want to be here under false pretenses, and what she wanted mattered. "I'll worry about Mom later. And I'm not going to do your mystery-guest thing."

"You what?" Scott yelled.

Scott never yelled. He had too many other techniques for getting what he wanted. She held the phone away from her ear for a moment. "You heard me."

"Listen, you promised you'd do it, and I need it done. In case you've forgotten, you'll have a great vacation on me afterward, along with a friend. This isn't fair. I can't go back to Advantage and tell them that my little sister chickened out, can I?"

"You tell them anything you want. I quit."

"Then I'll cancel your trip to Hawaii, and bill you for your room."

"You wouldn't."

"A deal's a deal."

"I'll pay my own bill."

"And sit in a strange inn for the next few days at your own expense? Why would you do that?"

So that she could simply enjoy her time with Luke, her conscience clear while she got to know the man. But what if there was no relationship to pursue with Luke? What if it turned out that she'd wasted all her money, and made her mother upset, simply to chase a dream?

Besides, she couldn't tell Scott her real reason for wanting to stay, especially if it turned out like so many of her relationships. The questions weren't difficult, and the forms shouldn't take long to complete, and if it meant so much to Scott that he was willing to lie to get a booking here, it had to be important. "Okay. I'll finish your survey."

"That's my sister," he whooped.

"It means that much to you?"

He didn't answer right away. "Yeah, it does. Thanks. And I'm sorry for lying to get a booking."

Her brother actually sounded sincere. Could he be going through some sort of seismic personality shift? No. Not Scott. "I've got to go."

"Stay in touch," he ordered, the old Scott back in charge.

LUKE SAT IN HIS OFFICE, staring out at the back lawn that swooped up the hill to a line of spruce and fir trees. Winter had been late in arriving this year, but if the weather report he'd just read was correct, Mother Nature was about to make up for it by dumping eight inches of snow on the region. The storm was slowly making its way up the eastern seaboard and had already brought traffic to a halt in parts of Delaware.

But with Christmas Eve two days away, he had bigger issues on his mind. He'd reviewed the menus for the entire week, remembering to keep the season festive while meeting the whims of his guests and the constraints of the impending weather. He loved the Christmas Eve dinner they held for the guests. Some of the recipes on the menu were from a local cookbook that his mother had given him when she and Dad had sold their beachfront condo on Kiawah Island, South Carolina.

"Hope I'm not late," Max Anderson said, coming into the office and closing the door behind him, a sheaf of printouts in his hand.

"No, not at all. I've just been going over our menus for the next week, and checking on the weather report."

"Me, too. I hope Jack's baby doesn't decide to arrive in the middle of a snowstorm."

"I've offered Lindsay and Jack the Hummer if they need it. I tried to convince him to stay home, but he said he'd wait and see what the weather was like." Luke remembered the day Ethan was born, how overjoyed he and Anna felt.

Max pulled up a chair next to the desk. "Well, we need to go over our menu contingency plan in case the storm causes delivery problems. "

They worked on how they'd manage in the event of a storm, should the weather make the roads impassable. Max was like a brother to Luke, and when Luke had taken the job at The Mirabel Inn, he'd convinced his friend to move up with him, leaving a hotel job he had in Virginia.

After three cups of coffee, Luke felt they were prepared for anything. Max had agreed to order additional essentials right away, just in case.

When they were finished Max leaned forward with a quizzical look on his face. "By the way, I just had a strange experience. I was walking past the library when I spotted a woman sitting near the window. She was running her fingers over the windowsill, and then she got up and walked around the room, checking the tabletops and the fireplace mantel." Max rubbed his head. "If I didn't know better, I'd say she was checking for dust. Thank God Mary was nowhere in sight. She's got little tolerance for anyone who dares to imply that the cleaning isn't up to par."

"That's odd. What did the woman look like?"

"She was around five foot five, with short dark hair, and she was wearing a pair of jeans and a bright orange T-shirt. The couples taking part in the Christmas Getaway event must be younger than I thought."

Luke had a pretty good idea who was loitering in the library. She should have been in his office with him, not out there drawing attention to herself. "I'll look into it," he said, getting out of his chair and heading for the library.

He didn't want it to be Marnie. He'd explained to her that it would be best if she didn't wander around too much by herself, and raise questions in the minds of the other guests. And what was she doing in the library checking for dust? Unease rose through him, followed by annoyance. Last night she'd been asking questions about the bar and now she'd been inspecting the library when she was supposed to find him after she finished up at the spa.

When he first reached the library the room appeared to be empty. Then he saw her over by the windows that overlooked the side lawn. The morning light caught the blue and crystal ornaments on the Christmas tree a few feet from where Marnie sat. The whole room glowed with a magical light, the air filled with the scent of pine and cinnamon.

She hadn't noticed him yet, her attention focused on the cell phone in her lap. She seemed so alone, her expression sad. He had a sudden urge to protect her from whatever made her feel so bad.

She turned, her eyes aimed directly at his. "I went

looking for you, but Amanda said you were in a meeting."

"And I was looking for you earlier so you could attend the meeting. All part of you being my assistant," he said, hoping she'd explain what she'd been doing in this room.

"Well, we're together now." She closed her cell phone, a hint of amusement capturing her eyes as she continued to look at him. Was she teasing him? The idea had its appeal.

What he wouldn't give to be able to sit down beside her and talk about anything and everything except work. How long had it been since he'd had a conversation that wasn't about the inn, its operation or its guests? And why did it suddenly matter to him?

That odd, totally unexpected feeling he'd experienced when she'd agreed to stay and be his assistant had left him perplexed by how easily she'd slipped into his life, his thoughts—and now she was making him want for things he hadn't missed before.

When she'd told him she wasn't married, that her brother had made up the story to get her a reservation, he'd been so damned glad he'd wanted to get up and dance. Marnie had turned his life on its end, and he was thankful for the distraction.

"This is an awesome room," she said, her gaze sweeping over the dazzlingly lit space, and coming to rest on the silver-and-blue tree.

"It is. Someone told me you were checking the windowsills for dust. Is there a problem? Or did Mary enlist your help?"

"No. I…I thought that while I was waiting I'd come in here and check it out. When you run a hair-and-aesthetics salon, checking for dust and dirt, straightening piles of magazines becomes automatic. Sorry if I caused you concern."

Her answer made sense and she seemed perfectly sincere. She was here, and she was trying to be helpful, and he could use her knowledge to improve the operation. "Forget it."

"I have a few notes from my visit to the spa. I've been checking email on my cell phone while you finished your meeting."

"Why don't we go to my office and you can fill me in on your spa experience?"

"I'd love that, but I need to make a call first. Do you mind? I'll just be a couple of minutes."

"Not at all," he said as he got up and started for the door. "I'll be in my office."

As he left the room, he spotted Brad Parker coming down the hall. Brad wasn't one of his favorite guests, too much of a bragger, but Luke appreciated the repeat business. "Hello, I hope your stay is going well."

"It is. My wife and I are just about to go into Wakesfield for a little lunch and shopping."

Brad looked distracted, and wanting to offer assistance, Luke said, "Can I help you with anything?"

"No, I thought I'd look for a book in the library, something to read," he said. Brad Parker didn't strike Luke as the kind of man who read anything beyond the sports section of the newspaper.

"You've come to the right place. The library has lots of reading material."

Brad glanced past him, a preoccupied look on his face. "Thanks."

Luke turned and watched him go down the hall toward the library, Jack's words playing through his mind. Had Marnie and Brad arranged to meet in the library?

Was Marnie's excuse about making a phone call simply a cover while she waited for Brad? Rolling his shoulders to ease the sudden tension he felt there, he went to his office and closed the door.

MARNIE COULD FEEL THE HEAT rising through her body as she sat glued to the chair in the library, surrounded by the breathtaking Christmas decorations. Luke suspected her of something, and she'd nearly been tripped up over the dust business.

He must have spies everywhere because she'd only checked a couple of surfaces before sitting down near the tree to take in the sheer beauty of the room. She loved all the decorating and baking that came with the Christmas season. No wonder her mother was bugging Scott to know where she was. This time of year she normally spent all her free time at her parents' house or out Christmas shopping with her mother.

Last week she'd decorated her salon to look like Santa's workshop and all her clients loved it, as did the children coming in for new haircuts for the many Christmas concerts and recitals taking place around town. But she had to forget about Christmas for the moment.

Just before Luke arrived, she'd had a text message from Scott asking her to call him right away. Could it be that Advantage Corporation had reversed their decision about the sale?

Her brother answered on the first ring. "Marnie, how's it going? How many of the questionnaires have you finished?"

She turned away from the door, and moved to stand by the window. "Three so far. Don't worry, I'll send them to you soon."

"Well, get a move on. Advantage wants to finish up earlier than planned."

"Scott, I need more time."

"I've got Mom breathing down my neck about where you are. I've got Advantage looking for results right away—as in yesterday—and you want to hang out at the inn and do some more navel gazing," he said, his disbelief on overdrive.

"I can always quit," she threatened.

"No, don't do that! Just get a move on. How's it looking, anyway?"

She lowered her voice. "For your information, I'm pretending to be the manager's assistant so that I'm not seen as a woman on the make, after somebody's husband. Then I had to correct your lie about us being married, and if I'm not careful, I could still be asked to leave. So now would be a good time," she said.

"A good time?"

"To thank me for saving your precious hide where Advantage is concerned."

"Oh, yes, thank you."

Was there a slight hint of condescension in his words? There better not have been. "And if that's not enough, the manager doesn't trust me, and the staff are reporting to him every time anyone sees me do anything suspicious." She peeked behind her to be certain no one had entered the room. "They're probably watching me now."

"Did you tell the manager you were working for me?" Scott asked, his tone stiff.

"No. But I had to tell him you and I are brother and sister not husband and wife. And thanks for making him think I'm a complete nutcase."

"What did he say?"

She chewed away at her new nail polish. "Not much."

"Why do you care what the manager thinks of you? You're there to do a job, and there's been a…a small problem which you took upon yourself to fix. But everything is fine, isn't it?"

"Sure, Scott. Everything is peachy, and I'm doing the survey work as fast as I can. Which reminds me, I'm expected in the manager's office. I've got to go."

"And you'll call me this evening and give me an update?"

"I'll think about it."

"Well, you may have lots of time to think because there's a blizzard headed your way."

Great! All she needed was to have Luke discover what she was doing there, and be unable to make her escape because of a snowstorm. As soon as she was finished in Luke's office, she intended to find a gas station. If she had to leave suddenly, she'd need a full tank of gas. "Thanks for the warning."

She slammed her phone closed and stared out the window. "Damn. What next?"

"Some things never change, Marnie."

She whirled around at the sound of Brad's voice. Had he been standing there all along, hidden so she couldn't see him? "What are you doing here?"

"I'm a guest, remember? Was that your brother on the phone?"

Did he overhear her talking about the questionnaire? He couldn't have. She'd been too far from the door, and she'd kept her voice down. "No."

"What are you doing here during this week? Are you married?"

"No, I'm not," she said. "I'm working for the manager for a couple of days."

"What about your salon?"

She didn't want to have this conversation. "I have to go."

He shoved his hands into the pockets of his jeans. "Suit yourself."

"And it would be a good idea if we made a point of avoiding one another. I don't want any trouble with your wife."

"Agreed."

She ducked past him, wondering what it was that she'd ever seen in him, how she could have ever thought she loved him. Marnie felt sorry for Cindy. Loving Brad was a losing proposition, at least in her experience.

When she reached the door to Luke's office, she knocked and was greeted by his welcoming voice telling her to come in. "Thanks for waiting," she said.

"As I was leaving the library, I saw one of our guests, Brad Parker, heading that way. Did you see him?"

Did he suspect that she and Brad had a connection? "Yes, but only for a moment." She sat down in the chair next to his desk, close enough to touch him.

He frowned, but didn't say anything.

To fill the awkward silence, she grabbed onto the first topic that came to mind. "My partner, Shane, and I co-owned a spa and salon called Total Elegance for ten years."

"And what was your area of expertise?" he asked.

"I was a hairdresser."

"It won't be easy to end that relationship, will it?"

She met his gaze and saw the sincerity in his eyes… and something more. "No, it won't be easy to leave, and that's part of why I need a little time to be sure that selling is right for me. We've agreed to everything, I simply haven't signed the papers. Shane wants to move on with his new bride. They're in love and he wants to make her happy."

"Do you feel you're in the way?"

Did she? "Yeah, a little. Selling my half of the salon has left me feeling a bit lost. It was so much a part of my life all those years."

"I know how it feels to care about a place, about a business. That's how I feel about this inn." His voice held a hint of melancholy. "The owners have never spent a day here, but they make all the major decisions on the financial viability of the inn, while I've put my heart and soul into this place."

Marnie could see the passion in his eyes, a passion she wished she felt for her shop. "If only I felt as strongly about my business as you do about the inn."

"But you don't."

She drew in a deep, cleansing breath. "No, I don't. Isn't that weird? I didn't sign those papers because I was afraid I might miss the salon, but hearing you talk about the inn…that's how I should feel."

"Then, there's your answer. You've made the right decision."

It felt so good to share her feelings with him, to hear him endorse her decision to sell. He may be a stranger, but she appreciated his opinion all the same. "Thank you for saying that."

"I was just telling you how I really feel," he said, leaning toward her, his arm resting on the corner of his desk.

He was close enough to kiss her. "Thanks," she murmured, hyperaware of his lips, the cleft of his chin and the rise and fall of his chest beneath his cotton shirt.

He took her hand in his, and interlaced his fingers with hers, sending a jolt through her. A day ago, she would've been happy with flirting and casual sex, but now she wanted—no, needed—to be with him, to share her feelings with him. To find the kind of intimacy that didn't revolve around bedroom gymnastics.

She'd never felt this way before and it frightened her. How could she have dated all those other men, nearly married Brad and never felt this kind of need, this sense that she had finally found the right one?

"I believe we're going to make a good team," he said, his breath hot on her cheek, forcing her heart to beat harder.

"Did you want to hear about my spa experience?" she asked, fighting to resist his mouth and what it offered.

Leaning closer, he kissed her gently, slowly, deliciously while his fingers traced the skin of her neck. She had wished for this sort of kiss all her life. This man—whose heart beat beneath her fingers—could, if he chose, claim her body and soul.

He eased away from her. "I've wanted to do that since you arrived here. Even when I still thought you were married." He gave her an apologetic smile.

His kiss left her wanting more of him, and she scrambled to regain her composure. This was moving way too fast for her. "Would…would you like to hear about the spa?"

"If you'd like to tell me, I'm ready to listen," he said, his eyes on her.

Her head spinning, her heart thudding from the loss of his touch, she swallowed hard.

She tried not to fumble her words as she went over her assessment, all the while fearing that he might be upset when he heard what she had to say. But he didn't seem to be bothered by the negative things she said about the spa. Instead, he leaned back in his chair, tented his fingers over his lips and studied her. "Is that all?"

She felt lost, discarded, missing his closeness. "What do you mean?"

"I wondered if there was anything else you had to tell me."

Was he talking about Brad? He couldn't be, and there was nothing to tell there, anyway.

Oh…God…in her eagerness to show him how smart and capable she was she'd rhymed off the survey points on the questionnaire she'd filled out for Advantage. Guilt began its slow assault on her mind. How could she be sitting here kissing this man while she still held her heartless little secret?

What if he'd had a mystery guest before, and then been confronted with the results? If he'd refused a promotion it might have resulted in the company sending someone to check up on him. What if he knew she was doing a survey because he recognized the points she'd listed? Or what if the cleaning staff had found the notes in her room….

She stared at the desk to keep from looking at him, waiting for his words of recrimination.

## CHAPTER FIVE

LUKE FOUGHT TO CONTAIN the rush of desire engulfing him. He should never have kissed her, especially when, instead of focusing on his work, all he wanted to do was to kiss her again. It had been so long since he'd felt like this, long enough to fear that he might be jumping too soon into something he couldn't handle.

And Marnie? What was going on with her? One minute she'd invited him to kiss her, and the next she was acting guilty about something. *Had* she stayed behind in the library to meet Brad? What if her real reason for being here had to do with Brad Parker? He didn't care for the man, but surely he wouldn't bring his wife to the inn so that he could meet Marnie on the side.

He took a deep, calming breath.

Had she returned his kiss to keep him from being suspicious of her? If she was here to meet Brad, he would be disappointed and hurt. Sure, he was attracted to her, but that was his problem.

But if she was here for some other reason, what could it be? So far she'd checked out the bar, the spa, and was seen checking out the library. Added to that, he'd offered her the job of being his assistant while she was here—the perfect opportunity to see what was going on at the inn.

Did she work for a rival company? Maybe another hotel company had heard about his success with the

Christmas Getaway event and had sent her to report back to them about it. The Chancellor and other inns along the valley were always vying for clients, and she had refused to stay at the Chancellor....

But what if he had it all wrong? He'd been working really hard, and he had a tendency to be suspicious of people's motives, thanks to his parents.

"I think it's time you came clean about why you're really here," he said. "It can't be much fun for a single woman."

Her brow furrowed, her eyes focused on the corner of the desk, she said. "I told you why I'm here. To enjoy the spa...and to think about my future."

*Look at me when you say that. I don't want to doubt you.*

"So why agree to pose as my assistant when you could stay at any other resort and have all the free time you need?"

For one long heartbeat he waited, hoping she'd deny his insinuation that she was there under false pretenses.

Her gaze flitted past him to the other corner of the desk. "I'm a good multitasker. I can do the job for you with time to spare."

She wasn't much of a liar, yet he really didn't have any proof that she wasn't telling the truth—just his gut. He rubbed his face to hide his frustration. She hadn't answered his question directly—a response that would've allayed his fears—and it made him angry. What was he going to do now? As long as he was suspicious of her, he couldn't allow her access to his office.

He lowered his hands, the enthusiasm of an hour ago long gone. "I have an important phone call to make, and a few hours of work that you really can't be of much help with. Why don't you take a break and go downtown, visit the shops, think about your…future."

She blinked, and smoothed her hair. "I've never been to Wakesfield."

"Our guests love the shops, and I can give you the names of a couple of restaurants you might enjoy if you decide to stay for lunch."

"Thank you," she said, standing up, her shoulders back and her head held high. Luke kept his eyes on the wall above his desk, at the painting his parents had given him as a graduation present, trying not to remember that his parents were off in Australia now, and that he'd still not received so much as a card from them.

What he wouldn't give right now for a brother or sister or some other family member to whom he could confide his feelings about Marnie. He badly wanted to believe her—to have a funny, sexy woman to spend the next few days with, someone he could share his plans for the inn with, and who would understand his enthusiasm for the place.

Working with her would have been the perfect cover for getting to know her.

He took a deep breath and refocused his thoughts with grim determination. He needed to concentrate on the job at hand, to make this the best Christmas in the history of The Mirabel Inn.

FIGHTING BACK TEARS, Marnie managed to make her way up the stairs to her room. Scott had warned her that a storm was headed this way, but she didn't care. Let it snow. In the meantime, she needed to talk to Julie, to gain a little perspective on her life and to hear how things were going back at Total Elegance. But most of all she needed to get some distance from Luke and how mixed up he made her feel. Julie was the woman to help her with that.

She dialed her friend's number, her spirits lifting.

"Hello, and how is inn life treating you?" Julie asked.

"It's great." She swallowed. "Fantastic...really."

"What's wrong?"

"Nothing."

"Marnie, it's me, remember?"

Suddenly, she couldn't talk about Luke without crying. And Julie would want all the details. But she couldn't explain everything that had gone on to Julie or she'd be on the phone all day. "How's life at the shop?" she inquired, squeezing her eyes shut to keep the tears at bay.

"You mean, how is life with Gina?"

"That, too."

"Well, let me count the ways I dislike the woman. She's told all the staff that if they have staff or work issues, they are not to bother Shane with them. She'll handle them. Oh, and she sent one of your best clients screaming out into the street when she botched her color."

"You're kidding! Who?"

"Ellen Parsons, you know the ex Mrs. Martin Jones who had come into the salon for a new look in celebration of her newfound freedom. She got a new look, all right." Julie's tone was wry.

"Well, you can pull her card. She won't be back."

"Ellen's not the only one not coming back. The two shampoo girls gave their notice. It seems the word's out that you're leaving, and people are beginning to take stock of what life will be like under the new regime."

"What can I do?"

"You can come back, but as your friend, I know that's

probably not possible, and I respect that. But I have to tell you Total Elegance is no longer elegant. I assumed things would get a little weird around here, but I hadn't expected it to go strange so soon. And Shane...his life is about to be totally ruined."

She heard the catch in Julie's voice. "I'm here for you if you need me."

"Why did he have to ruin his life? If only Shane would wake up and see what he's doing!"

"We both know that's not going to happen."

"Which means you'd better sign that agreement pronto. Given Gina's behavior, Total Elegance is about to go down the tubes."

"And you? What will you do?"

"I'm not giving up on Shane. I know you think I should, but I love him, and it hurts to see what's happening. I managed to track him down in his office the other day, and he and I had a chat away from dragon ears, and maybe it's my imagination, but he doesn't seem quite so infatuated with the woman as he was."

"Don't read something into his behavior that isn't there, please, Julie. I don't want you getting hurt."

"Too late. I'm already hurt. But I've made up my mind. I'm sticking around. I'm not going to give up if there's any hope that Shane might come to his senses."

"Would it help if I didn't sign until you had a little more time to get used to the idea that Shane and Gina are running things?" She had no idea what this would accomplish, but she needed to offer her friend any support she could.

"No, I believe that if you sign now, it might make Shane see that his old life is over, that he has to face the reality of Gina screwing up everything. Until now, he's had you and me to keep the show on the road. You signing the papers may act as a wake-up call."

"You're serious?"

"Never more. Have you got the agreement with you?"

"Yeah, I wanted to read it through one last time."

"Well, read it and sign is my advice," Julia offered to a chorus of shocked words in the background. "Gotta go and break up the wolf pack snarling at the throat of our esteemed lady of perpetual bossiness."

"Go get her, girl. And tell Shane I'm going to fax over the signed agreement, will you?"

"You're sure?"

"Yes. I can't buy Shane out and it doesn't make sense to delay it any longer. If you're right about Shane, you may still be able to save him from Gina."

"Are you sure you're okay?"

"I'm fine. Go back to work."

"Will you call me later and let me know how things are going?" Julie asked.

"I will." She closed her phone and climbed up onto the window seat with its fabulous view of the grounds and the mountains in the distance.

Chatting with Julie had made her feel a little better, but she worried about Julie. Her friend was still in love with Shane, which meant that she would be very unhappy the day Shane married Gina. But Marnie had done her best to convince Julie to forget Shane and find someone else, to no avail.

And she wasn't doing much better on the love front. Even though Luke was suspicious of her, and had made her feel guilty, she'd never been more attracted to a man in her entire life.

For now, she'd put him out of her mind, sign her agreement and fax it to Shane. After that she'd reward herself with a trip into Wakesfield. Scribbling her signature on the document, she gathered her bag, her coat and scarf and headed downstairs to see if she could send a fax.

In the office, she discovered Mary working on a laptop, a distracted frown on her face. "Excuse me, but would you mind if I sent a fax?" she asked.

Mary rose and came toward her. "No, by all means, and it's so nice to see you. Are you enjoying your stay so far?"

"Very much." What else could she say? It wasn't Mary's fault that she was completely confused by her relationship with Luke, if it could be called a relationship.

She fed the pages into the machine and dialed the fax number at the salon, and then waited for the document to feed through.

"You've made a big impression on Ethan," Mary said, shuffling some papers on Luke's desk.

"He's so sweet." *And so like his father in many ways.*

"Luke loves him tremendously, and he is such a good dad," Mary replied softly.

"Yes, it's so obvious."

"And what about Luke?"

Marnie felt her cheeks warm. "He's been really kind to me."

"I hope you don't mind me saying this, but Luke doesn't often show his feelings where people are concerned."

"What do you mean?" Marnie asked, downplaying her curiosity by pretending to be absorbed in the form generated by the fax machine.

"Well, he's been alone for three years now and I've often wondered if he'll ever smile again—a real smile,

I mean. Sure, he's always kind and solicitous with everyone, but I can tell he's still so sad."

Why was Mary telling her this? "I'm sorry to hear that. It must be very difficult to care for a toddler while trying to get over losing your wife."

"It certainly is. And a day doesn't go by that I don't wish he'd meet someone."

"I can understand that. After all, you're friends and you care what happens to him," she said, feeling suddenly very sorry for the man who, only a short while ago, had been driving her crazy.

"You could help while you're here." Mary focused her clear gaze on Marnie.

"How?" she asked, the catch in her voice betraying her.

"Be his friend. He needs someone like you. I see how much happier he seems just in the past day with you around. He likes you, and he told me himself that he admires the fact that you ran your own business."

Basking in the compliment, she smiled. "That's very kind of him."

"He wasn't being kind. Believe me, Luke takes business seriously, and he meant what he said." Mary heaved a big sigh. "Which leads me to what I really want to say. I see the way you look at him, the way he looks at you. Don't let it be wasted. We get so few second chances in life."

"But...I don't—"

"I've said enough, and I'm sorry if I offended you. But I'm the one who made the booking for your stay here at the inn. The man pretending to be your husband wouldn't take no for an answer. Luke told me it was your brother and that you'd apologized for the misrepresentation. I have no idea why you're here, and it's really none of my business—unless your being here could hurt Luke." Her tone was direct. "He's a little too old to be my son, but that doesn't stop me from wanting what's best for him."

*Did it matter to anyone that she might also have a few concerns, that her feelings could also be hurt?*

"I hope that Luke and I can be friends. I'd like that a lot."

Mary nodded. "Thank you. And for what it's worth, I hope you enjoy being his assistant."

Once she'd escaped from the office, Marnie bolted for the parking lot, snow smacking her face as the wind careened around the corner of the inn. Brushing off the melting flakes, she kept going. She had more on her mind than a little of the white stuff. Besides, it was the time of year for snow on the ground. Who wanted a green Christmas?

Reaching her car, she tossed her purse onto the passenger seat and started the engine. She climbed back out, swept the snow from the windows, and got behind the wheel again. She gunned the engine as she swerved out of the driveway and down the hill toward town. When she reached the outskirts of Wakesfield she was forced to pull over as her pent-up emotions got the best of her. A car drove past her and she saw Jack at the wheel.

"Jack of the great martini," she mumbled as huge dollops of tears spilled down her face and onto her chin.

*If I had any sense at all, I'd turn around and drive back to Boston.*

Luke had been kind and wanted to help her, and what had she done? She'd lied to him. And she'd done it while fully aware of how much she hated the men she'd dated who had lied to her. She was a complete hypocrite. She'd behaved terribly and all because of what?

Why had she put the one relationship with even the tiniest bit of potential at risk? To please her brother? She balled her fists on the steering wheel. Even if she still had a chance with Luke—which she highly doubted when he learned that she'd spied on his inn to get information for the owners, information that could cause him problems—he would never believe another word she said about anything.

She had experienced firsthand the agony of discovering that she'd been lied to by Brad. It had destroyed all her hopes and dreams, and her ability to trust.

She stared out at the dark clouds heavy with snow and wondered what she should do. If she went back and told Luke about the questionnaire, he'd be angry with her, which would mean the end for them. And when her brother learned that she had told Luke he would be furious. She was trapped.

"I'm tired of all this!" she yelled at the windshield. She wiped her face and leaned back, her head on the headrest, completely at a loss as to what to do.

What if the attraction was all in her mind? Luke had been sweet and kind, but that didn't mean his feelings for her ran deeper. What proof did she have that Luke cared about her? So far, all he'd done was look dark and suspicious at her. The kiss they shared could have been just two lonely people easing their loneliness. Had her longing for a meaningful relationship driven her to believe that a single kiss meant something? After all, he'd tried to get her to leave. When that hadn't worked, he'd been determined to keep her away from his married guests.

*What sort of man asks you to leave? A man who doesn't want you there, you ninny! What more does the man have to do to convince you that his heart isn't in the same place as yours?*

Her mind made up, she cranked the key and her car sputtered to life. She'd do a little Christmas shopping, search for a couple of new sweaters to replace the ones she'd lost in the basement flood and have a quiet lunch before doing what she should have done first thing this morning.

Pack her bags and go where somebody gave a damn about her.

Forcing her worries to the back of her mind, Marnie parked her car by a meter on the busy main street running through Wakesfield, and shopped for her nieces and nephews and four sisters-in-law. She didn't shop for her brothers—a gift certificate at their favorite men's clothing store in Boston was what was expected of her each year. She spent the rest of the time picking out a few new sweaters for herself.

When she reached a quaint little diner on the corner across the square from the post office, Marnie spotted the perfect window seat with a panoramic view of the street. Feeling ready for a break, she settled in with a glass of red wine and a hamburger while she listened to the Christmas carolers strolling in the square.

She wondered if Luke ever came here. Maybe he'd sat right where she was sitting now, and watched the same scene she'd been enjoying. A pang of yearning clutched her heart, tightening her throat. Taking a deep breath, she focused her attention on the throng of people outside the window when out of the corner of her eye she spotted Francine scurrying along the street and waved to her.

Francine smiled, bobbed her head and pointed at her glass of wine.

Marnie nodded and then waited for Francine to come in and join her. "How are you?" she asked as Francine took off her jacket and sat in the chair across from her.

"I'm great! Can't wait for Christmas. What about you?"

"The same, really excited about all of it," Marnie said.

After ordering her wine, Francine leaned her elbows on the table. "Wow! Did you hear the latest weather report?" she asked.

"No, I didn't." Marnie put her glass down, glad to have someone to chat with and take her mind off things.

"Luke asked as many of us as possible to stay at the inn overnight in case the roads are closed tomorrow. I came here to pick up a few things before I head back over there. Do you need a lift?"

"I have my car, but thanks. That's really kind of you."

"Well, to tell you the truth, it's a little more than kindness." Francine toyed with the cocktail napkin under her wineglass. "You're the hot topic around the inn."

Luke would love that, she thought ruefully. "Why?"

"We've haven't seen Luke look happier than he has in the past twenty-four hours, and we're convinced it's because of you."

If his scowling and paranoia were seen as a happier version of Luke, she'd hate to see what he looked like when he was sad. "Luke looking happier makes me a hot topic?"

"I have to tell you. Luke has never allowed a woman in his office, except for Mary Cunningham, that is. Not since Anna died."

"And that's the basis for your conclusion? That he let me into his office?" she asked, skeptical, but with just a hint of hope rising to the fore.

"You have to know Luke. For the past three years the guy has spent his days grieving his wife, and believe me it's not a pretty sight. He's moped around for far too long, and we all want him to find someone new."

"Am I the first suitable candidate who's come along?" She frowned in disbelief. "You're telling me there are no available women his age in all of Wakesfield?"

"Oh, yeah, there are. And lots of them are interested in Luke. It's just that he's not interested in them."

Well, maybe she could hope that there was at least a granule of truth in what Francine was saying, which reopened the issue of whether she should go back home, or whether she should stay and find out if there was any chance that there was something between them. The coward in her wanted to hit the highway. She pushed up her sleeve to check her watch. Three-thirty. Her hamburger forgotten, she looked outside and realized that she could hardly see across the square to the post office. "If I'm going to leave, I'd better get a move on."

"Leave for where? The inn?"

"Yeah, the inn," she decided. "At least for now."

"Do I detect a hint of indecision in your voice?"

She shrugged and took one more sip from her wineglass. "I can't see any reason for me to stay."

"You mean that business over your brother?"

"How did you know about that?"

"You haven't lived in a small town, have you? Or worked at an inn before, right?"

"No, I haven't," Marnie admitted.

"Trust me. Everyone knows everything." Francine smiled. "I'm glad your brother isn't your husband, and I'm even happier that you decided to stay after you told Luke the truth."

There really were no secrets in this town. "Why?"

"Because, like I told you. I want the guy to be happy. Anna was my friend, but she's not here, and she wouldn't want Luke to be so lonesome for so long."

ON THE WAY BACK TO THE Mirabel Inn, Marnie replayed Francine's words. Everyone wanted Luke to be happy and seemed to believe that she was the woman for the job. The question was, did Luke?

With "Rudolph the Red-Nosed Reindeer" blaring on the radio, and her ancient snow tires spinning and catching on the ruts created by the snow, she turned up the driveway toward the inn. What she saw when she took her eyes off the road took her breath away. The falling snow softened the edges of the imposing old structure while the floodlights gave a gauzy glow to the elegant windows draped with cedar wreaths. The front door held the largest wreath Marnie had ever seen, and beyond it, a tall Christmas tree glittered in the lobby.

Marnie brought her car to a halt, enchanted by the sight. With the snow swirling around the driveway and wrapping the lovely old building in magical light, The Mirabel Inn was the most beautiful Christmas scene she'd ever witnessed.

What a romantic spot for a Christmas getaway! Who wouldn't love to be wined and dined in a place with this much grace and style? What a brilliant plan on Luke's part. And she'd thrown a monkey wrench into it all by showing up at the door.

Suddenly it all came together for her.

She was spying on this wonderful place for her brother, who was taking orders from people who didn't work here, who had no personal involvement and whose actions stood to hurt someone she had come to care about. Meanwhile, she was living a fantasy life as she gathered the information that could damage someone's career. It wasn't right, and she was sorry for her part in it.

She was packing her bags and heading back to Boston. Whether she and Luke stood a chance with each other she didn't know, but she didn't intend to go on lying to him. She'd tell him the truth, explain that she needed to go home, and she'd give him her home number in the unlikely event he did want to see her again. Then she'd call Julie and let her know to expect her late this evening. It would mean driving for long hours in the snow, but she didn't care. All she wanted was to escape with as little personal embarrassment as possible.

She pressed on the gas, and the car fishtailed in response, nearly going off the narrow driveway. She turned the wheel to correct the swerve, and gently moved her car forward to park near the entrance. Thank heavens she'd be out of there soon, and safely on her way back to Boston and away from this storm.

As she turned off the ignition, she noticed a man stood framed in the open door, the light blazing around him. She looked up at him, realizing too late that it was Luke.

*Here's your chance.*

Mesmerized by the sight of him, she was unable to look away as he came around to her side of the car. As he opened her door a blast of snow covered Marnie, making her gasp. "Isn't this beautiful?" she commented, getting out of the car, forgetting all about her parcels and barely remembering to grab her purse.

"It is. Certainly not a night to travel," he said, his words whipped away by the blowing wind.

She gazed up into his face to see a look in his eyes she'd only ever seen on her brothers' faces before, when she'd first come home after her accident. A look that made her feel protected and warm, despite the icy air. "Is the weather report that bad?" she asked, following him to the front door.

"Worse, actually. It looks like we're in for a bad storm. I'll get someone to park your car. We've already had several cancellations for tomorrow, and we're getting organized in case there's a power outage."

What? She'd finally made up her mind, and she was about to be stopped by a storm? Not likely. "Guess I'd better hurry, then, before they close down the roads," she yelled at his back.

"Hurry to do what?" he demanded, stopping so abruptly she bumped into him.

He turned and grabbed her shoulders. "What are you talking about?"

"I…I think it would be best for everyone if I left."

He scowled at her as the snow created a mantle of white across his broad shoulders. "You are not leaving here tonight under any circumstances," he ordered. She saw the raw fear in his eyes. Was he remembering a storm three years ago? A storm that took his wife from him?

He put his arm around her shoulder and drew her close as they walked in step up to the door. "I was looking for you to tell you that there's no reason for you to leave—storm or no storm."

"Really?" Her heart jumped in her chest.

She was afraid to leave and afraid to stay, but a storm that threatened to close the roads meant she had no choice but to remain here. "I guess I'll just hunker down and wait for the snowplow tomorrow morning," she said, happy to know that he wanted her to stay.

"The plows may not be here in the morning, more likely the afternoon, but we'll see how much snow we get." He held the door for her as they walked together inside the inn.

Walking beside him, visions of spending a romantic

night in front of a roaring fire while snow swirled out-side the window sent her imagination into overdrive. But Luke clearly had something on his mind, if the set of his jaw was any indication.

She peered up at him to discover that he was frown-ing at something down the hall.

*So much for romance.*

She was nursing her bruised fantasy when he sud-denly stopped by the tree. "Marnie."

He said her name as if he wanted to say more, so she waited.

*Go ahead, set yourself up for a fall. You're an expert in that department.*

The grandfather clock broke the silence as it struck five o'clock. "Did you need to talk to me about some-thing?" she asked, still clinging to the hope that she might have a chance with him.

He brushed the smattering of snow off his shoulders. "No, it can wait until tomorrow."

Damn! She was losing patience with him. Couldn't he see that she was interested in him? Didn't he want a life outside of working long hours? Or maybe Francine and Mary didn't know everything there was to know about Luke Harrison.

Two could play this game. He didn't trust her. He'd said as much, and there was no obligation on her part to trust him. "Sure, fine. Tomorrow." She pushed her purse strap farther up her shoulder, spun on her heel and marched up the stairs to her room.

# CHAPTER SIX

LUKE TRIED NOT TO LET disappointment take hold as he watched Marnie retreat up the stairs. The truth was he didn't want her to go. For the past hour he'd feigned interest in the hall decorations, checked the dining room twice and basically stuck close to the front door, waiting for her to return. Even the staff had left him alone—waiting, he supposed, to see what he'd do when Marnie came back to the inn.

Then he'd blown it because he couldn't find it in his heart to let go of his fear that he wasn't ready for a relationship, that letting Marnie into his life was risky. After all, she had deceived him—although perhaps not intentionally—by letting him believe she was married when she wasn't.

As for the matchmaking efforts by the staff, he realized they were acting out of genuine kindness and a desire to see him happy. He appreciated their wanting him to be happy, but he was struggling to hold up his end of the bargain. A few moments ago, he'd shot a hole in their hopes by standing there like an ox, saying nothing. Was he afraid of being hurt? Or had he simply not been able to shake the feeling that there was something about Marnie's behavior that continued to trouble him?

Or was he simply out of practice when it came to making conversation with a beautiful woman? He'd never had a problem talking to a woman in his entire life. Actually, most of the time he didn't have to do much talking because the women did it for him. Anna was the first woman who had drawn him out, seen beyond his outgoing facade to find a man who had lived a pretty lonely existence despite the fact that he never lacked for women or friends.

For the first time since Anna's death, he found himself attracted to a woman, and he didn't seem to be able to do much about it. Why hadn't he simply asked her what he'd wanted to ask? What held him back?

"Daddy!" Ethan squealed, racing toward him, his arms flung open.

Luke scooped him up, hugging him close, pleased as usual to see his son. "What are you up to? Were you helping to make cookies again?" he asked. "How many did you eat this time?"

"I painted a picture for you. In your office," Ethan said, bristling with indignation.

Mary came along behind him. "I was about to get Ethan his dinner before I put him to bed, but he wanted to see you first."

"Daddy, we're having chicken fingers. You want some?" His bright smile returned, lighting the room.

"No, partner, not tonight." His gaze moved to Mary, who gave him a quizzical smile. He always ate with Ethan whenever he could, but tonight he was restless, edgy.

"Why?" Ethan placed his hands on his father's cheeks and pressed while he looked up into his eyes. "You like chicken fingers."

"I do, but not tonight," he said, trying to smile around his pinched cheeks. Luke seldom was able to resist the pleading look in Ethan's eyes. "Daddy's got something he needs to do tonight."

"Are you going out in the snow? Can I come?" Ethan asked.

"No, I'm not going out in the snow, and neither are you."

"All right," Ethan said, his eyes downcast, his voice full of genuine sadness. He pushed away, his signal that he wanted Luke to put him down. "See you later."

"Enjoy your chicken fingers," he called to Ethan as Mary took his hand and led him down the hall.

Ethan made a growling sound and smiled at his father over his shoulder.

He loved his son with every fiber of his being, a love that was as deep and powerful as it was unexplainable. He'd had no idea how much having a child could change his life until Ethan was born. He envied Jack and Lindsay. His friends had so much to look forward to with the impending arrival of their baby. He'd always planned to have a house full of children, and he certainly never planned to have Ethan grow up as an only child.

Unable to shake the unsettling feeling that he should have asked Marnie to have dinner with him, he headed for the bar.

MARNIE LOCKED THE DOOR, and dragged out her laptop and paperwork, prepared to tackle Scott's questionnaire once and for all. Pretty sad when a woman had to seek solace in a questionnaire, but that was how it worked in her world this snowy evening. She sure couldn't appear at the bar and upset the boss, or the bartender. No, never that. And yes, she was feeling sorry for herself, but she'd earned the right to a little self-pity.

She shuffled through the papers until she found the housekeeping one she'd started to fill out, and found a section on the air-conditioning unit. She put a call in to the desk to ask that someone come and check her air-conditioning unit. The questions on the form were directed mostly at how technician behaved, how long it took to answer the call, how long the technician spent in the room and what the result was as it pertained to the condition of the unit. Simple enough.

She was still reading over the questions when the technician announced his arrival with a light tap on the door. He introduced himself as he entered the room. "I'm Kevin Bailey. I'm not sure what you need checked on your air-conditioning unit." He nodded to the window and the snow fluttering over the glass.

*Idiot!* "I meant to say the heater. It's all part of the same unit, right?"

"Yeah," he said, glancing doubtfully at the unit under the window. "But according to my records here, the unit was checked two months ago. Did you have a specific problem?"

What was she supposed to say to that? There was no problem. "I couldn't seem to get the heat to turn on," she lied. She hadn't attempted to turn it any higher than the automatic setting, but come to think of it, the room did seem a little chilly.

She climbed on the bed out of his way as he took the cover off the unit and peeked inside, flipping a switch and poking around.

He opened his tool kit and withdrew a pair of pliers, then unhooked a wire out and examined it closely. "Hmm," he said, sounding puzzled. "The wire is frayed." He sat back on his heels and looked up at her. "It's possible that because this room is to be renovated, a full check of the system wasn't done, or someone was careless. Whatever the reason, you might have started a fire with this—" he held the wire up for her to see "—if you'd tried to turn the heat any higher."

"Really," she said, imagining what could have happened if she'd been there that afternoon, felt chilly and tried to turn up the heat before taking a nap.

"You can't stay in this room tonight. I'll have to shut the unit down until it's fixed. I'll speak to Luke about it, and I'm sure he'll find you another room."

She'd have to report this. The instructions on the survey emphasized guest safety and this was a major deficiency on that front. Darn! Given how well the rest of the inn was cared for, she hadn't expected to have something serious to report on his inn that could reflect badly on Luke's management.

"Thank you," she murmured, worried for Luke and what this might mean for him when Advantage got the survey results.

She closed the door behind Kevin and leaned against it for support. As much as she wanted to, she couldn't lie about what she'd discovered, but that didn't stop her from wishing she could. A hotel manager had to put the safety of his guests first, the same as any other business that catered to the public. More than ever, she wanted to give up on the survey, and enjoy the rest of her stay here, and face her brother's displeasure when she got back to Boston.

She was still leaning on the door when someone knocked.

Had they arranged for her to change rooms that quickly? "Who is it?" she asked.

"It's Luke."

Her heart jumping into her throat, she opened the door and stood back. "Did you come to show me to my new room?"

He gave her a quick nod before glancing past her. "Kevin told me what he found, and I want to apologize. The unit was checked, but obviously not carefully enough. We've had some cancellations due to the storm. Mary will arrange to move you down to an empty room for tonight. If our guests are able to get here tomorrow, we'll have to move you back up here. But in the meantime, they'll fix your unit and you'll get to experience the kind of luxury we're known for around the area."

His apologetic smile warmed her body in all the right places. "That sounds perfect."

"And I also want to invite you to have a drink at the bar with me."

"A drink?" A drink would almost certainly lead to dinner, and who knew where else after that? And now that fate had granted her a fancy room with the implied promise of a big bed, she gave her fantasy life full reign. He would ply her with liquor; she'd eat her fill of beautifully prepared food, after which they'd make their way upstairs hand in hand….

But before she went for a drink she needed a couple of minutes in the bathroom to get changed, apply a little makeup. She could be dressed in a matter of seconds. She glanced around and to her horror spotted the open laptop and the files containing the survey questionnaires scattered across the bed.

He mustn't see them. Wedging herself between Luke and the bed, she smiled brightly. "I would love to have a drink with you, but first I need to change my clothes and freshen up a bit."

"You don't have to dress up for me." There was that smile again.

"But I've been out shopping and didn't get a chance

to change, and it would just feel better. You don't mind, do you?"

"No, of course not. Meet you in the bar when you're ready," he said, backing out the door, his eyes aimed at the piles of paperwork on her bed.

When the door was safely closed behind him, she gathered up the forms and her laptop and put them away in the bottom of her suitcase. There was no way she wanted him to discover what she hadn't had the guts to tell him. Worse still, if he found out on his own...

She couldn't let herself think about all that right now. After all, she'd been invited for a drink, and she deserved to have a little fun in her life. Once dressed, she finished packing her things for the move downstairs and zippered her suitcase shut for good measure—just in case they decided to change her room for her while she was out.

Down in the bar, Luke settled on a stool and accepted the Scotch and soda Jack passed him. "You were right. She seemed very pleased that I asked her to have a drink."

"See? I told you. She was probably waiting for you to ask her."

Encouraged by Jack's words, he grinned. "You think so?"

"Absolutely. You should have asked her to have dinner with you when you met her at the door."

*Was he that obvious?* "So everyone knows I planned to ask her to dinner when I met her at the door."

"Why do you think the lobby was empty when you walked in with her?" Jack rolled his eyes.

"Well, I'll be damned."

"We're just looking out for your happiness, since you

seem determined to avoid it. Francine says that Marnie was asking about you when she was at the spa getting her massage."

"And about the operation of the spa, or so Francine told me. Francine says she likes her, finds her easy to talk to," Luke offered, taking another sip of his drink, remembering that he was the one who asked for Marnie's opinion of the spa's operation.

"Yes, everyone likes her around here."

"Especially Ethan."

Jack laughed. "If Ethan likes her, what more can you want?"

"There's still something about her that bothers me."

"Hot and bothered?" Jack asked, his voice edged with laughter.

"I'm going to ignore that for the moment."

"I'll let you off this once." Jack assumed a serious expression. "Are you talking about what went on here in the bar last night?"

"No. Well, maybe a part of it. But did you know that she was checking for dust in the library? And when I asked her about it she claimed it was simply a habit she'd picked up when she ran her salon."

"So, she likes to ask questions, and she checks for dust, so what? If you want my opinion, I think you're simply afraid to go out with her. You're making excuses, that's all."

Luke rubbed his chin as he stared at his friend. "Me? Scared?" he bluffed.

"Yes. You. Scared. When I saw her today on my way here she looked like one unhappy lady."

"And you think I'm to blame for that?"

"Possibly. She's a single woman sleeping alone at an

inn hosting a couples getaway, and you're the only un-attached male here."

"So, I win by default?"

"No! Look, get your head out of your business for once, and start paying attention to life. This woman is here. You're here. And you could do a whole lot worse than a beautiful, unattached woman who could prob-ably use a little cheering up."

"So, you're saying we're a couple of people desper-ate to spend the evening together?" Luke teased as he eyed his friend over the rim of the glass.

"Cut it out, man! I'm only saying that it's time you found a woman for yourself. No more eyeing mine," he kidded, polishing a wineglass before hanging it on the rack.

"How is my favorite woman doing, by the way? Any labor pains?"

"No, but I'm not taking any chances. I'm picking her up on my break and bringing her up here to stay the night. The last thing either of us needs when this baby decides to arrive is for her to be at home and me to be here, and the road between us to be blocked with snow."

"Why don't you go now before the weather gets any worse? I'll take over the bar until you get back."

Jack gave him a questioning look. "Are you sure? Your hot date is due to arrive any minute."

"My hot date can have a drink with me regardless of which side of the bar I'm on. Besides, you forget I have privileges."

"Besides working eighteen hours a day? What other privileges would you want?"

"I can have the chef send dinner over to my apart-ment after you get back."

"Wow! Are you serious?"

The idea appeared out of nowhere, startling him. Since Anna had died, he'd never invited anyone other than staff into his apartment. "Certainly. Why not?"

Jack whistled. "You... She must be special."

Was she special? Maybe... But whatever ended up happening with Marnie, he was willing to sit back and and let the evening unfold. "My apartment isn't an ideal hangout for anyone over the age of four, and it's not somewhere I'd normally take a date." Remembering her enthusiasm for Ethan, he didn't think Marnie would mind being around Ethan's toys, books and videos. "An adult could sustain serious injuries climbing over Ethan's stuff spread over every flat surface in the place," he said, ruefully.

"Hey, it's a start. I'm proud of you, my friend—"

Jack nodded toward the door. "You got company."

Luke turned, and felt all available blood rush south of his belt. Standing in the doorway was the most stunning woman he'd seen in a long while. Stunning and smiling at him. He stood, letting the napkin in his hand drop to the floor.

She moved across the room, her stride, the provocative angle at which she held her head, and the shimmering blue of her top joining forces to suck the air from his lungs.

"I didn't keep you waiting too long, did I?" she asked, sliding up onto the bar stool next to him.

He hadn't a clue what time it was, and he sure as hell didn't care. "No, not at all." Unable to take his eyes off her, he clutched the edge of the bar and sat down, his head buzzing as her perfume wrapped around him. "You smell great," he said.

*God! Is that the best you can come up with?*

"Sorry. I must sound like an idiot to you." He fidgeted with his glass and watched her face for a reaction.

She touched his arm. "I'm flattered that you like my perfume. Between you and me, I wasn't sure when I bought it…. So expensive."

The skin beneath her fingers tingled, charging his senses. The space between them seemed to sparkle with excitement. He hadn't felt like this for years. He quietly breathed in her scent as he grinned at her. "Worth every penny, if you ask me."

"I'll be sure to tell the salesclerk at Macy's," she said, her eyes alight with humor as they searched his. Her very kissable lips were only inches from his…memories of their last kiss adding fuel to the fire in his belly.

"Hello, there, Luke. Some storm we're having. Where's Jack?" Walter Pearson asked as he and his wife, Mae, approached the bar.

Luke slid off his stool and glanced around. Jack had disappeared. "I'm taking Jack's place here for a little while," he said, going behind the bar. "He wanted to go home and get his wife, Lindsay. She's days away from having their son, and he didn't want to leave her alone, and I can't really spare him here. So we compromised."

"She's going to stay here tonight?" Walter asked.

"We have five empty rooms due to cancellations, she and Jack will have one of those. I'm encouraging our staff to stay here if they want to. It might mean putting up cots in the spa and the library, but whatever works. It's one nasty night out there."

"No kidding! I was coming down the stairs and happened to look outside. All I could see was blowing snow, and the wind is something else. Does it snow like this often up here?"

"Not for a long time. The past few years we've actually had some of the mildest winters on record for this region. Not good for the ski hills, but much easier for the locals to get around."

He was so relieved to be chatting with Walter Pearson, it was infinitely less embarrassing than gawking at Marnie. Marnie didn't seem to be aware of how gorgeous she was, and he found that a very attractive quality. She had a whole lot of other great qualities, starting with how unassuming she was....

*I could really like this woman. Really. Like. Her.*

But he had paying customers who were eyeing him quietly as they approached the bar. He turned his attention to Walter's wife. "What would you like to drink?"

"I'll have a glass of red wine, please," Mae said.

"And I'll have a Scotch, neat." Walter Pearson put his arm around his wife's shoulders. The sweet retired couple had been coming to the inn for the past six years and always insisted on the same suite. Luke enjoyed their company, especially Walter's stories about fishing salmon on the Miramichi River in Canada, told late in the evening after everyone but he and Jack had gone to bed.

"Coming right up," he said, taking down a bottle of Talisker Scotch and opening a bottle of Napa Valley Merlot. As he chatted with the Pearsons about the weather, he kept stealing glances at Marnie. He loved the way she slid forward on her stool and watched him tend bar, a smile on her lips.

When Mr. and Mrs. Pearson were settled with their drinks at a table in the corner, he served the other waiting customers before returning his attention to Marnie. "And what will you have?"

"I usually have a glass of white wine, but I've never personally known the bartender before, so I think I should be more adventurous. What's that?" she asked, pointing to the second shelf where the specialty liquors were lined up.

"It's sour apple liquor. You drink it over ice or it can be part of a martini."

"I've never had sour apple liquor in or out of a martini."

He ducked his head to look under the counter. "Jack has a drink recipe file here somewhere. I'll make one for you."

"Why don't you have one with me?"

"I'm drinking Scotch. I don't think it would make for a good mix. Besides, my evening is just getting started."

"Oh…sounds interesting." She winked at him.

She was flirting with him, and he suddenly was having second thoughts about how the evening would go. What was wrong with him? He wanted to spend time with her… "Not interesting, more like…snow-packed. A drink with you will be the bright spot of my night. After that I have to check on the weather again, email the guests who canceled and advise them that I'll be in touch tomorrow as soon as we know the road conditions. Then I might find a few minutes for dinner."

"Why do you have to email the guests? Can't someone else do it?"

"They could, but I believe in having personal contact with all my guests. And sure, I could get Amanda to email them using my email, but that doesn't seem very honest. Besides, I want to stay in touch with them. They're important to the inn and to me."

Afraid he sounded old-fashioned, he busied himself with putting together the ingredients for her drink in a martini shaker. He poured it into a martini glass and slid it across the bar toward her.

"I always call my clients to remind them of their appointments. Or I did..."

Was she missing her business? he wondered. "So, you understand where I'm coming from," he said, relieved to be talking business.

"I do, and if I were a guest here I would appreciate hearing from you." Her glance was both shy and direct, and it occurred to him that he was really enjoying himself.

"I doubt anyone would start out without checking the weather first, but so many people rely on their cell phones and messaging systems that I don't want to take that chance. And then there's the snow removal, and keeping doors clear so that people can get out in the case of fire—"

Damn! He was babbling like a teenager on a first date.

MARNIE TOOK A SIP OF her martini as she listened to Luke's chatter. He seemed very worried about the storm, his concern for his staff and guests making her like him even more. "This is a delicious drink, sort of sweet and sour at the same time. I'd like to have the recipe," she said.

"That's Jack's department, but I'm sure he'll give it to you."

"Tell me more about Jack. You say he and his wife are expecting a baby."

"Yeah, their first. They've been trying for years, and they're going to be parents any day now."

Marnie saw the longing in his eyes, the vulnerability, and wanted to reach out to him. Instead she directed the conversation to other things, fearful that if she didn't, she'd find herself behind the bar, touching him, telling him everything would be all right. "So, he's bringing her here for the night?"

"They're seldom apart these days, with good reason. I've kidded him about moving in here, but I was only half teasing. I've never seen two people more in love," he said, his tone wistful.

Walter Pearson appeared at her elbow, his Scotch glass in his hand. "I think I'll have another," he said, smiling at Marnie before turning his attention to Luke. "Isn't it time you introduced me?" he asked, nodding at Marnie.

"Marnie, this is Walter Pearson. He's a notorious cribbage player."

"It's nice to meet you," she said.

"Don't get too friendly with Walter or he'll regale you with his fishing stories." The two men laughed as Luke refilled his drink and passed it to him.

"You two youngsters have a good evening." Walter raised his glance in salute.

"I take it he's a bit of a character," she said, watching him return to his seat.

"He is, but he's also a friend. He was once the head of Obstetrics at one of the hospitals in Boston…can't remember which one. He and Mae don't have any children but they've been involved in all sorts of work with underprivileged kids around Boston, and still are, I believe."

"That's so nice. To care so much about the welfare of others."

"It's the secret to success in any line of work, don't you think? Or at least that's how I see it."

As he stood across from her, she suddenly became aware of his height, the width of his shoulders under his sports jacket. She wanted to stay here and let him keep looking at her just the way he was now. She'd definitely lucked out. Maybe her bad luck in the man department was about to become history.

"Starting out, most of my clients in the hairdressing business were friends from school, or friends of my family. But after that, it was word of mouth that brought in new clients."

"So you were good at what you did, with a client list to prove it. And now you've decided to sell your business?"

"I faxed the signed agreement today. I haven't heard back from Shane yet." Then again, she'd turned off her cell phone and hadn't checked her messages....

"Congratulations. So, what do you want to do now?" he asked, and there was genuine interest in his eyes.

No guy in her life had ever asked her what she wanted before....

"Marnie?" he prompted.

She clutched the stem of her martini glass tightly. "I would love it if my family would let me run my own life."

"I take it Scott leads the charge on that front."

"He does, but the others are right behind him."

"Why? Have you ever done anything that would make them think you couldn't manage your own life? Or am I prying into something that's none of my business?"

If Luke had been anyone else whom she didn't know well, she would've changed the subject, but his interest was genuine. It showed in his eyes. "No, it's fine. It all started because my brothers were older, and they were all fantastic athletes in high school and university. They all went to the best colleges and graduated at top of their class. Then I came along, and I'm neither a great student nor an athlete."

"But you've got a successful business, and now you'll have a chance to start over doing whatever you'd like. Are you considering going back to school?"

"Not really. Making a commitment to go back to school means I'd have to be really sure about what I want to do in life, and I haven't had enough time to think that through. I'd always wanted to be a hairdresser, but that's not true anymore. And getting the offer to buy out my half of the salon is a fantastic opportunity that I don't want to miss. It's a chance for me to reconsider what I really want out of life. The trouble is, I'll be subjected to so much unsolicited advice from my family this Christmas...."

"And you're not looking forward to that."

"I'm not. Oh, and Mom expects me to play Mrs. Claus at her annual holiday get-together."

His dark gaze moved over her face. "I'm having a hard time picturing that."

"Me being Mrs. Claus?"

"Yeah, it doesn't fit somehow. The image of you as a little round woman..."

"I'll take that as a compliment."

"I meant it to be one," he said, his smile warming her all the way down to her toes. "Your family sounds close, involved in each other's lives. I realize that's not always a good thing...." He wiped the counter and straightened the swizzle-stick jar.

The silence between them stretched, leaving Marnie suddenly unable to think of anything but the improbable image of Luke sitting at her parents' dining room table. "Sometimes, I wonder if I would have been better off if I were a boy."

"A boy? You'd never make it as a boy," he said, his eyes teasing.

The fire his gaze ignited deep in her body threatened to rage out of control. She wanted to jump across the bar and rip his clothes off, run her hands over every inch of his body. Instead she drew a long, deep breath into her lungs and forced herself to be calm and smile up at him. "So glad you think so."

He leaned across the bar, placing his hands on either side of hers as they gripped her martini glass. "If you had been a boy this evening wouldn't be happening," he whispered, his lips so close, his eyes capturing hers.

She leaned forward angling her head, her lips parted. "My good fortune," she murmured.

## CHAPTER SEVEN

THE LOOK IN MARNIE'S EYES did something to his core. He'd forgotten that feeling, that sensation that life was about to begin, that the waiting for that one special person was over. He touched her neck, his fingers picking up the tattoo of her heart beating against his skin. He had so much he wanted to say to her, to share with her. But at this moment, he couldn't remember any of it. All he wanted to do was kiss her.

And he did—gently—the tingling awareness of need floating through him. He angled his head slowly toward hers, cupped her chin and pulled her face closer to his, aching for more.

But he had to remember where he was…his job. A quick glance around confirmed that they were all but alone—the one remaining couple in the corner were completely engrossed in each other. "It might be smarter for me to come around the bar," he said.

He heard the deep chuckle that started in her throat and rose past her lips, the sexiest laugh he'd ever heard.

"Please do, before I'm forced to jump over it," she said.

He rounded the bar, pushed the bar stool out of his way and reached for her, holding her arms, feeling the silky softness of her top as he slid his hands up toward the bare skin at her throat.

He fought the desire tearing at his gut. He was making out with a woman in the bar at his inn, a place he was expected to behave like a civilized person, totally in control, but all that was quickly being submerged beneath the ache that began near his heart. "Do you suppose the guests will understand this?" he asked, not really caring about the answer.

"I'm supposed to be your date, aren't I? Wasn't this the whole point?" She raised her face to his, her eyes aware.

"So true," he whispered against her throat, his arms going around her, his fingers eagerly caressing her back. He kissed her again, tasting her lips, enjoying the way her body pressed into his. He stiffened, blood roaring in his ears. Lust blurred his thoughts, as he pulled back, afraid that he might frighten her with his demanding, pulsing need.

He heard her quick intake of breath, and suddenly the lights in the room flickered and went out. Off in the corner, two points of light flared.

"What's going on?" she asked, her fingers clutching his lapels.

"Didn't know I had that kind of power," he said, joking to hide his annoyance at the interruption. "The power just went out and the generator kicked in. Nothing to worry about."

The words had no sooner passed his lips when Kevin Bailey appeared at the entrance to the bar and waved to him, a heavy frown on his face. "Or maybe there is," he said, nodding in Kevin's direction. "I'd better see what's going on."

He crossed the room to meet an anxious Kevin. "Sorry, boss, but there might be a problem with the generator. Can you come and have a look?"

He knew next to nothing about generators, but if they

needed to make a repair he had better have a look before calling someone to service it in weather like this. "Be right with you."

Trying to hide his disappointment as much as possible, he went back to Marnie. "Sorry about this, but Kevin needs me."

"Should I wait for you?"

"Absolutely. I'll be back as quick as I can." He searched the room. "Don't know who will tend bar while I'm gone."

"I can. I've had lots of experience doling out Christmas booze at the McLaughlan clan get-togethers." She gave him a lopsided salute. "You can count on me."

"Thanks." He hugged her close, her body fitting perfectly to his, reigniting his driving desire. "There's a flashlight under the bar if you need more light until the power comes back on."

MARNIE WATCHED HIM LEAVE. She wanted to have dinner with him tonight more than anything she'd ever wanted in a long time. She spotted another couple entering the bar, their arms linked, their eyes on each other. And Marnie was suddenly flooded with a sense of yearning so strong she could hardly breathe, reminding her that she was once again alone during the Christmas season.

The newly arrived couple leaned on the bar, and Marnie remembered that she'd offered to be bartender. "Good evening. What can I get you tonight?"

"A little more light, maybe," the man joked.

"I'll see what I can do." She reached under the counter, brought out a large flashlight and placed it on the bar.

"White wine for my wife, and I'll have a gin and tonic," the man said, settling on a stool next to his wife.

Marnie fixed the drinks and was about to check with the other couple sitting in the corner when Jack came into the bar with his very pregnant wife beside him.

"Well, hello. Did Luke leave you in charge?" he asked as he moved in beside her.

"He did. But now that you're here, I'll go back to being decorative."

"Don't quit on my account. I was just going to get a glass of sparkling water for Lindsay. She's going to take a table near the bar and keep me company for a few hours."

"That sounds nice."

Jack introduced his wife to everyone as they gathered around him. From the talk it was clear that everyone knew Jack and Lindsay, and about their baby. Marnie didn't mean to stare but she couldn't help it. Her four sisters-in-law were big during their pregnancies, but Jack's wife looked as if she could have the baby any minute.

While Jack chatted with everyone, Marnie lit candles on each of the tables, and placed extras along the bar, in between filling drink orders. Several of the husbands chatted with her as they ordered drinks or returned glasses. In a way it was comforting to mix drinks and pour wine. It kept her from thinking about everything else.

She was pouring a glass of Chardonnay when Brad and Cindy showed up. For a moment, she considered walking out. After all, Jack could take over. But walking out was not her style, and besides, she'd had her say where Brad was concerned. "What can I get you?" she asked, secretly enjoying Brad's surprised expression.

"Marnie, it's so nice to see you again," Cindy said, a smile of genuine pleasure on her face.

"It's great to see you, too," Marnie replied.

"I didn't know you worked here," Cindy said.

"I'm helping out," Marnie answered, which was the truth. And she was suddenly appreciative that the years of bartending at family functions had paid off.

"Jack's letting you behind his bar—you must be good." Cindy leaned on the bar. "I'll have my usual," she said.

"One dry martini coming right up," Marnie said, aware that Brad had moved closer to his wife.

As Marnie mixed Cindy's drink for her, the other woman chatted about her trip to Wakesfield. "Why don't you and I go shopping tomorrow…as soon as the snow lets up?"

Marnie was tempted to say she'd go, if only to make Brad uneasy. It would be payback, and so tempting. But when she met Cindy's hopeful glance, she remembered that this woman deserved to be happy, that if Brad made her happy Marnie had no right to interfere.

Regardless of how much Brad had hurt her, she was no longer interested in any aspect of his life. And with that realization came a sense of freedom. Having met Luke, she realized that Brad had never been the man for her. "Cindy, that sounds great, but I'm working straight through until Christmas Eve."

"Well, maybe another time," Cindy said, looking at her husband with love in her eyes.

Another couple arrived at the bar and stood next to Cindy. They were obviously acquainted with one another and Cindy and the other woman immediately struck up a conversation.

Feeling completely calm and in control, Marnie turned to Brad. "What can I get you?"

"I'll have a Scotch…and thanks, Marnie," he said, softly, his gaze contrite.

"Not a problem," she said, reaching for the Scotch. "I hope you have a wonderful stay here."

"We will." He took the glass from her hands, his gaze locked on her. "And I hope you enjoy your stay, as well."

"I will." She turned from him to another couple, thankful that she'd seen Brad Parker for what he really was that night years ago.

A little later several of the couples drifted off to dinner, while others wandered into the bar from the early seating. But still no sign of Luke.

"Here, let me take over," Jack said, scooting around behind the bar. "Have you had dinner yet?"

*Where was Luke? What could be keeping him?*

"No, but I will. I hope Luke's okay."

"I'm sure he is. Why don't you have some dinner, and come back and sit down with Lindsay? She's worried she might go into labor tonight."

"Oh, dear. Well—"

Mary Cunningham appeared at the archway leading into the bar, her gaze sweeping the room until her eyes met Marnie's. She nodded and wove her way past the people standing in small groups. "I've brought you the key to your new room. I've moved your things, and tomorrow your old room should be ready for you again. I assume Luke explained all this to you," she said, handing her a large, ornate key.

Marnie's heart stuttered in her chest. She'd forgotten all about the room change and her things being moved. Then she remembered she'd hidden her computer and her papers in the bottom of her bag, away from prying eyes.

Mary stood waiting, staring at her. Did she expect

Marnie to leave with her? Had Luke sent Mary to deliver the key? What she wouldn't give to ask where Luke was and when he'd be back. It would be a simple inquiry, and one she had every right to make, but her pride wouldn't let her. Luke was busy, and she didn't feel she could interfere. She was a stranger here. A helpful stranger, but still a stranger.

But why couldn't Luke have spared a few minutes to come and tell her he'd be busy all evening? "Thank you, Mary. Would it be possible to leave Mr. Harrison a message?"

"Certainly."

Suddenly, she wanted to go home to her family, to the security of people who loved her. "Please tell him I'll meet him for breakfast tomorrow morning around eight."

She was tempted to tell him she'd be leaving as soon as the road was plowed. Although she handled seeing Brad again tonight with as much savoir faire as she could muster, she was tired of feeling like the odd person out, of being the one who had to adjust her life to please everyone else.

"Would you like to order room service this evening?" Mary asked, her expression kind.

Why not? Her brother was paying the bill, and she hadn't eaten since early that afternoon. "Sounds lovely. Thank you for suggesting it."

"Why don't I walk with you? Show you to your new room?" Mary asked, following along beside Marnie as they entered the main hall.

With the snow pelting the windows, she glanced down at the number on the key. "No, I'll be fine," she said, and started toward the stairs.

As she unlocked the door, she understood why Luke

was so hesitant to put her in the room on the third floor. Even in the emergency lighting, this room was spectacular with its four-poster bed, fireplace and bathroom with a Jacuzzi and marble shower. The room also had a bay window that—if there hadn't been such a horrific snowstorm blowing outside—would have offered a panoramic view of the gardens beyond the back patio.

She ordered from the menu and settled in to wait for her dinner, and her first opportunity to face the reality of having signed the agreement to sell her business. Despite the fact that she was leaving a huge chunk of her life behind, she now realized she didn't want to work in a salon anymore, with or without Gina's interference. As proud as she was of her accomplishments, it was definitely time to move on to something new and interesting.

When her steak and Caesar salad arrived a few minutes later, she decided she had earned a little luxury and settled in to enjoy her meal. Sinking into the wingback chair after dinner, she turned on the propane fireplace and watched as the flames swooped up then died down to a quiet burn.

As she sipped her glass of Merlot her gaze moved around the room, from the ornate dressing table, to the satin drapes and the flat-screen television, she wondered what it would be like to work at an inn like this. She'd never considered the hospitality industry as a career. But why not? When she got back to Boston she'd look into some courses.

In the meantime, she needed to get her rest if she was heading out tomorrow morning. The driving wouldn't be easy, and she didn't have the best snow tires in the world.

She finished her wine and pushed the trolley outside her door.

With the roar of the wind outside, she showered, got

ready for bed and climbed up into what reminded her of a giant nest with its voluminous pillows and thick, fluffy duvet.

Sinking into the epitome of comfort, she closed her eyes.

## CHAPTER EIGHT

THE NEXT MORNING, MARNIE awoke to complete silence. The windows were encrusted with snow, sparkling like diamonds in the pale morning light. Climbing out of her bed, she crossed the room to have a look outside. From what she could see, the entire patio had disappeared under the snow.

She'd never seen so much of the white stuff. A snowfall like this and Christmas only days away, the inn and Wakesfield would be guaranteed a white Christmas. Brimming with enthusiasm, she showered, dressed and went down to breakfast. As she reached the lobby, she heard the animated chatter of guests whose only topic of conversation was the storm—now being described as the storm of the decade. The word was that all the roads were closed, and the people at the weather center were calling for more snow today.

Now Marnie had no choice but to stay another day. She also had no choice but to keep her mystery-guest status hidden until she could leave. But all her concerns were swept away when she realized that because of the storm she had nothing to do today but relax and enjoy herself. Wow, for the first time in years she'd be free to do whatever she pleased.

When she reached the dining room, she chose a table near the windows that looked out on the patio, marveling at how much snow was packed against the windows, yet how cozy it felt. Sipping her coffee, she glanced around, only to spot Luke standing near the door.

As he started across the room toward her, a smile of pleasure on his face, she was reminded of the incredible connection between them. She couldn't define it, but she didn't care. She was simply filled with delight that he was here and about to join her.

"Good morning. I trust you slept well in your new room," he said, pulling out the chair next to her and sitting down.

"I did. I didn't wake until about an hour ago. What a lovely room. I can see why you get so many repeat guests here."

His smile wrapped around her, his eyes searching hers. "I'm sorry about last night, but we had our hands full keeping the snow away from the doors and dealing with the power outage. I had intended for you and I to have dinner together." He rubbed his face, his exhaustion evident in the lines around his eyes. "I survived the night, fueled by coffee and adrenaline. A shower this morning helped me regain my sanity."

"I understand. Really," she offered, his fresh-scrubbed scent sending a flood of neediness through her. His closeness, the way he leaned toward her, the sense that his attention was directed only at her, made her want to reach out and touch his hand where it rested on the linen tablecloth.

"The good news is that you won't have to give up your room and go back upstairs tonight. There is no hope the road to the village will be cleared because a tractor-trailer unit got stuck last night, and they're still working to get it dug out. On top of that, the highway going south is blocked. Rescue vehicles and plows are trying to reach those vehicles stranded on the highway."

"I hope they get to these people soon," she said, shivering at the thought of being stuck in the snow overnight.

"Everyone's hoping they can, but with more snow in the forecast, it isn't looking very likely. They may get the people out, but the cars may take longer."

The server appeared, poured coffee for Luke and took their orders.

"Where's Ethan this morning?" she asked.

"He's discovered Lego. Evelyn, the pastry chef, brought him a box filled with pieces that her son played with when he was little, and Ethan has them scattered all over the apartment. The evening shift couldn't leave last night, so one of the cooks stayed with him all night, and is still there this morning."

"What happens now?"

"We'll try to keep the inn going until the roads are cleared. We have enough food and the guests seem to be getting into the spirit of it all. Several have even volunteered to help shovel."

"So what am I doing today? As your assistant, I mean."

"Not much. I've already emailed guests who were planning to arrive today, and mostly I'll be making sure that we're ready for the next round of snow due to start sometime this morning." He glanced toward the windows. "I'd say it's about to start again soon."

"Do you have any office jobs I could do? I'm good at paperwork."

"I'll ask Amanda at reception if she needs help. In the meantime, if you're interested, I do have some plans for changes to the gardens around the back of the inn next spring. You might like to see those, and if you have suggestions…"

He wanted her advice? "I'd love that."

*You'd love anything that brought you more time
with him.*

When they finished their breakfast, she followed
Luke to the office. He pulled several large blueprints
out of a drawer and spread them on his desk. As he
began to talk about them, she witnessed firsthand the
care and attention he'd put into the planning, how his
face lit up when he told her how he'd worked with the
landscape people to design a maze of cedar trees that
would add an interesting walking exercise for his older
clients who were no longer able to hike.

"This could all come to nothing if Advantage Corp
has its way. There's talk they're going to sell one of the
inns they own in the area, that someone from head office might make a site visit, but so far there's been nothing confirmed."

Luke didn't know that the inn was going to be sold.
Scott had told her they planned to sell it, confidential
information that she wasn't allowed to disclose. If it got
out, Advantage would suspect Scott of being the source,
and his agency's relationship with Advantage would
suffer. "I don't know why they would want to sell this
place. It's beautiful," she said in a lame attempt to hide
her dismay at the realization that she had to keep quiet
about what she knew.

"It is beautiful, and I love it here. I hope I never have
to leave. But if the inn doesn't produce the profit margin
their shareholders are looking for, and corporate bonuses
are tied to profit levels…" He shrugged.

She felt so guilty she wanted to climb under the table.
She was not only working for the people who planned
to sell the inn, she was helping them prepare it for sale,
and in the process she would hurt someone she cared for.

Why had she gotten involved in this? She understood

better than most people how difficult it was to run a successful business, and how running a business takes a great deal of personal commitment. If only she could back out of her promise to Scott....

She wished she could tell Luke what she was really doing here, and find a way to help him. With the lessons she'd learned running Total Elegance, she had lots of ideas that might prove useful. But none of it mattered if Advantage was determined to sell. If only they wouldn't...or couldn't.

"Running a company isn't easy these days. In a way I'm glad to be out," she said, more to make herself feel better than anything else. Right now, she was feeling like a traitor.

"It couldn't have been easy to start up a business on your own."

"I had a great partner—until he fell in love."

"Oh, yeah?"

She nodded. "Shane and I worked really well together. We spent long and sometimes difficult hours finding ways to keep the business afloat. Luckily we were both hairdressers, so in the beginning we focused on that, but as the clientele grew we had to expand our services, and that meant having someone to look after the business side of it. So when we added massage and aesthetics, I took over managing the salon."

"So why did you decide to sell?"

"Because the work had become too routine, too predictable for me, while Shane still loved what he was doing. When Shane met Gina, I couldn't see myself working with her. Gina's not my kind of person. She likes being in control, and too many bosses can ruin a business."

"And she wants to be the boss."

She nodded, remembering Julie's remarks about Gina, and wondering how her friend was making out.

"I intend to own my own business someday." Luke rubbed his hands together. "I'd love to buy this inn if Advantage decides to sell, but they'll want a lot of money for the place." His gaze moved slowly around the room, his expression one of sadness.

"You'd be really good at running it," she said. And she could be the one to hurt his good reputation if the owners took some of her comments as condemnation of his management skills. Would her responses to the questionnaires influence their decision as to whether they offered him another position?

Luke was the kind of guy she enjoyed being around, talking business and sharing ideas. Her brother and his money-grubbing client could destroy this man's dream.

When the phone rang, Luke answered it, his expression going from interest to anxiety in quick succession. He hung up, folded the landscaping plan and put it away. "I have to go."

Wanting to ask what had caused him to look so worried, but afraid she might be intruding, she said, "And I have to make a phone call."

He shoved his hands through his hair. "Nothing wrong, I hope."

"No, but my mother is probably looking for me," she said, trying to disguise her lie behind a bright smile. "I turned off my cell phone when I got here."

"Okay." He glanced at his watch hurriedly. "I'll meet you for lunch, and we can talk a bit more. I'd really like to hear your perspective on starting a new business." His distracted tone was unnerving.

*What was happening? Had that call been from the owners? What had gone so wrong?*

Whatever was going on, she couldn't do anything to help him, or surely he would have asked her. One thing she'd learned about Luke: he was a man who valued his privacy, and she wouldn't attempt to interfere. "See you," she said. Waving goodbye, she slipped from the room.

Armed with renewed determination to block Advantage's plans by any means possible, she practically ran up the stairs. She was on her way to the third floor when she stopped. Turning around quickly, she headed to her new room. She needed to talk to Scott.

CONFUSED AND CONCERNED, Luke wanted to simply sit in his office and talk to Marnie, but now he had a bigger issue to cope with, than the storm even. Jack had called to tell him that Lindsay was in labor, and the snowplow headed for them had had a breakdown. Jack was trying to get ahold of Dr. Pearson.

The sky outside his office was obliterated by the massive swirls of snow. Due to the rising winds and zero visibility the search and rescue helicopters were grounded.

The phone rang again.

"Hi, Luke. Me again. Dr. Pearson isn't in his room or the dining room. Lindsay's contractions are only five minutes apart and I need a doctor. Do you have any idea where he might be?"

"I doubt he would've left the inn because there's literally no place to go. He wasn't among those shoveling last night. Maybe he's out there now?"

"Damn it! Where in hell could he have gone?" The tension in Jack's voice made his words harsh.

"Try to stay calm. We'll find him." The last thing they needed was a medical emergency and no medical personnel available.

He headed out the door.

MARNIE CLIMBED INTO HER oversized bed and snuggled down while she waited for Scott to answer his phone. "Hi, sis. How's the storm?"

"We are completely snowed in."

"Too bad. Mom's really putting the pressure on to know where you are, and I can't hold her off much longer. Any chance you can be out of there before Christmas Eve?"

"None. There's more snow coming," she answered proud of how she'd managed to keep the smug tone out of her voice.

"Bummer. I need you back here, or I'll have to tell another lie to Mom, and I don't want to do that."

"Then tell her the truth—I'm up in the Berkshires and snowed in."

"Don't think that will do. She needs you there to help her, and she's blaming me for you not being around. She and Dad have decided to go all out with a big cocktail party the day after Christmas, and you're on to be the greeter. Anyway, I told her you'd be home tomorrow, probably late in the day."

What she wouldn't give to spend one Christmas without being clucked at and sighed over because she was single, dateless and without any prospects—three major sins in the McLaughlan family. "I probably can't make it home that soon."

"And when will your survey work be finished? Have you still got internet access?"

"I don't know. Scott, why are we even doing this survey if Advantage plans to sell the inn?"

"I explained that to you at the salon. They want to be able to tell any potential buyers that the inn is operationally sound, that it's a turnkey operation with no hidden problems."

"Wouldn't the potential buyer want to do their own evaluation?"

"Of course, but this is Angus McAndrew we're talking about. He's a perfectionist to the core. Marnie, I needed this done yesterday. I want Advantage as a client, and this is their test. If I deliver for them, I'm going to get a whole lot more business from them."

"You have lots of business already."

"In case you haven't noticed, there's a recession going on out there in the world. Companies are cutting back, spending less, and it's affecting us as much as anyone."

Marnie wanted to help her brother, she really did, but she couldn't hurt Luke in the process. "Scott, I hate staying here under false pretenses. These people are kind and caring, and I'm spying on them."

"Not really. You're simply doing a survey of their operation."

"Without telling them!" she said, exasperated that he didn't seem to understand what was going on with her. But how could he? She hadn't told anyone how much she cared about Luke. She hadn't even told Luke, for that matter. She drew in a deep breath. "I'm coming home as soon as the roads are cleared, which may not be for another day or so. But as much as I don't want to do your survey work, I will try to finish it before I leave."

"Thank you so much. I really appreciate it, sis."

She got off the phone. What if she didn't make it home for Christmas? What if she ended up staying right here with Luke? No family pressures, no list of things to do to prepare for a party she didn't want to attend and no hiding from all the questions directed at her over her sale of Total Elegance. It sounded like a dream.

Feeling an urgent need to get out of the room, away from her mixed-up feelings, she pulled on all the warm clothes she could wedge under her winter jacket and started downstairs. She reached the bottom and, not being able to see her feet with all the layers she'd bundled on, she aimed her cumbersome body at the front door, then tripped, only to be caught up in Luke's arms.

"WHOOPS!" LUKE STEADIED HER, feeling the heat of her body through the bulky clothes she was wearing. But her bulky clothes couldn't hide her appeal. What he wouldn't give to spend the rest of the day with her, without any distractions....

But that was wishful thinking, and there was no room for it in his life...at least for now. "Where are you going in such a hurry?"

Her eyes were looking straight into his, her breath coming in short gasps.

"I'm going outside to see if I can help them shovel. I need the exercise and I want to be useful."

Reluctantly he let go of her, already missing how she felt in his arms. "You're just the person I'm looking for," he said, recognizing the hidden truth in that statement. "I need a favor."

"Sure. Anything." Her eyes were wide with concern as she pushed her cap back from her face.

"Lindsay's in labor, and there's no chance we can get her to a hospital. Dr. Pearson and his wife are going to have to deliver a baby here and probably in the next few hours." The emotion of the moment momentarily choked him up. Lindsay was the sister he'd never had and if anything happened to her... "It would be great if you could watch Ethan. The staff, and many of the guests, are busy shoveling snow or getting some rest so they can work again tonight. The snow has grounded helicopters, the road is still blocked and there's no choice but to deliver the baby here. It would mean so much to me if you could care for Ethan at least until after the delivery."

She pulled off her mitts and took his hand in hers, her fingers gentle against his skin. "I would love to do that. And if there's anything else I can do, please tell me."

Her eyes were warm and caring. He was exhausted, worried and needed to be cared for. "Thank you."

Her lips worked as if searching for the right words while her gaze never left his face. They stood there, sharing a moment of deep understanding, which left Luke feeling reenergized. She put her arms around his neck and hugged him to her, a hug meant to ease his worry, and it did. But it was also a hug that told him she cared, that she would be there for him. He held her tight against him, seeking her warmth, her reassurance, and for that instant he didn't feel alone, stranded in some emotional wasteland.

"Where is Ethan?" she asked.

"Playing Lego in the apartment. I'll walk you over."

"No. I'll find my way. You go do what you can for Jack and Lindsay. They need you."

"I will, and thank you."

"Luke, I know you're worried. They're your friends, and if there's anything I can do…"

She left the offer unfinished, but he knew from the deep concern in her eyes that she meant what she'd said. That she understood how hard it was for him to face the possibility that, should anything go wrong with the delivery, there was no one to call that could assist them. That Lindsay and her baby were facing an uncertain few hours, and all anyone could do was wait and hope.

For the first time in his career as a manager accustomed to dealing with people, he had no words to express how he was feeling, as emotions he'd lost touch with rose through him. In just a few words she'd lifted his spirits, and offered him hope that everything really would be okay.

He was the first to walk away, not because he wanted to but because he needed to escape from the sure knowledge that he felt closer to Marnie than to any woman since Anna. He longed for that deep feeling of closeness, that mutual contact that said so much without a word being spoken.

# CHAPTER NINE

MARNIE WATCHED LUKE LEAVE, resisting the urge to go after him. She'd seen the pain in his eyes, and felt a connection to him that made her heart rise in her throat.

A baby was about to be born in an inn that was completely cut off from the outside world, and all that stood between success and complication was a retired obstetrician and a former nurse, a duo who had no instruments to work with and no other qualified person to call on to help. She shivered.

Thank heavens Luke hadn't asked her to help with the birth. She'd be about as helpful as a kite in a windstorm. But she was good with children, thanks to all the time she'd spent babysitting her brothers' children. She hurried on down the corridor toward the apartment, peeling off her layers of clothing as she went. She found Mary with Ethan—who'd taken over the entire living room with Lego blocks—under the supervision of Henry, who met her at the door with a joyful bark.

"Thanks for coming so quickly," Mary said, an expression of relief on her face. "You'll probably be with him for the rest of the morning or longer. One of the men is shoveling the snow away from the garden doors that open onto the patio, and when they're done, you can take Ethan outside for a while. His snowsuit, mitts and boots are on the chair by the door."

"We'll have fun, won't we, Ethan?"

"Yep," Ethan said without looking up.

"And I've got to run. If we're about to have a new baby in our midst, I need to get to the attic and find some of Ethan's clothes."

"They didn't bring any with them?" Marnie asked.

"No. I suspect Lindsay was so anxious to be with Jack last night, she didn't think of bringing baby clothes. It really isn't a problem as Anna saved all of Ethan's baby things. Luke asked me to go to the attic and find some newborn things. I'm sure there are cloth diapers, receiving blankets and a bassinet as well up there. Anna and Luke had planned to have a second baby real soon."

"They must have been so happy," Marnie said.

"They were. Luke has been so lonely these past years, while his parents are off traveling the world, blinded by their selfishness. Those parents of his, what a pair!" She snorted. "Sorry, I didn't mean to unload on you."

"Not to worry. I'm here to provide whatever help I can." She gave Henry's ears a good rubbing, and was rewarded with doggy groans of delight.

"I hope you don't mind me leaving you like this."

"Not at all." Marnie shed her outdoor clothes, aware that she was inside Luke's private home. "Don't worry. Ethan and I will do just fine. Right, Ethan?"

Ethan smiled his father's smile as he came toward her, trailing a huge misshapen hunk of blocks. "I made a truck," he said in a proud voice.

"Is this a truck?" Marnie inquired, kneeling down to the little boy's level.

"Yes! You can help." Ethan nodded as he passed her his attempt at a Lego truck and went back to the pile of blocks. "Here." He pointed to the Legos.

"Okay, let's see." Marnie sat on the floor, taking in the sight around her. There were toys scattered every-

where. Luke had turned his apartment's living room
into a playroom.

She spotted a table next to the propane fireplace. On
it were several framed pictures. Curious to know what
Anna Harrison looked like, Marnie rose and went to the
table. Her eye was immediately drawn to a photograph
of Anna, her long dark hair held back by silver combs, as
she sat holding Ethan, a beautiful blue afghan wrapped
around his infant body, her face resting against her son's
cheek, a look of complete happiness lighting her face.

The photos all held so much joy, so many poignant
memories for a man who'd lost his wife in the days leading up to Christmas. And now, with Christmas so near,
how sad he must feel.

She tried to imagine what he'd lived with the past
three years. Her own family had had it so easy. Her
brothers were all happily married with eight beautiful
kids among them. Except for her accident, life had been
good to the McLaughlan clan.

Ethan raced across the room, nearly knocking over
the photo display. "That's me." He pushed his finger
against the glass of the closest photo.

"Aren't you handsome." She ruffled his hair, and he
grinned up at her.

"Okay, let's get back to work," she said, returning to
the huge mound of blocks.

Ethan knelt beside her, his eyes wide with interest.
"I want a snowplow, too."

"Let's see what we can do." Marnie began assembling
the pieces to build something resembling a snowplow as
Ethan lugged over his half-finished truck, but her mind
was on Luke and his friends, and whether or not they
had delivered a baby yet. How must it feel to be having
a baby under such circumstances?

Would she ever have a baby? She'd always believed that fate would determine whether or not having children was in the cards for her—after she finished proving to everyone, including herself, that she had what it took to succeed in business.

But as she worked side by side with Ethan, seeing the enthusiasm with which he hooked each block together, she wanted this—all of it—in her life.

Ethan gave a huge sigh. "I'm thirsty."

As if on cue, Henry got up and ambled toward them from his spot at the door.

"Then let's get you something to drink."

She followed him into the kitchen to find him standing with the fridge door open next to the cold shelves, his hands on a bottle. "Can I have apple juice?"

She lunged for the fridge, and lifted the glass bottle of apple juice from his eager fingers in the nick of time. "I'll pour it for you."

Before she could close the fridge door, he'd opened the cupboard next to it and took out a plastic cup. "These are all mine." He waved at the array of plastic cups and plates, along with spoons and forks that were available for him to choose from. What a great idea, having everything Ethan needed where he could reach it. She poured his juice, which he drank noisily, and then they returned to his Lego.

An hour later he requested a peanut-butter sandwich for his lunch, and showed her where to find the bread, peanut butter and jam. Marnie made one for herself as well, and they ate together at the kitchen table with Henry looking on hungrily. With lunch over, they continued building with such intensity that Marnie lost track of time.

Suddenly, Ethan stood up. "Let's go," he yelled, heading for the door.

"Hey! Wait for me," she called, picking herself up off the floor and chasing after him.

"I want to go out."

Henry got up again, wagging his tail so hard his whole body shook. Ethan buried his face in the dog's neck. "Henry can come with us," he announced.

"You mean out in the snow?"

He nodded vigorously, a large curl bouncing on his forehead.

"Okay, then we need to get your snowsuit on, and your mitts and hat—"

"No!" Ethan scowled and cocked his tiny fists on his hips. Henry barked in support of Ethan's cause.

"Ethan, it's too cold to go out without your snowsuit on. Look, I'm going to put on my mitts and hat and jacket." She pointed to the pile of clothes on the chair by the door.

"Not me." He pouted.

"That's too bad. You stay here then, and I'll take your truck and snowplow outside."

"No! I want to come with you." Henry yawned and ambled toward the door, looking up expectantly at the doorknob.

She knelt down and gently held Ethan's tiny shoulders in her hands. "If you want to go outside with me, you have to get dressed."

He dropped his chin to his chest.

"It'll be so much fun. There are huge drifts of snow out there."

His head snapped up. He leaned closer, peering into her face. "Can I shovel?" he asked in an enthusiastic whisper.

"You sure can, but first we have to get our outdoor clothes on," she said, mustering her most persuasive tone of voice.

He grabbed his snowsuit and dragged it over to her. She helped him get dressed and put on her outdoor clothes, then followed him out of the apartment. Ethan lugged his Lego truck and snowplow out to the patio, Henry trailing after him. Ethan whooped in delight as the falling snow hit his cheeks. Someone had shoveled out a huge section of the patio that was rapidly refilling with snow. Ethan went over to the corner of the patio, and put his Lego creations down on the snow-packed ground.

He tried moving them through the snow, but they kept getting stuck. "You help," he ordered, and she squatted beside him.

After a few frustrated moments of trying to make the Lego truck haul snow, Ethan gave up. "Dump truck." He pointed to the opposite corner, and Marnie realized that his metal dump truck was probably buried where he'd left it the day before.

"Okay, give me a minute." Down on her hands and knees she used her hands to dig away the snow from the spot where she estimated his truck should be. Henry joined her, snorting as he buried his nose in the cold snow.

"I'll help you." Ethan rushed over and fell into the huge drift she was working on, squealing as the snow rose in a cloud and rained down on him.

He climbed out of the drift and wrapped his arms around her neck, laughing. Henry barked in delight as he circled them. Then Ethan pushed back and held her cheeks in his hands while he peered into her eyes. "I love you," he whispered, his cold nose pressing against hers.

Her heart stilled and her breathing stopped. Tears pooled under her eyelids as she fought back the feeling she'd long buried. Who could wish for more out of life than to hear those words spoken by a child? "I love you, too, sweetie," she said, smiling at him as she brushed snow off his hat and kissed his cheek.

"Okay." He wiggled out of her arms—the moment over—and began digging for his dump truck once more.

Accompanied by Henry's enthusiastic barks, they dug together, and finally Marnie discovered that the ground beneath where she was working was dirt and not patio stones. "We're nearly there," she said to Ethan, who let out a whoop and began digging harder. They were both on their hands and knees digging rapidly when Marnie heard a familiar voice.

Ethan stopped. "Daddy!" he squealed, and backed out of the corridor of snow their digging had created. Henry shuffled past Marnie in hot pursuit of Ethan.

"I figured I'd find you here."

"Up," Ethan ordered.

*Wouldn't you know? I'm on my knees with my butt in the air when the man of my dreams returns.*

Marnie backed out of the tunnel and stood, swiping at the snow crusted on her pants and jacket as she glanced up into Luke's face.

"I see Ethan has put you to work and Henry's assisting."

Luke had circles under his eyes, his hair uncombed, and his smile was one of weariness. But he'd never looked more handsome, more human or more vulnerable. Seeing him this way did something to her. She let the feeling flow over her, warming her soul. "Yeah, they've kept me busy, but it's been fun. It's so pretty out here."

"With Ethan in charge, I'm surprised you got a chance to do much looking around," he said, exhaustion shaping the lines around his mouth.

"Just a quick peek." She smiled at him, hoping he'd smile back.

He didn't.

Henry put his front paws up on Marnie's leg and nudged his nose under her hand. "Is everything okay? Is the baby okay?"

"Yeah, he's great and so are the parents." Luke hugged his son and touched his bright red cheek lovingly. "Everything is just fine," he said, his tone filled with a mixture of relief and sadness.

There was something bothering Luke that went beyond his concern over his friends and their baby. "Let me stay here and watch Ethan. You're exhausted. Why don't you take a break?" She reached for the little boy, who hugged his father's neck, pursed his lips and glared at her in response.

Luke held his son tighter as he met Marnie's anxious gaze. "I'm… I… Their joy at having a baby…"

The yearning imprinted on his face did it for her. In that moment she felt connected to him in an inexplicable way, sharing his unspoken wish for a child. "The perfect Christmas present, a healthy baby boy," she said. "Will they be able to get home tonight?"

"I doubt it. The plows aren't making much progress." He squinted up at the sky. "And the weather service says we're in for at least another six hours of this."

HE SWALLOWED OVER THE unwelcome sensation that he was very close to tears. He couldn't cry in front of his son, or Marnie. Tears and the emotions driving them had never been welcome in his family growing up, and old habits held them in check now. "It is the perfect Christmas present, and I've never seen my friends happier."

"How's Dr. Pearson?"

"He's great. He and his wife were fantastic. It was as if they were in their own world as they did all the things they had to do."

"You were there when the baby was born?"

"No, only when they were getting organized, but I waited outside, in case they needed anything. Francine was there to help Mae. She was the one who told me the good news."

She touched his shoulder. "What does he look like?"

"He's got reddish hair. Other than that I couldn't see very much of him." Emotion clogged his throat at the memory of seeing his friends so happy, a memory that left him wanting to feel that special kind of joy again.

"Do they have a name for him?"

"They're calling him James Edward after Jack's brother who was killed in Iraq."

"What a beautiful gesture."

"It is. Jack and James were only a year apart, and Jack had just returned from a tour of duty himself when the family learned that James had been killed in a suicide attack."

"I'm sorry for their loss."

"But what a nice way to remember James," Luke said.

"So, what happens now? I mean until the storm stops."

"We've set up a temporary nursery in one of the empty suites, and Mary found Ethan's bassinet up in the attic. I'd forgotten it was up there." He pressed his face into Ethan's neck to hide the tears stinging his eyes.

*Stop this! You have an inn to run, a major snowstorm to deal with and so many people depending on you.*

She reached for Ethan. "Let me take him. It will be dark soon, and I'm sure he's hungry. I'll get his dinner ready."

She was being so kind and yet she hardly knew him. Looking into Marnie's eyes as she stood waiting, he wished he didn't have so much to worry about. Marnie's kindness, her warmth and his growing feelings for her had made him see the emptiness in his life.

He felt so tired, so drained. All he wanted was to spend time with son. "Marnie, I'll take Ethan into dinner and get him ready for bed. I haven't seen him all day, but thank you for everything."

She lifted her hand from his arm, her smile focused on Ethan. "You're welcome."

"I know this is asking a lot, but could you possibly help me with something else?"

"Sure, anything," she said.

"I need someone to work the reception desk. Some of the staff who couldn't stay last night weren't able to get back to do their shifts. Would you mind?"

"No, of course not. I'll change and go over there right now." She opened the door and went inside, Henry on her heels, the snow blowing through the door behind her.

MARNIE SHOOK THE SNOW off her boots and yanked them off her feet, carrying them up the stairs with her. She avoided making eye contact with anyone as she made her way to her room. Tears blurring her vision, she pulled off her clothes and changed into dry ones, as a stark realization formed in her mind.

More than any other time in her life, she wanted someone to love, and she wanted a marriage like her parents had, one based on mutual love and respect. And she wanted a relationship with Luke, a man she hadn't been honest with, and knew beyond a doubt that should he learn the truth, he'd reject her.

She had to make a decision soon. If Scott was right, Angus McAndrew would announce the sale of the inn, possibly leaving Luke without a job. And if the survey she was working on cast his managerial skills in a bad light...

She should tell him what she knew about Advantage's intention to sell the inn. But if she did, and it impacted Scott's business relationship with Advantage...

She felt she had to support Scott, after all, he was her brother and he had always been good to her. But with Luke now in her life...

She knew what her decision had to be. Luke had to be told the truth. He needed to know what Advantage's plans were for The Mirabel Inn, not just to ease her conscience, but also to give him an opportunity to prepare for his future. If Advantage dropped this news on Luke without any warning, how would he feel?

Luke had alluded to the possibility of the inn being sold, but hadn't given any indication that he had a plan should it be true.

But what if she finished the survey purely for Luke's benefit, to alert him to any problems she found, wouldn't that make the dreaded job of telling him easier? He might be able to correct any deficiencies immediately, and she wouldn't have to report them.

While she figured out how to tell Luke, she headed to the reception desk. She arrived to find a weary Amanda waiting for her.

"I haven't had a wink of sleep in almost twenty-four hours. I'll show you the basics, including how to do a reservation, and then I'm off to bed somewhere...."

Amanda showed Marnie what she needed to do, and

it looked relatively easy. The computer booking system was very much like the one she had installed at Total Elegance, so that part would be easy. The switchboard also seemed straightforward, and all she had to do was read up on the various packages the inn offered should someone want to make a reservation. As she settled into the job and began to feel comfortable, she pulled the questionnaire out of her bag and looked it over. She'd given the inn top ratings for each category listed except when it came to the visibility of the staff name tag, a minor problem she'd spotted on her first day here.

She sighed in relief. There was nothing in the survey that could hurt Luke. The damage to the wiring in her old room had been fixed right away. The issues with the manicurist's technique were mostly a matter of retraining that could be done very easily.

The evening settled into a routine, broken only by the wind howling outside the massive front door. She wondered if Luke was getting some rest after putting Ethan to bed. She hoped he was.

She had one call for a reservation, and other than that, the evening was quiet. The generators kept the lights on, but Kevin came by the desk to say that unless the storm eased by tomorrow morning, they could face a total blackout as the fuel tanks feeding the generator were running low on fuel.

At ten o'clock, Marnie passed the keys over to the night watchman. Despite the blizzard outside, and the sense of isolation, Marnie felt at home in this place. There was something so solid and enduring about it. When she reached her room, she fell into bed, at peace for the first time in a very long time.

# CHAPTER TEN

THE NEXT MORNING THE STORM had fizzled to a dusting of snow drifting through the morning air. The plows were out in force, clearing the roads leading to the interstate. Marnie was on the reception desk once again, fielding calls from staff trying to get into work and people wanting to speak to Luke. She'd taken several reservations for the ski packages in January, and she was really enjoying the work, and loved feeling useful. She could get to like the hospitality business. Several of the guests came by to chat about the weather, when the roads might be cleared and how cozy the inn felt with all the snow packed around it. Everyone was in generally good spirits, and talking about this evening's Christmas Eve dinner that was part of the Christmas Getaway event.

Meanwhile, the questionnaires on the reception desk and the booking system were finished. She was about to put the material in her bag when Luke appeared with two coffees. She hurriedly put her notes away.

"Thought you might need a caffeine hit," he said, holding out a mug of coffee to her.

She took a sip, delighted to find that Luke had added just the right amount of cream and sugar. A man with devastating appeal who remembered what she took in her coffee. "There are lots of similarities between working here and working in a salon. There are the bookings, the phones to answer and…"

"Does the salon include babysitting and bartender duties?" he asked, chuckling.

"Not yet, but we keep evolving," she offered, wishing he would make a move, to demonstrate that he was still attracted to her. That he still wanted her to have dinner or lunch with him, go to the moon, to the movies, she really didn't care.

A Christmas Eve kiss would be perfect, especially if he was going to be as busy today as he had been all of yesterday.

She waited, sipping her coffee, meeting Luke's gaze, and…and nothing.

Her feelings for him ran deep, but wasn't it time for a little show of response on his end? He'd left her waiting for him in the bar, but he'd had the perfect excuse. He'd gotten her to babysit Ethan because his friends had needed him. As much as she wanted him, he'd been too preoccupied with his own life to make room for her. When they were together, most of the conversation had revolved around his issues, and she was more than willing to be helpful—her best role actually—but needing her help was a long way from demonstrating that he cared.

Luke leaned on the desk, his muscled arms a tempting display. "I need to talk to you about something."

*No words about missing me. No stolen kisses like the night at the bar. Not even a word about this being Christmas Eve. Just the same old words he always used when he thought she was hiding something.*

He was acting as if they were simply friends, and maybe that's all they were. Maybe she'd read more into his behavior than was there. But they were together for a few moments on one of her favorite days of the year, the day when all the final Christmas preparations were completed. She could be generous and hope he was about to offer her some other role than being supportive. "Sure, what is it?"

"Would you be willing to help out with the changes you identified as being needed at the spa?"

Disappointment curled its cold tentacles around her chest, squeezing any hope from her. Had she been fooled into thinking he cared because she cared so much? Or had he simply taken advantage of her generosity?

Whatever the case, she needed to decide what she should do. There was always her life back in Boston, her Mrs. Claus suit and all the uproar her brothers would create over the sale of her business.

If only Luke had given her a reason to be helpful. Wasn't he taking her role as his assistant a little far? After all, it was Christmas Eve. "Today?"

"If possible. I'd like to go over how the changes should be implemented."

She forced back the hurt, the longing, dredging up her pride to rescue her. "I have…had some of the same services in my salon, I'm well aware of the key components in a professionally run spa. Mostly, the issues relate to product type and use, and I can easily make a few notes for Francine and provide a copy for you."

"That would work, thank you. Would you like to see the new baby?"

*Had she misread the situation that badly? Was she that desperate to fall in love?* She could feel her cheeks growing hot with embarrassment. "Are you sure?"

"Absolutely. Lindsay is bringing him down to lunch. The staff wants to see him, and of course you're invited. By the way, thank you for looking after Ethan. I didn't really get a chance to thank you enough for what you did yesterday, but I really do appreciate it."

"You're welcome." Those few hours were some of the best she'd had in months, and she'd felt so much a part of Luke's life, but he clearly didn't feel what she was feeling.

He stood before her, a faint smile on his face, and humor in his eyes. "Would you like to have lunch with me? Ethan's been asking for you. It seems he's quite impressed with your snowplowing capabilities."

Was the only way to this man's heart through his son? "You mean my ability to bury myself under a snowdrift."

He laughed and the sound drew her into his space, lifted her spirits and made her wish that they were a couple. All these years while she'd been working to build up her business, other people had been making a life with someone they loved, having children and connecting in a way that really mattered. Meanwhile, she'd been working in a business she loved, but a business that left her feeling unfulfilled at the end of the day. The only living things that needed her back at her house in Boston were a fern and her overweight tabby, Prince. "What time is lunch?"

He checked his watch. "In about fifteen minutes. I'm going to find someone to replace you on the desk so you can meet me in the dining room."

Seeing the baby, getting to spend time with Luke was great, but so far it wasn't leading anywhere. "Fine." She smiled up at him, searching for some genuine affection in his eyes and coming up empty.

DESPITE LUKE'S EXHAUSTION, he was suddenly energized at the prospect of lunch with Marnie. It was amazing how easily she fit into his life, how much he had begun to rely on her, and he'd only known her for a couple of days. Could life really change that much, that easily?

He checked his cell phone for messages, and for the first time in over twenty-four hours there weren't any. He was settling into a table in the dining room, relieved that the power had come back on an hour ago, and the emergency generator could be shut down for repairs. It had taken all of Kevin's skills to keep it running and he owed the man a bonus.

But if the owners decided to sell the inn, everything he'd worked for would be relegated to the past. Anger, deep and primal, boiled up inside him at the thought that people who lived somewhere else, who cared nothing about the inn and its employees, were in a position to threaten everyone's livelihood and happiness with one indifferent signature.

He was still angry when Marnie showed up with Ethan trailing along behind her. As they approached the table, his anger evaporated. His heart rose in his throat, his breathing ceased and he was filled with the sense that he belonged with Marnie. The three of them together enriched his life, and gave it meaning. He held the chair for Marnie.

"I found someone who says he's hungry," Marnie announced as she helped Ethan into the chair next to him before sitting down.

"Dad, I want macaroni," Ethan said, wiggling forward in his chair and tilting his cheek up to his father for a kiss.

Luke kissed his son's smooth skin, offering him a moment to calm his expectations. As much as he liked Marnie, and as much as he enjoyed her company, he didn't know her very well. And a woman like Marnie almost certainly had a life she was eager to return to in Boston…possibly someone special who had to be wondering when she'd return for Christmas Eve.

And as of today, she was free to leave the inn with only a goodbye.

"So, where's the man of the hour?" Marnie asked, her eyes bright with enthusiasm.

"He must be having his lunch, but I'm sure he'll be here soon."

"Babies are so sweet." Marnie spread her napkin on her lap. "Unfortunately, there are no babies in my family right now, just a rowdy bunch of teenagers."

He remembered those first days after Ethan was born, his scent, his cry, the way he took over their lives by simply being there. Luke beckoned the server over to hide his discomfort around a topic that evoked a sense of emptiness in him.

They placed their orders with special attention to Ethan's request for extra cheese on his macaroni, and lots of ketchup. She had just left when Jack and Lindsay arrived with James, accompanied by the curious glances of the guests at other tables.

They sat at the table reserved for them next to Luke's, as Jack helped Lindsay and James into the chair closest to Marnie.

MARNIE COULDN'T BELIEVE how relaxed Lindsay looked as she sat there, holding her son after what had to have been an exhausting twenty-four hours. "He's beautiful," Marnie whispered, reaching out to touch the tiny fingers peeking out of the blue blanket wrapped around his tiny form.

"Thank you," Lindsay murmured, her full attention on her baby as she tucked the blanket around James's face, his lips pursed in sleep.

Marnie had to confess she wasn't very good when it came to discussing the birthing experience, but she was sincerely pleased that Lindsay seemed to have come through it very well. "I'm so glad everything went okay."

"Me, too." Lindsay gave her a grateful smile. "We're very lucky, Jack and I. And James is...everything we could have hoped for."

She cradled the baby close to her body, her fingers gently stroking his cheek. "And what about you? I hear from Luke that you took over with Ethan like a pro."

"I've had lots of practice with my nieces and nephews, and Ethan is so much fun."

"Yes, he is." She rested James on her shoulder, steadying him as she patted his back. "You've been really kind to Luke, and we want you to know how much we appreciate you. He needs someone like you in his life." She spoke quietly, her expression conveying her sincerity.

She glanced over at him, but he was engrossed in conversation with Jack. "Thank you for saying that."

"You're welcome, and I mean it," Lindsay said.

"Daddy, where did Lindsay get the baby?" Ethan asked, his voice rising well above everyone else's.

"Can't wait to hear how you get out of that one, Harrison," Jack teased.

"Why don't you give it a try? It's your baby," Luke countered.

"Ethan, James is a Christmas baby," Marnie blurted, and exchanged quick glances with Luke and Jack. They both gave her a nod.

"Like Baby Jesus?" Ethan asked, excitedly rubbing his hands together as he peeked around Marnie at the baby in Lindsay's arms.

Marnie looked to Luke for support. "Yes, a little like that, I guess."

"And a bit of a Christmas miracle," Lindsay added, smiling.

"Will you put him under the tree?" Ethan asked.

"No, I don't think so." Lindsay grinned at Jack.

"Will you be here when Santa arrives?"

"We'll be here on Christmas Day to see what Santa brought you, Ethan." Jack took James from Lindsay's arms and held him upright against his shoulder, nuzzling his cheek.

"Will Santa bring James's presents here?" Ethan asked, his expression now one of concern.

"Santa will find James at his house," Jack said.

Ethan slumped back in his chair, a look of satisfaction on his face. "I want Santa to come. How much longer, Dad?"

"Just one more sleep until you get to open your presents," he said.

Ethan turned to Marnie. "Will you be here with me when I open my presents?"

The question took her completely by surprise, which she quickly did her best to hide. Until she had a better indication from Luke that she was more than a reliable assistant, the question of Christmas was pointless.

"I'm not sure, Ethan. Besides you'll have lots of other people here to play with at Christmas."

"But, Daddy! I want her to play with me when Santa brings my train," Ethan howled.

"Is Santa bringing you a train?" Marnie asked.

"Yes! Daddy promised me."

"Marnie has to be home for Christmas at her house." Faced with the fact that she could leave whenever she wanted, he was more aware than ever of how much he would miss her. How much he needed her in his life.

"We wrote a letter to Santa, and asked for Thomas the Tank Engine train," Luke said to Marnie, meeting her questioning look.

"Yeah! Thomas!" Ethan squealed as he got off the chair and ran to the window. "Is Santa coming in the sky? Can I see him?"

"Not yet, buddy. But soon." This would be Ethan's fifth Christmas, and although Luke loved seeing his son's happiness over the season, Christmas still held a sense of loss for him. Would having Marnie here change that? he wondered.

Yet he did have family here at the inn. And he was now the godfather of a beautiful, much-anticipated little boy.

"Christmas here must be so special," Marnie said, her voice trailing off as her eyes met his.

Physical desire engulfed him, and a deeper, more immediate need held him captive. In that instant he realized that if she was willing to stay, he wanted her there with him. For better or worse, no matter what life held for him over the next few months, he wanted Marnie here with him.

He wanted another chance at happiness. "Would you like to stay for Christmas?"

She remained perfectly still. "I…I'm not sure."

"Is there anything I can say or do to convince you to stay here with us? I realize you have a family back in Boston, and they'll be expecting you. But if there's any chance you'd consider it…" He shrugged, his dismal attempt to say what was on his mind and in his heart falling flat as a pancake.

She squinted at him. "Would I be expected to do anything?"

Luke glanced from Jack and Lindsay, who both smiled and shrugged, then back at Marnie. "No, definitely not. You would have absolutely nothing to do. Unless you wanted to do something, that is, like snowshoeing, or cross-country skiing, or downhill skiing at one of the downhill skiing resorts nearby, or playing with Ethan…. I'm doing it again, aren't I?"

"You are." A huge grin lit her face. "But you're in luck. I've never had a responsibility-free Christmas since I was a kid."

"Seriously?"

"Seriously."

"Then, as far as I can tell, you deserve a Christmas here at the inn."

His words were met by clapping from Lindsay and Jack, which made Marnie giggle, and happiness flooded over him. Yep, he was happy and he intended to stay that way.

MARNIE'S FEET BARELY touched the stairs as she all but floated up to her room. She felt absolutely wonderful, delighted and happy, the excitement of Luke's invitation hovering in her mind. An invitation that had made it impossible for her to concentrate. She changed into her best pair of jeans, in honor of a day that suddenly held such promise.

During lunch, the plows had done their job, and everything was back to normal. All she had to do was decide if she would stay another night here tonight— Christmas Eve. If she was staying, she had to explain her change of plans to her parents. It wouldn't be easy, but somehow she had to find a way. She was as much a fixture at her parents' house during the holiday season as the eight-foot tree in the living room.

She sighed. She didn't mean to be ungrateful. But this chance to be with Luke was important to her, and yet she still felt a responsibility to her family around their Christmas celebration.

And what if Luke had made the offer as a thank-you for babysitting? Maybe he was simply being nice? She shook her head at the thought. She was picturing the way he'd looked at her when he'd asked her to stay when her cell phone rang.

Shane?

"Hi, how are you?" she asked.

"When are you coming home?" he said, not responding to her question.

"We've had a storm up here, and they're just getting the roads cleared today, so I'm not a hundred percent sure when I'll be back in Boston."

"I got your fax, but I need to talk to you about the business."

"Shane, it's no longer my business—"

"I know," he said. "But, you see...a bit of a problem has developed since you left."

She really didn't want to hear about his problems with Gina, but he was still her friend, and she cared about him. "What's going on?"

"We've... A few employees have quit."

So Julie was right. "Quit? Why?"

"Between you and me, I think it's because Gina's being a little...bossy. She doesn't mean to be. It's just that she's new at the job, and she does things a little differently from you. I tried to convince them to give her a chance."

"Did you talk to Julie about this? She's really good at dealing with people."

"I did. She's been great." His long sigh filled the line. "I had no idea how much Julie knows about this business.... Guess I hadn't given it much thought before because you were here."

"You're really lucky to have Julie there, and she really wants you to succeed."

"Yeah, she told me that, but she says it's for me to decide how to manage the place."

The silence on the line was punctuated by the sound of Shane tapping his pen on a desk, clear evidence of his anxiety. "Marnie, I realize we spent hours working out the agreement between us, but I assumed that Gina would be good at managing the place, the way you were, and I'd be able to concentrate on styling. I was wondering if we might rewrite the agreement to have you stay on and manage the salon."

God himself couldn't work with Gina, and everyone in the salon had come to that conclusion about three weeks after she'd arrived. And sure, she'd like to help Shane. They'd been good partners, but now he had another partner. And with his new partner came a new set of problems.

She and Shane were friends. He'd help her out if she needed him, but she couldn't get caught between Gina and him, no matter how much she cared about Shane. No, she couldn't go back there regardless of what he offered. It was over for her. A few days ago, she couldn't have said those words with such certainty. But today... she had plans for a different life.

"Shane, I'm flattered that you'd want me to come back—"

"I take it you don't want the job," he interrupted, sounding defeated.

"Shane, if I were you, I'd run this whole management thing past Julie."

"Meaning?"

"She's very bright, and she really cares about you and your success."

"You don't think she'd leave me, do you?"

"I can't speak for Julie, but why don't you talk to her, get her input?"

"Now that you say that, Julie has been so great these last few days. She's been such a good friend through all this—the whole changeover with Gina and everything. I had no idea that Julie and I have so much in common. Did you know that we both like country music?"

So they'd been talking—that was a really good sign. Dare she hope that there was still time for Shane to come to his senses and see how Julie trumped Gina in every category that mattered? "There are a whole lot of really nice things you don't know about Julie."

"She's pretty special."

"Maybe it's time you really paid attention to her. She's one smart lady."

"I couldn't agree more, but let's get back to you. Is there anything I can say to change your mind?"

"No, sorry. But it has nothing to do with you or the salon. It has to do with me. I'm thinking I'd like to manage another kind of business."

"Have you been looking?"

"No. I've been having a break, and I discovered something. I don't want the life I have in Boston anymore."

"You're kidding! What will your family say?"

"I haven't told them, but I will, as soon as I know for sure what I'm going to do."

"So you're about to break away from the family. I'm so proud of you."

"Yeah, I love my family, but they need to let me be for a while."

After a moment's pause, he said, "Love ya, gal. You know that. I wish you'd come back here with me, but you deserve to find your place in this world."

Tears blurred her vision. In all the time that she and Shane had discussed business, argued and sometimes fought, there had always been room for honesty between them. Maybe she should have told him what a pain Gina was to work with, but would he have listened? She didn't think so. "I'll come see you right after Christmas. I promise."

"Can't wait. We'll do dinner, maybe a movie, like old times."

Had Shane begun to see Gina for who she really was? And if he had, would it change anything? No. She and Shane were friends, but only friends, not business partners. And that wouldn't change. "Like old times. And Shane, have a great Christmas."

"You, too."

"I plan to."

She hung up the phone, and pushed the questionnaires aside to make room for her to stretch out on the bed and consider what she'd said to her ex-partner. She'd told Shane the truth. Her plans no longer included being involved in the hairdressing business, not his or anyone else's. All she wanted now was to spend time with Luke, get to know him better and see if they had a future together. And his invitation to spend Christmas with him was a great way to start. Wow! She still couldn't believe that he'd asked her....

She'd stay for Christmas, offer him any help she could to get his whole operation running even better than before, and she would come clean about the survey and about Advantage's plans to sell the inn. He deserved to be prepared, and he might find someone to finance an offer to buy the inn if he had the opportunity. She was still thinking about how she'd tell him, what she'd say and how she'd say it when someone knocked on the door.

She opened the door to Luke, who was standing there, smiling that smile of his that did it for her. "Hi, come on in," she said, happy to see him, to smell his cologne and, most of all, to see that he had come alone.

This was a day for celebration, and never more than this instant. Was he about to share his plan for how they'd celebrate Christmas?

"I came to ask if you could help out at the reception desk for a couple of hours."

*Not exactly what she'd wanted to hear, but then again, he could have called, and instead he came all the way up the stairs to ask her in person....*

Oh, how she'd love to wrap all her limbs around this man and let him carry her to her bed—but there would be lots of time for that later. She'd see to it. "Absolutely. Just give me a minute." She ducked into the bathroom, pulled a comb through her short hair, touched up her lipstick and checked her appearance in the mirror. She opened the door, ready to walk as seductively as her jeans would allow, right to the spot where he stood, and breathe in his sexy cologne before she headed down to reception.

"What's this?" he asked, anger simmering behind his words.

She stopped, blinked and stared at the papers he held in his hands. Survey forms. Oh. No. This was it. No turning back. No way out now. "They're question-naires."

"Who asked you to fill them out?" His voice was eerily quiet.

"Scott. It's a contract he has with Advantage Cor-poration."

"You're working for the owners. You went behind my back and collected this information without telling me. Your brother's marketing research company is being paid—and so are you—paid to spy on me."

"No! I never meant to spy on you. I was only doing a favor for Scott. I didn't want to do it. I told Scott that, but he needed me. It was all last-minute, and he really needed me," she repeated.

"And you never stopped to think that I might lose my job here as a result of this, have to give up my friends and move my son from the only home he's ever known?"

She shook her head, gasped for air, tears spilling over her cheeks. "I never meant to hurt you, or Ethan or anyone else. I didn't know you when I came here, but if I had I never would have taken this job, I swear. You have to understand that. I would never do something to hurt you. I—"

"Have the results gone to the owners?"

"No. Scott's been on my case to send them to him, but with the storm and all that's been happening, I haven't had a chance to send him anything—"

"I can't believe you'd do this to me. I don't see any reason why you should remain here any longer. And you don't have to worry about your bill. Your brother left his credit card number when he made the reservation."

"Don't! You need to listen to me. Luke, I didn't do this to damage your career. I could have sent those results, but I didn't."

"You will, but that's not really the point. The point is you deceived me. I trusted you with my work. I allowed you access to my office, and all the confidential information in there. I even trusted you with my friends and my son." He shook his head in disbelief. "Why would you do this to me? To Ethan?" The hurt in his eyes pierced her.

She'd made a terrible mistake and now there was no way out. "Luke, please let me explain."

"There's nothing to explain." With that, he walked out of the room and slammed the door.

The door rattled in its frame, the sound shattering Marnie's hope. She'd never felt so awful in her entire life—so scared, so afraid that she had lost everything she'd ever dreamed of. She'd let her need to please her brothers and her family, to return their kindness, and to prove herself worthy of their respect, keep her from telling Luke the truth.

She stared at the door, at the room, at the window framing the mountains outside and knew without hesitation that this was where she wanted to be; here, with Luke and Ethan. She'd finally found what she wanted, and in one swift act of cowardice, she'd let it go.

But there was still a chance, wasn't there? If she explained why she did what she did? If she could make him see that she cared for him, more than she'd ever cared for any man in her life…

She yanked open the door, and took the stairs two at a time, nearly knocking over another guest as she raced to Luke's office, determined that he should hear her side of it before he kicked her out—or before her courage deserted her.

When she burst into his office, he was sitting behind his desk, his head in his hands. When he glanced up at her, his eyes were hard. "What do you want?" he asked, his voice devoid of all feeling.

## *CHAPTER ELEVEN*

BETRAYAL BURNED THROUGH Luke as he stared up at Marnie—the woman he'd allowed to get so close enough to him, to who he was and what he cared about that she'd made a fool of him. And he had been a fool. A fool to believe what she offered—her sweet, sexy presence in his life, her companionship and helpfulness. All of it a sham while she spied on him. But worse of all, he'd let himself believe that there was someone out there for him who cared about him, and in whom he could trust.

She closed the door softly behind her. "Luke, I came to apologize."

"Apology not accepted." The boulder trapped in his chest barely allowed him to get the words out.

She stood at the door, her hands clasped in front of her. "When I came here, I was doing a job for my brother. I owed him a great deal because of my accident. My whole family has always seen me as needing protection. They mean well, but it has made my life difficult at times, especially when I've felt inadequate around them. I was determined to prove that I could do the survey work to please my brother Scott. And I admit, in the beginning I didn't give any thought to who might be hurt by how I answered the questionnaires, or what sort of purpose the answers might be used for."

He waited, keeping his eyes trained on his desk.

"I hadn't expected to care about anyone here. Then

I met you and Ethan. I was here for James's birth, and you needed me—"

He heard her sudden intake of breath, but he couldn't look at her and feel something he knew to be false. He had already spent the past three Christmases mourning the loss of Anna; he refused to let himself feel any more loss…any more pain.

"And so now you're saying you care." He gripped the desk to keep from lashing out at her.

"Yes, I do. Very much."

He heard the quiet sincerity in her voice, and wished the circumstances were different between them. "So, if you cared, why didn't you tell me what you were doing?"

"At first it was because my brother said he really needed Advantage as a client, and I felt I had to help him."

"At first? And now?"

"I was going to leave here the day the storm started. I was going to go home and tell Scott to find someone else to do the survey. But when the storm came, and I couldn't leave, and then I spent time with Ethan, and got to see the new baby, I started to feel part of something so special. Like I was accepted here, not as someone's daughter, not as someone's sister. As me. Everyone was so good to me. I was going to tell you about the survey and maybe we could use what I found to improve your operations. I wasn't going to send it to Scott."

"Why?"

"Because I care. Because I know what this place means to you. And now it's special to me, too. The Mirabel Inn is the most beautiful place I've ever been. I never suspected that coming here would be the happiest time of my life…." Her words faded to a whisper.

He looked up, his eyes meeting hers, the worry and

sadness he saw there tearing at him. He was mad as hell at her, but would he have done things any differently? Like her, he would've tried to do his job, as she had done. And hadn't he asked her to stay even when he knew Scott had lied about the husband and wife thing? So why did he blame her? He didn't want Advantage to get a report about his management skills, and she said she hadn't sent it. Besides, what did it matter what the owners found out? If Angus McAndrew and his team intended to sell The Mirabel Inn, the new owners would have their own plans for it, which may or may not include him.

He shook his head to remove the memory that flashed across his mind. Three years ago, he'd sat in this same office, struggling to come to grips with his pain. The funeral for Anna was over and he was faced with the reality that he was alone with his son because of his wife's behavior.

"Are you all right?" Marnie asked.

"Funny how women can turn the world on its end."

She came across the room and slid into the chair beside him. "Not just women do that," she said gently.

"Meaning what?"

Marnie took a deep breath, her eyes searching his face. "Fifteen years ago I had an accident, a careless mistake on my part that resulted in two really difficult surgeries and months of rehabilitation. My dad warned me about my driving, but I didn't listen."

"What's your point?"

"Francine told me about Anna, and how you wanted her to stay in Boston, to not try to drive home in the storm. How she didn't listen and you blamed—"

"Damn! Does everyone have to weigh in on my life? This is none of your business." He closed his eyes. He didn't want to yell at her. "My life is not what we're discussing here."

She tilted her chin up in defiance. "She didn't listen, in the same way that I didn't listen. The same way so many people don't listen to the advice of the people who love them."

"So, what's your point?'

"Did you ever consider that maybe Anna drove home in that storm because she couldn't bear to be away from you and Ethan for another moment? That maybe it was her love for her family that made her do what she did? Not her disregard for your warning about the roads? Did you ever consider that until you forgive Anna, you won't be able to love someone else?"

Her words stung. His breath stopped. "You don't know anything about my relationship with Anna, and of course she wanted to get home. I wanted her home, but—"

"It's about more than getting home. It's that feeling that your day isn't complete until you feel someone's arms around you. That your life isn't whole if you're not with them. It means that sometimes we act irrationally. And sometimes we need forgiveness."

Was she right? Was his unwillingness to forgive Anna standing in his way of him finding happiness with another woman? And if so, was Marnie asking for forgiveness for what she'd done? Was she waiting for him to forgive her, as well as Anna? He wasn't sure about anything anymore. "It might be better for everyone if you went back to Boston."

Her eyes shiny with tears, she got up slowly. "You want me to leave?"

"If what you say is true, I'm not ready for a relationship."

Marnie smoothed her hair from her face, and touched the neck of her shirt nervously. "Luke, there's something else I didn't tell you."

He sighed, bracing his hands against his desk. "Out with it."

"One of the reasons Advantage wanted the survey done was to satisfy a potential buyer. It seems the purchaser wanted to know that there were no problems, either financial or operational. I assume that they'd seen the profit and loss statement for the inn, and wanted to have an outside party on-site to evaluate the facility."

"So they're selling The Mirabel," he said, sadness and dread filling his heart.

"It would seem so, but since I'm not completing the survey, they'll have to get someone else to do it."

"Given what I know about them, they won't waste any time."

"Well, at least, they can't do it while you have no vacancies."

SOMEHOW MARNIE MANAGED to make it to her room and close the door before she lost it—tears streaming down her face, her chest hurting as she forced air into her lungs.

What a mess! She'd made Luke angry, and lost her chance with him. Now, she had to tell Scott what she'd done, she owed him that much. He answered on the first ring.

"Tell me you're finished and you're on the way home."

"I'm coming home, but the survey isn't finished."

"What? Why not? You've been snowed in with nothing but time on your hands."

"I can't finish it."

"Look, Marnie, we've been through all this. You

don't want to report on the inn because you have…feelings for the manager. I understand, but as long as he doesn't know what you're doing—"

"He does. I told him."

She waited while Scott huffed and puffed about the need for the survey and his shrinking client list, but she couldn't care less. Her life was in tatters, and she had nothing to look forward to except coming home and being part of Christmas, minus the Christmas spirit. Scott's problems paled in the face of what she'd lost.

"Mom's going to call you today. I couldn't hold her off any longer."

"Tell Mom I'm on my way, but tell her I've turned off my cell phone."

"She won't believe me. You never turn your cell phone off."

"I will now." With that she clicked the phone closed and began to toss her clothes into her bag, dumping the underwear out of the drawers and pulling her laundry bag from the bottom of the closet. Her cosmetics were next, and she was about to zip the bag when someone knocked on the door.

Her pulse slowed. Luke? She hurried to open the door. Mary Cunningham stood there with Ethan at her side. "He's been asking for you."

"Luke?"

Mary looked startled. "No. Ethan. He wants to play outside with you."

She tried not to look at the sweet little face peering up at her. "But I…I can't."

Ethan reached up and took her hand. "I want you!" he demanded.

At least one of the Harrison men wanted her. And

how could she possibly resist those eyes? "Okay, but I can't play very long."

He pulled on her hand. "Now!"

The kid was beginning to sound just like his father. "Okay, let me get my jacket and stuff on." Ethan and Mary stood in the doorway while she got dressed.

"Are you leaving?" Mary asked, glancing around Marnie's room.

"Yeah. I've got to get back to Boston this afternoon." She couldn't believe how close she'd come to spending Christmas here—a dream with no chance of coming true.

She glanced around the room, the tall windows with the white light coming in through the frosted panes. Her bright blue top she'd forgotten to pack draped over a chair. All the memories this room held for her... "Okay, big guy, let's go."

"Thanks," Mary said, sighing. "Oh, by the way, Henry is waiting to go out with you. He's down by the patio doors."

"Would you like me to walk him?" Marnie asked.

"No, he's been walked, and he won't run away on you. He always stays with Ethan. You and Henry are best buddies, aren't you?" Mary asked, patting Ethan on the shoulder.

"Henry loves me." Ethan squared his shoulders, glancing from one woman to the other with a grin that would soften the meanest heart.

"I really appreciate this. We're so busy today with getting the Christmas Getaway guests settled in for the evening activities."

"It's not a problem."

She took Ethan's hand and went downstairs with him, listening to his excited chatter about playing in the snow, and as she listened, all she could think about was that this was over for her. This was the last time she'd play outside with Ethan, or walk past the dining room, or greet the other staff members she'd gotten to know.

She really should say goodbye to Francine when she came back in from playing with Ethan. She liked her so much and would miss her, but not nearly as much as she would miss Luke and Ethan.

She blinked to keep from crying and made a big deal out of getting Ethan's mitts on before she opened the patio doors. Henry barked in canine delight as he waited, his nose pressed to the glass of the door.

"There. We're ready, aren't we?" she asked the dog, rubbing his glossy coat.

"Go!" Ethan pulled on the door handle in vain. "Out, please," he said, turning his sorrowful look on Marnie.

"Okay, off we go," she said with all the bravado she could muster.

Ethan squeezed past her through the door as he and Henry raced each other into the snow. Outside, the air was crisp and the wind swirled a plume of snow up past the windows of the inn. The lights on the fir tree by the corner of the patio glowed like sugarcoated jelly beans through the snow-covered branches. Someone had cleared the patio of snow, creating an outdoor playroom.

"My truck." Ethan shuffled over to the huge yellow dump truck sticking out of the wall of snow. His arms flailing at the snow, he yelled over his shoulder. "Help me dig."

Marnie knelt down beside him, and dug his truck out of the drift. As she watched the little boy playing with his truck, accompanied by his gleeful chatter about Santa, cookies and Christmas, she felt overwhelmed by a sense of loss. This would be the last time she played with Ethan, and she was so sorry to be leaving him. Forcing back her tears, she filled her mitts with snow and dumped them into the back of the truck.

UNABLE TO CONCENTRATE on his work, Luke was about to shut off his computer when the phone rang. When he answered, a voice boomed, "This is Simon Mandel."

Luke didn't recognize the name. "How can I help you?"

"I called to compliment a member of your staff."

"Thank you, Mr. Mandel, we always appreciate hearing compliments about our staff."

"I booked a ski package at your inn the other night. A woman name Marnie something made the reservation. Can't remember her last name, but her first name stuck because I'd never heard it before. Anyway, she was so friendly and went out of her way to explain everything to me. I had planned to book with another inn and was just calling for a price comparison, but Marnie convinced me to book with you. That's one smart lady you've got there, and I ought to know. I'm in retail and I don't need to tell you how hard it is to hire good people who understand the customer's need to feel appreciated."

Remorse knotted Luke's stomach. Marnie would never know how much this client appreciated her. A few hours ago, he would have searched her out, told her about what the man had said. But he'd made the decision that sent her packing, and now... Now, he wished he could tell her about the compliment, about how much he appreciated her helping them in a pinch, and doing such a good job for him. And she had done a good job, the other staff had corroborated that, but he hadn't told her that, either. He'd let her leave here without ever acknowledging that she'd made a difference to the inn and to him. "I'll be sure to tell her," he lied.

"You do that, and you tell her I'm looking forward to meeting her in person in February."

"I will," he lied again.

He hung up, wishing he could take back what he'd said to Marnie. Part of the reason he'd accomplished nothing since she'd left his office was that he'd mulled over what she'd said, and despite the fact he was still angry, he had to admit that she was right. Anna would have wanted to get back home to him, to Ethan. Sure she should have waited for the storm to pass, but she loved them, and she would have wanted to be home to tuck Ethan into bed and then watch *It's a Wonderful Life* with Luke as they'd planned to do.

As much as he resented Marnie's words, she had made him face the anger he felt toward Anna. But once again, he'd been too proud to confront how he felt, so he'd taken it out on Marnie.

Had he used his grief to protect himself from ever caring for anyone again? Marnie wouldn't have said the things she'd said, unless she had feelings for him. Why didn't he just admit his mistake and bring her back?

There was no time to lose if he wanted this to be a special Christmas, one he would remember for the rest of his life. He prayed he wasn't too late, that she was already gone...probably halfway home to Christmas with her family.

*You didn't even say goodbye to her, or wish her a merry Christmas.*

Feeling like the biggest jerk ever he left his office in search of her. He got as far as the dining room when he heard Ethan crying. He strode quickly in the direction of the sound, his heart pounding with anxiety. At the hall leading to the patio, he saw his son clinging to Marnie's neck, the tears staining her cheeks. As he approached, Henry slinked past him down the corridor.

Relief flooded through him at the sight of her standing there holding his son. Until this moment he'd had no idea how desperately he would've missed her if she'd gone back to Boston.

"No!" Ethan screamed louder, snow sliding off his snowsuit and creating puddles on the floor.

"Ethan, honey, please don't cry, or I'll be crying with you." She untangled his arms from her neck and lifted his chin.

"Please stay," he whimpered again, burying his face in her neck, his tiny shoulders shaking as he sobbed.

There was such gentleness in the way she held his son, the curve of her arm offering support to a little boy who obviously didn't want Marnie to go.

*Face it. You don't want her to go, either.*

Suddenly aware of him, Marnie lifted her head. "We were outside playing in the snow, but I have to get on the road, so I had to bring him in. I didn't mean to make him cry, but he wanted me to come to the apartment and play Lego with him."

His chest aching with loss of what might be if he could overcome his fears and reach out to this beautiful woman, he finally managed to find his voice. "He's going to miss you."

He took Ethan in his arms, the dampness of his son's clothing penetrating the dress shirt he wore. He didn't care. Nothing mattered except to soothe his son, and to find the words that would make this woman standing here so tentatively in front of him stay in his life.

"I'll miss him, too, but that's life, I guess." She shrugged, her eyes brimming with emotion.

"You're really good with kids."

"Thanks," she said weakly.

He rubbed his son's shoulders, wanting to take Marnie in his arms and beg her to stay. "I was actually hoping you hadn't left because I have something…a message to pass on to you."

"Not my brother again!" She groaned.

"No, a Mr. Mandel, who called to compliment you on the way you handled his reservation."

"He did? That's great. I remember him. He sounded like a really nice man who wanted to take his entire family on a skiing vacation, and needed three rooms with two double beds in each. He also wanted the spa for après ski recovery. I gathered from what he said that his wife and he have taken up skiing to please his family more than anything. So, he was happy with what I put together for him." She stopped. "I'm babbling! This is so embarrassing."

"Maybe a bit," he conceded. "However, he was filled with praise for how you handled his requests."

"I should get him to talk to my brothers—proof that I can do something well," she said, a sardonic look on her face.

"But you owned a successful salon, and that takes a heck of a lot of skill and hard work."

"But that's not how success is defined in the McLaughlan family."

"Well, for what it's worth, I think your family are job snobs."

"That's an expression I've never heard before." She looked straight at him, the corners of her mouth turned up in a quizzical smile.

"My word for the day, and it describes people who subscribe to the belief that unless you have a high-profile

career and an Ivy League education, you're not a success. I have a cousin who's a job snob."

Her rich, deep laugh made Ethan frown. "I'm hungry," he announced.

"You're always hungry," Luke said, laughing with
Marnie as he put Ethan down. "I suppose I'd better find
him something to eat before he corners the pastry chef
for more sweets. Would you like to come with me?"

An uneasy silence stretched between them as he
searched for the words that would erase the memory of
his earlier brusqueness.

She raised her eyes to his, her expression guarded.
"I've got to go. Mary had asked me if I'd play with Ethan
one last time." She forced her gaze past him, her eyes
glistening. "I couldn't refuse, but now I have to get on
the road. Thank you for having me here." She focused
her attention on the wall behind him as she brushed
past him.

Luke felt as if he'd been punched in the stomach.
She was walking away from him. He couldn't let her
go. He needed her there with him. "I want you to stay,"
he blurted.

She stopped and stared up into his face. "I'd like that,
but I'm not sure if it's the right thing for either of us."

His heart plummeted. He had to find the words that
would change her mind. "Could you be a little more specific? I'm not good at this type of thing."

"I need to know that if I stay it means you're willing
to see the potential in us. I've never felt like this before,
but I also know that you're still angry with your wife,
and that means you're not ready for a relationship."

No… He'd been alone long enough. "But I am," he
said, his voice breaking.

She touched her fingers to his lips. "Don't say that

until you mean it. I need to be honest with you. I don't want to start another doomed relationship. My record when it comes to relationships gets a failing grade, and that's not likely to change with a man who still has issues. If this hurts you, I'm sorry, but I need a relationship based on honesty. And ours didn't start out that way. I've told you the truth now, and I really believe you need to face your own truth. I can't live in her shadow. If this is too much honesty, I'll understand."

Was his inability to let go of his anger at Anna the reason why he was still feeling so lost, as if he was living outside his life?

He had been angry at what Marnie had said about not being able to let go, but the anger had allowed him to see himself through someone else's eyes. He didn't want to be angry anymore. He wanted to love again, to know the thrill of being with someone who lit up his life. And if he let Marnie go, he'd never have the chance to find out if this woman, with her great laugh and her infinite ability to make him smile, to encourage him to face life, was the woman for him.

"Will you please stay? It's Christmas Eve, a time for miracles." He chuckled at that. "If you stay I promise you a very special Christmas."

She moved so close to him that her perfume clouded his senses. He reached for her, pulling her into his arms. "Say you'll stay."

"I will," she whispered.

His lips sought hers, gently at first, tasting her, breathing in her scent. But when her arms went around his neck and she pulled him down toward her, her tongue on his, his reserve faded. He pulled her tighter, sliding his hands over her hips, forcing her against his erection, his body flooding with heat as her hands tightened around his neck.

He held her, his fingers in her hair, her body pressed to his, the thrill of once again being alive to another person aroused him so much he came dangerously close to dragging her off to his room, the stairwell, anywhere they could have a few precious moments of privacy.

"Daddy!" Ethan pushed against his father's legs. "I'm hungry!"

Startled, Luke sucked in air, banking his need as he kissed her once more—lightly this time, nuzzling her cheek, and hearing her sharp intake of breath. "Meet me for dinner around seven?"

She kissed his jaw, her lips lingering. "Sounds perfect."

His body thrummed from the touch of her lips on his skin. "Christmas Eve is the busiest day of the holiday. So much has to be done around here. And we're having a traditional Christmas dinner. I'm afraid that, as my date, you'll have to share the hosting duties."

She leaned back into his embrace, a teasing grin on her face. "Another date?"

"And more whenever you like."

"I'll have to move back to my old room. Mary tells me all the guests are on their way here now."

"Have I told you I have a certain fondness for that room?"

"No, you haven't," she said, laughter in her voice and a mischievous smile on her face.

"It was where I stayed while they renovated my apartment."

"So you've had a few encounters with the walls."

He laughed, a laugh that cleansed and warmed him. "I have."

"Daddy!"

"I'm coming, big guy." He took Ethan's hand. "See you later?"

"I wouldn't miss it for the world."

## CHAPTER TWELVE

ALL HER LIFE SHE'D DREAMED of a man running his fingers through her hair, in just the way Luke had done. The men she'd dated had wanted to run their fingers somewhere else. Not that she didn't want to have sex with Luke—she did—only this time it would be with the man she loved.

As she gathered her bags to move back to her tiny room, she marveled at what a rollercoaster ride the past few days had been. She'd have to call her mother, and tell her that she wouldn't be home for Christmas, a call that would fill her with guilt. Yet somehow, she had to make her family understand that she needed to be with Luke, without letting them launch into their stories that proved how impulsive she was around men, how little she seemed to know about picking the right man, and on and on and on…

She sighed as she put her makeup back in its case and checked her appearance in the mirror. Then she lugged her bag up to her old room, put things away and closed the door.

When she reached the bottom of the stairs and started down the hall, she heard music. Someone was playing the piano, a beautiful rendering of Beethoven's "Moonlight Sonata." Curious to see who it was, she slipped into the dining room, and made her way over to the far corner. She found Luke playing the baby grand piano nestled in behind a folding room divider. Ethan was sitting beside him with his face turned up to his father adoringly.

Luke finished playing and smiled up at her. "Ethan came to share my coffee break, and we decided to play the piano together. How's your afternoon going?" he asked, resting his arms on the top of the piano.

"I didn't know you played the piano."

"What's that old cliché? There's a whole lot you don't know about me."

"Marnie!" Ethan shimmied off the piano seat, throwing his arms around her legs.

"I've got you," she whispered as she lifted him up, hugging his little body next to hers. "Can I sit next to your dad? I'll hold you on my lap?"

He squeezed her cheeks between his hands. "Yes!"

"Ethan, why don't you try for your indoor voice, please," Luke said, suppressing a grin.

"Do you play often?" she asked, sliding onto the bench beside him, keeping her arm around Ethan.

"I don't, but somehow this afternoon it just felt right to be down here at the keyboard."

As he began the opening bars of Beethoven's ninth symphony, Marnie couldn't help but notice his fingers, their length and their controlled touch on each key. She listened, feeling the emotional thrust of the cascading notes until the melody faded and Luke lifted his hands off the keys.

"I used to play the piano before I started Total Elegance. It seemed there wasn't any time for the piano after that. I really miss it, especially the songbooks from the Big Band era."

Appreciation flared in his eyes, his gaze fixed on her. "I prefer classical. My all-time favorite is Beethoven."

A blush moved up her neck to her cheeks. "You were playing 'Moonlight Sonata' when I came in," she murmured, as he turned toward her, his lips inches from hers. She had an overwhelming urge to kiss him.

"Is music the way to your heart?" he asked gently.

"Music is the way to anyone's heart, isn't it?" she countered, feeling suddenly vulnerable. "And yes, music is very close to my heart."

"What else is close to your heart?" he asked, the innuendo in his tone leading her to have thoughts of bed—his bed.

*Careful. Take it slow.*

"Peanut-butter cups, long walks and *The New York Times,*" she offered.

"I'm impressed, especially the peanut-butter part." He played a few quick chords. "And my favorite Sunday morning occupation is reading *The New York Times* in bed."

Visions of the two of them in bed together, reading the paper filled her mind. "Mine, too."

His fingers halted. "Want to play 'Chopsticks'?" he asked, his fingers once more moving languidly over the ivory keys, his dark eyebrows arched in challenge.

"'Chopsticks'?" she said. "I can do better than that."

She adjusted Ethan on her lap, ready to show this man her one social skill.

"I'm waiting." He moved over on the piano bench, letting her settle in front of middle C.

She began the opening bars of "Moon River." Ethan plunked his hands on top of hers and began to sing off-key in unintelligible words.

"Want to play a duet?" she asked him, kissing Ethan's cheek, and he immediately responded by smacking a kiss on her cheek.

The sound of Luke's laughter enveloped her—carefree laughter, the kind that turned heads and caused others to join in. Completely happy to sit here and play the piano with Ethan on her lap, she slowed the tempo of the melody, as she adjusted his fingers over hers.

"What does that music make you think of?" Luke asked close to her ear, sending a thrill through her.

*How utterly content I am right at this moment. How easily I could stay right here for as long as you want me to.*

"I'm thinking that Ethan and I make a great duo, don't you, Luke?"

"You certainly do." He grinned.

"Okay, Ethan, let's show your dad what we can really do."

"My cue to get out of the way," he said, getting up off the bench and going to stand next to the piano.

HER SMILE WENT STRAIGHT to his heart, filling him with a need so strong he wanted to make love to her right then and there. Fighting the urge to send Ethan off to be with his babysitter, Luke leaned on the piano instead, and listened as Marnie guided his son's fingers over the keys in an unhurried rendition of "Tennessee Waltz." It had been so long since he'd felt like this, this feeling that someone special loved the piano the way he did.

Ethan tilted his head up and smiled at Luke, and all he could think about was how much he needed this. How thankful he was that he'd managed to convince her to stay with him, if only until tomorrow. He couldn't let himself consider how he'd cope when she went back to Boston, which she'd have to do sometime soon, leaving him to feel her absence.

"The dynamic duo," he said, trying for a lighthearted tone he didn't feel.

"That we are," she said, switching to a few chords with Ethan's fingers clinging to hers.

"Daddy, I love Marnie." Ethan planted a noisy kiss on her cheek without removing his fingers from her hands.

She looked startled for a moment, and then pleasure swept across her face. "I paid him to say that. Trying to get in good with the boss."

"You're already in good with the boss." He came around the piano and slid back onto the bench beside her.

"Daddy, go away," Ethan said, elbowing him.

Luke wished they could continue like this, that he didn't have to go back to the reality of overseeing the Christmas Eve preparations. What he wouldn't give right now to be able to stay where he was, to feel what he was feeling for the rest of his life. He took Ethan into his arms to hide the raw emotions rolling in his chest. "Love you, buddy—" Luke pointed in the direction of the door where one of his staff stood ready to take him back to the apartment "—but Charlene's waiting for you over there. See?"

Ethan scrambled out of his arms and ran across the room, making the edges of the tablecloths flutter as he passed them, before throwing himself into the woman's arms.

Watching Marnie from the corner of his eye, he made a decision. "Hope you don't mind me asking you something."

"Sure," she said, acutely aware of how good his body felt pressed ever so gently along hers. "Ask away."

"Have you ever considered having children?"

She glanced up at the ceiling, studying the chandelier, stalling for time. What could she say to that? That she was afraid? That it didn't matter so much what she wanted, but what life dealt her? "Having children is a huge commitment."

"You're ducking the question."

"If I were lucky enough to have children, I'd want to be home with them full-time at least until they went to school. I know that lots of mothers work full-time while they raise their family, but I couldn't do it." If she were ever blessed with a child she would keep her child close.

His fingers encircled her hand, his touch as he traced a line over her palm, making her skin tingle. "The way you are with Ethan…you'd make a great parent." His voice was low, sexy and went straight to her heart.

She wanted to tell him that she loved kids, would love to have kids, but there were some issues too painful to share. "I want a career, and I'd love to have kids, too. But it's a lot of responsibility…and maybe I've waited too long."

"I'm not convinced." He slid his arms around her, his mouth searching for hers. Unable to resist him, she leaned into his embrace, touching his chin, angling her fingers into the open neck of his shirt. His lips moved along her cheek, close to her ear. "But right now, we have a more urgent matter to attend to."

Oh, God. Was she about to get her wish? Were they headed back to her tiny room? "And that would be?"

"Want to play a duet?"

Why did she always have to be wrong? And when would she get her wish? "What did you have in mind?"

"How about 'I'm Dreaming of a White Christmas'?"

"You got it," she said, her gaze going to the windows and the snow outside.

"No kidding! Okay. Follow my lead," he whispered,

placing his hands carefully on the keys as his gaze held hers.

She followed his notes with tinkling high notes on her end of the keyboard, harmonizing with him, as they sang the song's verses together.

Caught up in the moment, Marnie's spirits soared with each note. She'd never done this before with a man. Piano had been her mother's idea, and she'd gone along with it to make her mom happy. But now, she wished she could go on making music with Luke forever. As the last notes rose then faded, she met his gaze and saw the raw need in his eyes.

"That was awesome," he said. Without touching her, he kissed her lightly, the tension in his body matching hers, and then pulled her into his embrace. Her head was spinning with the sensation of being held so tenderly. With his arms encircling her, he whispered. "We have an audience."

She pulled away. "There goes your story about me being your assistant."

He held her fast. "Maybe we can drop the story and go for the real thing."

"Meaning?" She held her breath.

"Marnie, I'm feeling so different. As if suddenly my whole life has changed, and you're the reason. Why don't we go somewhere private? No one will miss us."

His breath on her neck was hot, demanding. "Are you sure?"

"Yes. I've worked my butt off the last couple of days. I can disappear for a few hours and no one will blame me for taking a little time for myself."

She wanted him to make love to her. But she didn't want a casual fling. Yet, here he was waiting for her to say yes to his offer....

"Why are you hesitating?" he asked.

"Because I don't want… I need to believe we have something—"

"I can't promise you that everything will work out between us, but I want it to." He sighed. "You mean a lot to me. I'm happy when you're around."

"What are you saying?"

"You… We deserve the chance to know if what we're feeling for each other is real. I've seen those feelings in your eyes, and I feel the same way."

"But I'm a born loser when it comes to love."

"You're hung up on ideas about yourself that aren't true. I understand how your track record when it comes to relationships could make you shy away from anything new. But if you never give it a try, you could miss out on something incredible."

"And what if we start a relationship, and Ethan gets attached to me, and then something happens between us? He doesn't deserve to be hurt again."

"Ethan has a whole group of people here who love him, and look out for him. They'll be there for him no matter what happens."

"How can you be so sure?"

"Are you looking for excuses?" he asked, exasperated.

"I…I don't know."

He held her shoulders in his powerful hands and looked her straight in the eye. "I'm not worried about you and me. In my opinion we're meant to be."

She shook her head, focusing on anything but his face.

He touched her chin, raising her eyes to his. "Are you willing to give up on us so easily?"

The hurt in his eyes tore through her with the force

of a hurricane. This very kind, gorgeous, sexy man was offering her the chance to share his love, and he had a son she adored.

*Go ahead, do your usual thing. Make a joke. It's how you usually get out of an emotional situation.*

"Stay right here. I have to go make a phone call. I'm sorry, but it can't wait. "

He stared at her, not moving, not saying a word, then grasped her head with both his hands and kissed her hard this time, before pulling away. "I'll be waiting."

Marnie got up, and fumbled her way out of the dining room, past several guests who smiled at her. She ignored them. She couldn't seem to clear her thoughts, her pulse pounded in her head. All she wanted was to get up to her room before she embarrassed herself by crying. She'd waited so long for a chance with a guy like Luke. A guy who made her feel valued…cherished… special. But most of all, he offered her what she'd missed out on all these years—the opportunity to have a real relationship.

## CHAPTER THIRTEEN

SHE'D NEVER DEFIED HER MOTHER, not openly at least. What a sad thing to have to admit at the age of thirty-five. But that had been her life…so far. She'd always complained about her family running her life, her brothers' interference, but Luke had made her realize that she had *allowed* her family to control her life.

She was aware that her family was especially protective of her, all because they were concerned about her health, but their concern after her accident had become a habit of constantly weighing in on her life and how she lived it. Still, she hadn't fought back or stood up for herself—until she'd decided to sell her salon.

It was time to call her mother.

When Eleanor McLaughlan answered, there was impatience in her voice. "Honey, you haven't called me all week, and I was worried. Scott said you were coming home today, and I've been waiting. Have you forgotten what day this is?"

"Christmas Eve."

"Where are you? Your brothers and their families are due here later this afternoon. I need you. I have your Mrs. Claus outfit all ready. We agreed—"

"We didn't agree, Mom. You just assumed I'd show up."

There was a moment of silence in which Marnie suddenly wished she could simply pack up and go home, erase the flat line of her mother's lips and once again be the person in the family whom everyone could always rely on.

"Well, yes, of course your father and I have expectations of you, and your brothers do, too. You're part of this family, and part of our Christmas tradition. Have you forgotten we've got everyone coming over after church tonight, and you're the one who leads the Christmas singing?"

"No, of course I didn't."

"Then, tell me what's going on with you. Why did you leave home without saying anything to your father and me? How am I supposed to host our Christmas party without you? And what's this about you selling your business?"

Guilt made her stomach pain and her head throb. She'd let her mother down by not doing what was expected of her. How easy, how completely automatic, it would be to utter the words that would appease her mother—to go home to her old bedroom at her parents' house over Christmas, and get the requisite cashmere sweater and Guess bag.

How easy and how awful.

And it would continue to be that way for as long as she allowed it. If she didn't take control of her own life, she'd soon be booking a room at her parents' seniors residence so she could continue her daughterly duties. Visions of her and her parents playing cribbage or bridge or some other game popular with the retired set popped into her mind.

She might not be an athlete, and she hadn't graduated from college, but she shouldn't have to do her family's bidding. She was a successful businesswoman who had earned the right to make her own decisions. "Mom, I won't be home for Christmas," she said.

"You what!" Her mother's voice held a mixture of anger and disbelief.

"I've been away trying to figure out what I want to do with my life now that I've sold my business. And I think… No, I've *found* what I want to do."

"Oh, for heaven's sake!" her mother said, indignantly. "Why don't you wait and discuss it with the family when you get here?"

"Mom, what I do with my life has to be my decision."

"Why are you acting so…so unlike yourself, honey? Why didn't you postpone your decision to sell your business until we had a chance to talk it over with you?" she asked, her voice taking on that familiar tone suggesting that once again Marnie hadn't quite reached the goal set for her.

"I've met someone." Marnie swallowed against the flood of feelings engulfing her. She wished Luke was beside her, to offer support. But Luke didn't know she loved him.

She closed her eyes, letting her feelings for Luke wash over her, a smile forming on her lips. "I'm in love for the first time in my life. Genuinely, truly in love with a man who has a little boy."

Eleanor gasped. Marnie could picture her fingers flying to her throat, clutching her single strand of Mikimoto pearls, her look of shock as she peered over her half-glasses at Dad. "But, Marnie, how could this happen so fast? How do you know him? Where does he live? What does he do for a living?"

"Mom, slow down. His name is Luke, and he's—"

"Why not bring him here for Christmas? The family needs to meet him."

"He can't come, because he runs an inn, and he has to be here for Christmas. And I want to be here with him and his son, whose name is Ethan. I've been staying at his inn, and there was a snowstorm, and I helped him out. His best friend and his wife had a baby during the storm."

"What an emotional time for you, honey, but maybe that's all this is. Simply an emotional reaction to the circumstances?" she asked, her voice warm and soothing, the implication clear. The only daughter of Mr. and Mrs. McLaughlan could not possibly be right about something they had no input on.

Her fingers tightened around the phone. "No, Mom. It's not like that at all. I love him. Please understand. I've never felt like this."

"Marnie, you know your father and I worry about you, and want you to be happy, but are you certain about this? I mean it's so fast. You're often so quick in your decision making, and sometimes it's had a negative influence on your life."

She wished her mother could behave differently toward her, just this once. She knew it wasn't going to happen, and it made her very sad. She closed her eyes, steeling herself against her mother's disappointment. "Mom, I won't be there until probably the day after Christmas. I'll call you."

"By all means," her mother said, her words stiff.

Marnie got off the phone, awash in sadness. Why did every important conversation with her mother leave her feeling inadequate? Why couldn't her mother try to be happy for her?

Her cell phone danced in her hands causing Marnie's heart to pound. This call was bound to be from her father, her mother's trump card when it came to getting Marnie to do her bidding.

Instead, it was Scott. It had been a long time since she'd welcomed a call from him. "Hey, what's up?"

"Marnie, I've got good news," Scott said.

"Good news for you or for me?"

"For you. Advantage Corporation has decided not to go through with the survey after all."

"Well, I have news for you, too. I decided not to turn in the results."

"Really? Why?"

"Because it felt too much like spying on someone I care about. I couldn't do it. I was going to tell you today."

"That's it? So, you've been sitting up there surrounded by luxury, enjoying a great vacation? Is there something you're not telling me?"

"It's a long story. Mom can fill you in on the details."

"You've been holding out on me, haven't you?"

"It doesn't really matter. I won't be home today."

"Do Mom and Dad know?" Scott sounded shocked.

"Yes. I just got off the phone with Mom."

"What did she say?"

"Oh, you know. The usual stuff."

"Well, I guess there isn't much more for me to say. One great thing came out of all this, though. Advantage wants me to make a proposal for their next major ad campaign."

"Did they say any more about their plans for the Mirabel?" she asked.

"They're on their way there now."

"On Christmas Eve? You've got to be kidding. Who does business on Christmas Eve?"

"Welcome to a new world of decision making, my dear sister."

"Does Luke know?"

"The manager? I assume so."

Why hadn't Luke said anything? What if he didn't know? "I've got to go."

"Wait! When will you be back in town?"

She couldn't think about that now. She needed to get to Luke. "Soon, I hope. Talk to you later."

"Merry Christmas, Marnie."

"Yeah, you, too," she said. It might not be a merry season for Luke, and she had to find him. "I've got to go."

LUKE HAD TRIED TO WORK on his cost projections for next year, but his mind wouldn't cooperate. All he could think about was Marnie, why she'd rushed off and hadn't returned. He was pacing and worrying about her when the office phone rang. Relieved to have a distraction, he answered.

"It's Angus McAndrew here. I need to speak with Luke Harrison."

Oh…no. "Speaking."

"We've been going over the financial reports you sent us, and we'd like to meet with you. I realize it's the holiday season and all, but this can't wait. We have a board of directors meeting the first week of January."

Luke's stomach tightened in anticipation of the board's decision. "When would you like to meet?"

"We're on our way up from Boston now, and we should be there in a couple of hours. I have my accountants and acquisitions people with me."

"Are you planning to put the inn up for sale?"

"Yes, that will be part of the discussion."

Anger toward this man who could be so uncaring not to see what he was doing to Luke's life, not to mention the lives of all his staff, wiped all other thoughts from his mind. If there was even the slightest chance that he could convince McAndrew to let him make a counter offer, he'd do it. But he needed money to make a bid for the inn, and that meant finding a backer. "I'll be here," he said.

The conversation ended with the usual pleasantries, and he couldn't wait to get off the phone. He twirled his steel pen in his fingers. He'd try his father first. He might know someone interested in financing the purchase.

His father's cell phone went immediately to voice mail, and he left a message. As he hung up, someone knocked on the door. He rose to answer it. Marnie stood there, her eyes wide. "Oh, Luke, something's happened," she said, a frown drawing her eyebrows together. She slid into his arms, hugging him close. Love swelled through his chest: love and need and want and all the emotions he'd ever felt for a woman, as he enfolded her in his arms.

"I just got off the phone with Scott. The people from Advantage Corporation are on their way here."

"I know. They called here a few minutes ago." He continued to hold her close, to soak in the feeling of her in his arms, a wave of yearning sweeping through him.

She rubbed his back as she nestled her body against his. "What did they say?"

"They're coming to talk about the inn, about selling it."

"No. Does that mean you still have a job?"

He tightened his arms around her, seeking reassurance. "I assume so, but it will ultimately be up to the purchaser, and they may bring in their own manager.

Or Advantage might offer me a job at another one of their hotels."

"Where would that be? I mean, would you have a chance at a job somewhere else around here?"

"They have a group of boutique hotels spread out all over the world. It could be anywhere they have a position they think I could fill," he said with as much enthusiasm as he could muster.

She gazed up at him, her eyes searching his. "Would you move?"

He shook his head. "I can't leave here. My life is here. Ethan loves it here, and these people are my family." He had no other family, none he could count on, at any rate.

"Maybe they'll decide not to move you until they have a buyer."

"That's possible."

"Is there another option? Anything else we might be able to do?"

He eased out of her arms, aware of the anxiety in her eyes, and wished he had another choice. "Unless you have a couple million or so dollars hidden away somewhere, there's not much we can do. The owners will be here soon. They'll look over the facility, probably offer me a position elsewhere, then leave and go home to their families for Christmas."

"We have to come up with something." She began pacing the room, her hands on her hips, her firm breasts pressing against the soft fabric of her white T-shirt. His body hardened. He wanted to make love to her. And not the slow and easy kind of loving, but the kind that left them both panting and wanting more.

"Marnie, stop pacing for a moment," he said. "I have something to ask you."

She stopped. "I'm listening."

Determined not to let her duck the question this time, he took her hands in his. "The last time I saw you, you needed to do something before we could talk about us. Did you get it done?"

"I did." She searched his face. "I talked to my mom, and I had an epiphany, you might say."

"Don't do this to me, woman."

"I…" Her fingers wrestled with his. "This is probably not the time or the place, and you have so much on your mind right now."

She was driving him crazy. "Out with it."

She squeezed his fingers as a smile blossomed on her face. "I love you."

He ran his hands up her arms, along her neck, savoring the feel of her skin beneath his fingers, anxiety circling his mind. "You love me?" he asked. "How can you be sure?"

# CHAPTER FOURTEEN

IT WAS DÉJÀ VU ALL over again.

A few minutes ago in her room with her mother as her only witness, she'd confessed to loving Luke Harrison. Then she'd traipsed down here expecting him to be overjoyed.

She'd expected him to say that he loved her, too. By the way he held her, by the look in his eyes, she believed he felt the same as she did, that they were meant to be together. She had imagined that Luke's feelings for her ran as deep and as strong as hers did for him, but she'd confused lust for love.

That's all this was really about.

If only she'd kept her big mouth shut. In her silly rush to tell him, she'd never entertained the possibility that he'd be less than thrilled with her confession.

She'd taken the stupid-in-love approach, and confessed her feelings to a man who obviously didn't share them, and she'd been too intent on her dream to see what was right in front of her.

She was aging, growing old and desperate. She was desperate enough to think that a man as handsome as Luke might find an unemployed hairdresser with chipped nails and an overprotective family loveable.

Had she really expected him to say those three little words after only three days of knowing each other, during which their opportunities for intimacy had been thwarted by everything else going on?

Her cheeks glowed red. Tears of humiliation pricked beneath her lids. She turned away, feigning interest in an impressionist painting of water and trees on his office wall. Messed up water and trees, messed up like her.

*Concentrate on the gentle scene in the painting. Take a deep breath. Get your act together and figure out how to get out of this room without making another blunder.*

"Marnie, look at me."

She had no intention of facing him. She had her pride to consider. "I have to get back to my room."

He turned her around and slowly tilted her face up to his. "You can go to your room after I'm done."

Not "I'm sorry." Not one whisper about love, about anything remotely related to an intimate relationship. Just a direct order—like she was a member of his staff.

She wasn't going to let him boss her around. Not a chance. She raised her eyes and stared directly into his.

Would she never learn? Her mother and her family were right. Her impulsive behavior had resulted in regret, again.

She gently disentangled herself from him. She needed to get away. Away from the humiliation of believing in something that would never be. "I've got to pack."

"Is this your answer? To run away whenever you're faced with real feelings?" he demanded, leaping past her and blocking the door.

"Please don't pretend to care, and don't worry about my bill. As you said yourself, you have Scott's credit card."

"What's gotten into you?"

She didn't answer him, nor did she look him in the eye. She seemed to be studying the front of his shirt.

"Marnie, do you have any idea what your words mean to me?"

Her gaze slowly moved up his shirtfront. "My words were a mistake. Forget I said them." She moved to one side, making it plain she planned to escape past him.

He stepped in front of her. "Not so fast. You haven't answered my question."

"Your question. I make a complete fool of myself and you're worried about me not answering your question." She snorted, and this time her eyes locked on his.

Her beautiful green eyes, luminous with suspicion, searched his, as passion welled up in his heart, shattering his reserve. He struggled to find his voice, his heart drumming in his chest. His brain wouldn't function; he couldn't find the words to say what he so desperately needed to say.

His hands holding her arms began to tremble. He cleared his throat. "Marnie, I love you. That's why I was so surprised when you said it. And yes, I'm sure I sounded like I didn't believe you or didn't feel the same way, and I'm sorry if what I said hurt you."

Her eyes closed, and two small rivulets of tears trickled slowly from beneath her lids, meandering down her cheeks. But it was her sigh, so filled with longing and raw emotion, that was his undoing. He pulled her against him, holding her chin in his eager fingers, his lips moving over hers. His mouth brushed hers, hesitating on the sensitive skin at corner of her mouth, eliciting her sudden intake of breath. He took her head in his hands and kissed her lips, the heat of her body fanning the fire already threatening to burn out of control.

She returned his kiss, her body seeking his, pressing into his erection and forcing a groan of pleasure from him. He trailed his lips along her jaw toward her ear, relishing in the soft tenderness of her skin. His hands cupping her head, he eased her face back, tilting it up so that he could look straight into her eyes. "Marnie, I love you. I loved you the moment I met you on the front step. I didn't recognize it as love because I was too wrapped up in my own selfish concerns to acknowledge my feelings, which shows you just how dumb I can be. But from the first—that instant I saw you—you've been all I can think about."

Again her incredible green eyes searched his, a slight smile tugging at the corners of her mouth. "I was so sure you didn't like me. You were kind of rude, you know."

"Why do you think I delivered your dinner that night?"

"I don't know—all that was going through my mind was that you'd see my pink bustier."

He laughed in a way he hadn't laughed for a very long time.

"What's so funny?" she asked.

He inhaled her scent, clinging to the moment, wishing they could stay like this forever. "You know those yellow shoes caught my attention first, but you really had me going with that pink bustier. You wouldn't be wearing it now, by any chance, would you?"

"Sorry to disappoint, but today's offering is a standard C-cup utility model."

"I'll take whatever you're offering." Giving in to the happiness her smiling face held for him, he kissed her mouth again, lingering, alive in the moment. He was no longer alone, but held in his arms the one person he'd found who could relight his life.

She sighed deeply and her body arched to conform to his. "I meant it when I said I love you. But standing here like this is driving me crazy. Could we take this somewhere? Maybe my attic abode?"

"We can take it anywhere you want," he said, his arms circling her waist, happiness bubbling through him. He kissed her again and again, wanting more of her with each taste.

A gentle tap on the door startled both of them. "Are we doomed never to have a moment alone?" he moaned as he moved her away from the door, keeping her body as close to his as possible. "Who is it?"

"It's Amanda. I'm sorry, but I need to speak to you. It's urgent."

Marnie took a seat in the guest chair near his desk while Luke opened the door. He threw her a knowing glance. "Come in."

Amanda entered the office, a worried frown on her face. "There are three men in business suits waiting in the library. Were you expecting them?"

"Did they give their names?"

"They did, but I didn't catch them. One of them passed me this." Amanda gave him a business card with Angus McAndrew's name on it.

"The CEO of Advantage Corporation is here," he said.

"They're here already?" Marnie asked, a slight tremble in her voice.

"So it appears." He turned the card over in his hands, his mind racing over how the meeting would go, who the potential purchaser was, what his future role would be.

"Who are these people?" Amanda asked, her worried look switching from Luke to Marnie and back again.

"This man who gave you the card runs the company that owns this inn."

Amanda's eyes widened. "The owners? What does that mean? Why are they here today of all days?"

"Let me talk to them and see exactly what's on their minds."

"Do you want me to show them in?" Amanda asked.

"No, I'll meet them in the library in a couple of minutes."

He closed the door behind Amanda before turning to Marnie. "Whatever happens in the next couple of hours, I'm not letting you go, so don't get any crazy ideas about packing your bags again," he warned, kissing her.

"They're a bunch of mean-spirited grinches to show up here at Christmas and drop bad news in your lap."

"So the sooner I meet with them, the sooner we can get back to our first Christmas together."

She put her arm around his waist, the warmth of her body his defense against his dread. "How can you be so calm?" she asked.

"Because I have you now." Luke let the air he'd been holding in his lungs escape in a long, tired sigh. "And as much as I'd like to continue this, it's time for me put my manager hat back on."

Marnie's hands rested on his chest, her expression one of determination. "I'll be here when you need me."

"I'm lucky you dropped into my life when you did."

"Dropping in is a specialty of mine. Don't forget to call when you're done."

"I'll call you the second they're gone."

"I'll be waiting." She stepped out of his arms, and went to his desk to jot down her cell-phone number. Bringing it over to him, she said, "I'll probably be in my room, but just in case I'm not, here's my number."

He studied the piece of paper in his hands, a sense

of calm settling over him. "You'll be the first person I'll call."

She gave him the thumbs-up. "It will all work out, you'll see."

"Based on what?"

"Based on the fact that we love each other, that we're going to deal with things together from now on, and that includes the three suits sitting in the library."

"Gotta love these feisty women," he said, kissing her hard on the mouth, his lips claiming hers, his body hardening. Then he released her and watched her leave the room.

Staring at the door, he wished he could let them stay out there a little longer to cool their heels, but he would only be postponing the inevitable. With a heavy sigh, he pulled on his tie and jacket, smoothed his hair and went down the hall to the library.

## CHAPTER FIFTEEN

MARNIE COULDN'T GET her legs to move fast enough as she rushed toward the library. She had to see what these men looked like. During the years she'd spent running the salon, she'd come to accept that you could learn so much simply by observing a person without them knowing—how they sat in a chair, how they stood, their expression, whether they made nervous hand movements, how easily they smiled.

She rounded the corner, her mind intent on her mission, and stopped short. The library with its fireplace bracketed by poinsettias and with the sun streaming through its tall windows, looked like something out of a fairy tale.

Except for the three men standing near the windows with their Brothers Grimm expressions.

Wouldn't you just know? Not a smile or a soft angle among them, and it appeared as if they were all wearing the same tie. She squinted into the sunlight to get a better look. They *were* all wearing the same tie. Talk about slavish obedience to the man—the man being Angus McAndrew. The triplets of Wall Street—Boston-style.

How she wanted to go in there and say something, do something, anything, to relieve her worry over what they were about to do to Luke. Indignation burned in her chest, and her jaw tightened at the prospect. Was there anything she could do? Anything she could say?

She peeked in at them again, and saw that each man held a BlackBerry in his perfectly manicured hands.... *Nice manicures,* she admitted grudgingly. She was staring at the three of them when, from down the hall, she heard Luke's deep baritone voice.

She stood perfectly still...there was something she could do. Something that might help Luke.

She retreated into the alcove by the stairs and waited for Luke to go by, and was about to head up to her room when he moved back down the hall to his office with the suited threesome in tow. The four men walked in silence toward Luke's office, Luke walking in front with the alpha dog, Angus McAndrew, while the Ken dolls brought up the rear, leaving behind a cloud of expensive colognes.

She waited for them to enter the office before scooting down the hall behind them. When she reached the office door, she hesitated, torn between wanting to listen at the door and wanting to get upstairs so she could put her plan into action.

She was about to move on when she realized the door was slightly ajar, and she could hear the men's voices quite clearly. She glanced up and down the hall, only to see Mary coming her way.

*Darn! She didn't want to be seen as a nosy eavesdropper, but she couldn't resist the opportunity, either.*

"Hi, Marnie—"

Marnie held her fingers to her lips as she moved a few feet from the door. "Luke's in there."

"With the three men?"

She should have known that the inn grapevine would be working double time on this one. "Yes, and I'm worried," she whispered.

"I am, too," Mary whispered back.

"What should we do?" Marnie asked.

"I'll keep people away from here, and you see what you can hear," Mary murmured so quietly Marnie wasn't sure if she'd heard her right.

*A woman after my own heart.*

"Thanks," she mouthed, and moved closer to the door, while Mary took up her post farther down the corridor.

LUKE LED THE MEN INTO his office, and realized too late that there were only three chairs. Oh, well, he might be better off standing for this meeting, anyway. "Gentlemen, please have a seat," he offered, moving to the filing cabinet at the back of the room. "Can I get you anything? Coffee? Tea?" He could use a drink of Scotch right about now.

"No, thanks," two of them said.

"I'll have a wee dram," Angus McAndrew said with a pleasant smile on his face.

"Certainly." Luke took a bottle of single-malt Scotch and a crystal glass from the top of the credenza that rested along one wall, and poured Angus a drink.

Angus took a sip, an appreciative gleam in his eyes. "Wonderful. It's been a long drive up here," he said, settling into the best chair in the room.

"Yes, I hear the roads are still pretty snow-packed, but the plows are working to clear them."

"I should hope so, because we had a couple of narrow misses on our way here. But that's winter in the northeast," Angus said, his gaze moving about the room. "Do you not have another chair? I'd like to get right down to business since we have a long drive back, and no one wants to miss Christmas Eve."

Idly, Luke wondered what Christmas Eve would be

like at Angus's house. Would he treat his family like employees? Or did he have a whole other side no one in his company would ever see? "I'll stand, if you don't mind."

"It wouldn't be right for you to have to stand while we discuss business," he said, his bushy eyebrows flexed over his eyes. When Luke refused to budge, the man sighed and continued. "Luke, we're here to discuss the future of The Mirabel Inn and its relationship with Advantage Corporation. After a full review of our assets, and in light of our shift away from smaller holdings—those under one-hundred rooms—the board has come to a decision." His tone was urbane, congenial and without a hint of personal involvement, with words that were code for changing the landscape of the company. Words used by people who cloaked their callous behavior in socially polite language. "So, you're planning to sell The Mirabel." A spasm knotted Luke's stomach.

"We have a potential buyer who has begun to put limitations on his bid. It's the main reason we felt we needed to come up here today."

"Go on," Luke said, suddenly interested. If the buyer they had was backing out, he might have a chance at putting in a bid. He didn't know where he'd find the money—there having been no return call from his father—but he'd wait and see what Angus had to say.

"While we're negotiating with the buyer, we need to discuss your place within our organization."

They were about to disassemble the life he'd made for Ethan and himself with one short speech to him about his value to the organization.

His anger toward these people who didn't give a damn about him or his life threatened to get the best of him, and he realized he had to get away from them, if only for a few minutes. "I'll get a chair and be right back."

Pushing open the door, he nearly ran headfirst into Marnie, her eyes huge with surprise. He closed the door quietly behind him. "What are you doing out here?"

"Nothing. I was just on my way to the—to my car."

"Without a jacket in this weather? You were listening at the door, weren't you?" he accused her.

"Well, someone left it open a tiny bit, and I couldn't help it. I'm worried about you."

He couldn't look into her imploring eyes, aware of how much he loved her, and how their future together could now be in jeopardy. He had to focus on finishing the meeting, and getting these men back on the road to Boston.

"Marnie, please do not get involved in this," he said.

"Did they tell you who the buyer is?"

He shook his head, longing to hold her, a reprieve from all the harsh reality playing out in his office. "I need to get a chair from the reception desk," he said, gathering all his reserves to walk past her down the hall.

On the way back, she reached for him. "Luke, I've got to do something, but I'll be right back, I promise. Wait for me, and please don't worry. I've got a plan."

"A plan?" he whispered. "The only thing that will save the inn is if we can find a buyer."

"There has to be someone out there who would see the inn as a great investment," she whispered back. "Let me work on it."

In the midst of this unsettling event, he'd found an ally, a friend, and someone he could rely on. He no longer felt isolated from the world around him. "I love you," he whispered.

"Ditto," she whispered, her smile consuming her face.

Inside his office, the room felt stuffy. The scent of men's colognes was overpowering. "So, you were saying that you're going to sell the inn." He set his chair down along the wall near the door.

"Yes, we are, but we want you to know that your position is safe here until the purchase is finalized." Andrew crossed one long leg over the other, and checked the knife-sharp seam on his pants.

No one's position was safe during a transition, regardless of what these men said. "Do you have an offer pending?"

The man hunkered in the corner—his nervous gaze flicking from his BlackBerry to a spot on the wall behind Luke's head—spoke up. "In the event our buyer doesn't go ahead with the deal, a photographer will be up—" the man grimaced "—January second."

"Well, that answers most of my questions," Luke said, angered that these people couldn't wait until after Christmas to come up here. If they'd waited until after Christmas, thus giving him and the staff a chance to enjoy the holiday, this decision might be easier to accept.

"There's so much going on within the company at the moment. I felt we needed to come here and see you personally," Angus said.

How could these three men sit there with their smug expressions and not care what they'd just done to him and the rest of the staff? They might be able to ruin his Christmas, but that didn't mean they could take up any more of his Christmas Eve. "I understand, but right now, I have a Christmas Eve celebration to host, and as you said earlier, you need to get back to your own families." He rose and started toward the door.

Angus caught up with him. "Luke, I'm sorry to have dropped this news without giving you a heads-up first, but the company is going through so many changes at the moment, many of which I've had to address rather quickly."

*Your stupid excuse doesn't cut it.*

"You do what you have to do."

"And I mean it, Luke, this job is yours at least until the new owner takes over. And you have my word that I will personally recommend that you be retained as manager in one of our hotels."

*And you expect me to believe you?*

"I appreciate that," Luke said, holding the door open for them.

Watching them troop out, his courage deserted him. He suddenly felt completely exhausted and bereft. He was certain the staff would be waiting to hear the outcome of the meeting, but he didn't have the heart to break the news to them right now. He simply didn't have anything left to give anyone.

All he wanted was to find Marnie and make love to her, to forget everything that had happened in the past hour. Closing his office door, he picked up the phone and called her room. No answer.

Where was that piece of paper with her cell-phone number on it? After searching for what seemed like forever, he found the scrap of paper, dialed her number, his spirits lifting at the expectation of hearing her voice, a voice he needed to hear more than anything in the world.

The call went to voice mail.

# CHAPTER SIXTEEN

MARNIE HAD BEEN ON HER WAY to her room, her hand on the newel post, about to ascend the stairs, when Jack intercepted her.

"Mary just told me what's been going on. Can we talk?"

She didn't want to talk right now. She had to come up with the money to buy the inn. "I can't. I mean I have to get to my room and call my brother."

He frowned. "What for?" he asked, his tone wary.

Marnie could understand him being suspicious. Jack had to know about the survey by now. "I… We need to see if we can line up some financing for this inn. Do you think Luke's parents would help out?"

"Luke's parents have been indifferent all of Luke's life."

"Indifferent?"

"Yeah, you know. Luke spent most of his childhood away at boarding schools, and even now, with Christmas here, there hasn't been a peep from them. Not so much as a card."

"No gift for Ethan?"

"Not unless it was held up by the storm."

"When was the last time they were here to visit?"

"They were here for about two weeks after Anna died."

"That was three years ago."

"And they kept talking about Anna's accident until Luke couldn't listen anymore."

They sounded like a totally useless set of parents, but if they could help in other ways... "Do you think there's any chance they'd be willing to loan him money?"

"According to Luke they live beyond their means. No spare cash, I assume." Jack gave her a grim look. "Marnie, you're a smart woman with lots of business experience, but a piece of advice."

"And that would be?"

"Don't go messing around in Luke's life. He doesn't like it. The inn may be for sale, but Luke will make it through this. He's tough."

"But if I know someone who might be willing to back him, should he decide to put in a bid, would that be a problem? He can't lose this inn, it means everything to him."

Jack touched her arm. "You don't know the half of it." He shrugged. "If you know someone..."

"When Luke comes out of his office, tell him I'm in my room."

"Doing dirty deeds?" He winked.

"The dirtiest of dirty. I'm going to see how much cash I can wheedle out of my family."

He looked at her with a mixture of skepticism and amusement. "You know what?"

"What?"

"I see why Luke likes you so much. You're pretty damn special, going out of your way like this to help him."

"He told you he likes me?"

"Luke's a changed man since you came on the scene. We've all noticed how much happier he is, how much more engaged. And I've been told that you and Ethan are buddies."

"Best buddies. He is the cutest little boy."

"He's a huge favorite around here. Of course now that we have James, he'll have some competition."

"How is James, by the way?"

"He's great! Lindsay is spending all her time either sleeping or feeding him. I've been relegated to errand running and grocery procurement." He smiled. "But I'm about to be granted a reprieve. Lindsay's mother arrives tomorrow."

"It all sounds wonderful…"

"Hey. Is that a sad tone I hear? It better not be," he teased. "With a man like Luke ready to beat down your door you've already gone where few women have gone before." Jack moved to the bottom of the stairs. "Marnie, trust me about Luke, will you?"

"I will," she said. Somehow she had to convince her brothers to do what they could to help her. If she succeeded, it would be the miracle of all Christmas miracles.

BY THE TIME SHE REACHED the third floor, she was even more determined to do what she had to do. Her family would reproach her for being impetuous, but she was ready for them.

Her happiness was at stake.

Marnie closed the door to her room behind her and picked up her cell phone. Scott answered on the first ring. "I want to talk to you, Liam, Gordon and Alex as soon as possible. I've got something I need you to do for me."

"Sounds intriguing. Tell me more."

"Not right now. I have to talk to all four of you to-gether. Can you line up a conference call?"

"You do realize that it's almost time for Santa Claus to do his thing."

She'd completely forgotten. "Oh, sorry," she said. "I'll bring my presents to everyone the day after Christmas."

Scott whistled. "Hey, it sounds like you're on a mission."

"I'll tell you all you need to know as soon as you line up the conference call."

There was what could only be described as a loaded silence on Scott's end of the line. She was just about ready to give up and say something funny to break the awkwardness when he spoke. "Marnie, there's something I want to tell you before we talk with the other three."

"What's that?"

"I realize that I've sounded pretty domineering over the last few years. And there were times when you were annoyed with me."

"Tell me about it." She snorted.

"I have a confession to make. You know how much we all worried about you when you had to have heart surgery as a kid, and how the whole family got into the whole protection racket, as you called it, after your accident."

"How could I forget? So what's your point?"

"Me and Liam, and Alex and Gord… We'd been raised to look out for you. It just became a natural way for us to think where you were concerned. Then when the accident happened and you were sent to hospital with so many injuries, all four of us were terrified that you wouldn't make it."

"Why didn't you tell me this before?"

"I don't know. Being big dumb jocks has its draw-backs, I suppose."

Her heart warmed, and tears welled up in her eyes. Deep down, she'd always adored Scott, the brother who had always been there for her, who had protected and cared for her, and who now had the grace and class to tell her the truth about how he felt. "What happened to make you see things differently?"

"Mom. She called me after she talked to you. In case you're interested, yours isn't the only conference call we four have been on recently."

"Mom talked to you guys about me?"

"She did. She said we needed to cut you some slack. She even admitted to relying on you too much, especially at Christmas. Then Dad got on the phone and talked about how much he was waiting for all of us to come home for the holidays, how much they were look-ing forward to seeing all of us. It was a pretty teary scene. And all because of you."

"I'm going away more often if one little vacation can produce this kind of change in the way you all see me."

"Yeah. We made a mistake by insisting on oversee-ing your life. It's not going to happen again."

"Does that mean you're not going to do a background check on the next man I bring home?"

"Well, we might slip up now and again, but we're going to do our best to change."

"I love you guys," she said, smiling through her tears.

"Before I hang up and get the conference call orga-nized, I want you to know that I've always loved you best."

"Scott...don't make a confession you'll regret," she warned, trying for a teasing tone and failing miserably.

"I'm serious. Now get off the phone, and I'll call you

back as soon as I can round up your brothers. Oh, and by the way, hope you're having a great time. That man, what's his name?"

"Luke."

"I hope he's worth it."

"He is."

"Well, then, I'm really pleased you've found someone special. You deserve to be happy."

A lump the size of a golf ball formed in Marnie's throat. "The age of miracles is not over," she said, fighting to maintain a light tone in her voice, all the while wishing her brother was within hugging range.

"Talk soon, Peanut. Whoops! Sorry!"

"It's okay. Just this once," she said, feeling closer to her brother than she ever had in her life.

LUKE COULDN'T STAND it any longer. Marnie wasn't answering her room phone, and her cell phone kept going to voice mail. He had to talk to her, to tell her what happened and what it could mean for both of them. He headed for the stairs, almost running into Jack, who was coming out of the library.

"Whoa! What's up?" Jack asked, looking a whole lot like he had a secret he wanted to share.

"I'm on my way to find Marnie. You haven't seen her, have you?"

"As a matter of fact I have. She and I chatted for a bit, and then she took off to her room, as if she was being chased by demons. I hear that the Advantage people were here to deliver some bad news. Sorry that this had to happen, and especially right at Christmas. What a bunch of jerks."

He wasn't surprised that Jack would be up to speed

on everything. "You've got that right. But maybe this will turn out better than it seems."

"Do you mean Marnie?"

"How did you— What have you been up to?" Luke gave him a glowering look, eliciting a chuckle from Jack.

"I haven't been up to much, but Marnie is. She's on the warpath. You're one lucky man to have a woman like her in your life."

Luke was on the verge of denying the implication of Jack's words, and then reconsidered. Why should he deny his feelings for her? "Yeah, I'm lucky, all right." He shoved his fingers through his hair, trying to figure out how much he should tell his friend. "I'm lucky in so many ways, especially in the way she loves me."

"I knew it! You two are in love. I told Lindsay last night that there was something going on between you two. My wife owes me a date with her, just the two of us."

Luke nodded his head, soaking in Jack's words, feeling them to his core. That was it. He and Marnie were meant to be together, to be there for each other through thick and thin. "We are in love. All this time, I thought…" He grimaced at the memory of all those evenings he'd spent with Jack, going over what happened to Anna, trying to put it in the past, and be a good dad while trying to juggle his work life. "You know what's been going on with me since Anna died, all I've had to deal with. But it's as if I've been given a second chance to be happy, and it's so…"

"You deserve every second of it."

"It's as if everything is new, so much to look forward to," Luke went on, realizing for the first time that Marnie had set him free of the past.

Jack clapped him on the back, a smile lighting his rugged features. "Go tell that woman how you really feel. She deserves to know, and you've both earned the right to be happy."

"Tell Marnie what?" Marnie asked from halfway down the carpeted stairs.

Jack winked at Luke. "It's now or never, my friend."

MARNIE SCURRIED DOWN the remaining steps, trying to be cool, wishing she had long hair to flick off her shoulders. Slowing at the bottom of the stairs, she clutched the newel post and waited for Luke to cross the couple of feet of carpet separating them.

This man of hers was so gorgeous, and how she loved the expression on his face right now—half joy, half humor. "Were you and Jack talking about me?" she asked, teasingly.

The smile in his eyes would melt icebergs. "Guilty as charged," he said, covering her hand with his where it rested on the post, his fingers gently massaging hers.

"How did your meeting go?" she asked, worried for him.

He shrugged. "As expected. They made their announcement about selling the inn and left."

"So, what's next?" she asked, struggling to remain calm and poised, while his touch held the power to buckle her knees.

"Why don't we go back to my apartment? We've got a lot to think about."

She slipped her hand into his as they walked down the corridor past the spa to his apartment door. "Luckily, Ethan's not here right now. Mary's got him helping her and Charlene to double-check all the linens for the Christmas Eve dinner. Max has been swearing and cursing all day, which means that the meal will be a masterpiece."

She could hardly wait for this evening, as she hoped to be able to tell him her brothers would back his purchase of the inn. "This is so exciting. I've never spent Christmas Eve at an inn," she said.

"There's so much going on," he hedged.

Her heart skipped a beat. "Want to fill me in?"

He moved so quickly he practically dragged her down the hall. "This time I'll be careful that all the doors are closed. Far too much of my life seeps from beneath a door, I swear."

"I'm all for closed doors," she offered, feeling his fingers on the small of her back as he maneuvered her into his apartment ahead of him.

The sun slanted through the windows in the dining room, highlighting the row of photographs on the wall, and the pile of toys in the adjoining living room now arranged in a path leading to the kitchen. Over in the corner of the living room was a beautifully decorated tree covered in gold and red ornaments and strings of popcorn. She stopped to take in the sight. "Someone has done a lovely job decorating the tree."

"Mary did it. She and Ethan worked here for hours the other day. She loves him so much."

"What a great group of friends you have in your life."

"They really are."

"Should I make a pot of coffee?" she asked, turning to him just in time to be kissed. An excited kiss filled with determination, sending her thoughts whirling over the possibilities. He led her to the sofa in the living room, and pulled her down beside him. "First I want to tell you that I've come to a decision."

"You have?"

He snuggled her into the crook of his arm, his powerful body pressed against hers. She leaned into him, her fingers tracing the edge of his shirtfront.

"Until The Mirabel sells to whomever—and that doesn't seem to be a certainty as yet—I'm going to look for another managerial position nearby. Leaving here is not my first choice, but I figure that the new owners, whoever they turn out to be, will want to put a management team together that they're familiar with. That means that my time here is limited, and I want to find a new inn to manage as soon as possible. I'm even considering buying a smaller inn and setting up my own business."

As she listened to him, she barely managed to contain her excitement. Within a few hours she'd be able to present her own plan to him. A plan that involved her brothers providing at least part of the financial backing for her and Luke to purchase The Mirabel, a plan that would allow Luke and Ethan to stay right here with her and his entire hotel family.

She listened as he talked about his prospects, the potential for a new job, his words coming fast. He went on to talk about helping Ethan with any changes that might be necessary. As much as she wanted to, she didn't dare interrupt him with her own thoughts. And if what Jack said was true—that Luke didn't like people messing around in his life—she might regret putting forward her ideas too quickly.

Besides, she was perfectly content knowing that he loved her. He'd said so, even told Jack about how he felt. But a new relationship was a very tenuous thing—she'd had firsthand experience in that department.

"I believe my plan will work, don't you?"

He referred to it as his plan—not theirs. He hadn't

mentioned how she would fit in with his plan, what her role would be. She eased out of his arms, wanting to gain a little perspective on what was going on. She hadn't expected him to have a plan already in place. She'd believed he'd want to discuss all the options with her first so they could make a decision together. Wasn't that what couples did?

"Why don't we go over all the possibilities?"

"Like what?" His voice didn't hold much enthusiasm.

"Maybe there's an investor willing to offer financial support so you can buy the inn?"

"Who were you thinking of?" he asked skeptically.

His tone hurt. Why did he sound so surprised that she might have an idea about what to do? Weren't they supposed to be in this together? She loved Luke and Ethan, and she had built her hopes on the idea that he felt the same—the same depth of love and commitment.

With dread seeping through her mind and blocking her voice, she got up and went over to the tree, needing to put a little space between herself and Luke. She knelt down, and saw the gifts wrapped and ready for tomorrow morning. She could almost hear Ethan's squeals of delight as he opened each gift. More than anything she wanted to be part of Luke's Christmas as they planned their future together. She wanted to wake up tomorrow morning filled with happiness and hope.

But if Luke talked only in terms of what the sale of The Mirabel meant to him, their future as a couple was in serious doubt. Feeling spent, she sank to the floor and stared up into the tree.

"Marnie, what's going on?" Luke moved to sit beside her on the floor, putting his arm around her shoulders. "Did I say something to upset you? I didn't mean to, you must realize that."

His tone was so sweet and concerned. She couldn't tell him she felt left out of his life, his plans. She couldn't risk discovering that her impetuousness had once again gotten in the way of her happiness. "Christmas is such an emotional time for me," she said, trying to tamp down her feelings.

If Luke wasn't interested in her plan, she'd have to make some sort of explanation to her brothers when they called, and once again she'd be exposing her life and her feelings to another round of her family's discussion and dissection of her life.

She looked into his eyes, touched his chin, felt the warmth of his skin and decided that one way or the other she had to tell him how she really felt—no hiding behind humor or self-deprecating behavior. She loved Luke too much to hide behind anything. If he really loved her, he would want her to share what she was thinking, and how she saw their life together. If he didn't... It was better to face that now.

"I've been thinking over what you said, and what Advantage intends to do. Have you considered having a partner? Someone who could help with the financing and management of The Mirabel?"

"Have you someone in mind?" he asked, his eyes going from narrowed slits to slowly widening in surprise. "You and me?"

"Why not? Don't you think we'd make a good team?"

"I do, it's just that you have a life back in Boston, but I didn't realize that you—"

"That I cared enough to stay here?"

*Just when she needed her guy to sweep her off her feet, he shows off his insecurities.*

"It's all over the inn that we're in love, that the owners were here and are going to sell the inn. It only makes sense that you and I do something about the situation."

"So where do we go from here? We can look for an inn to purchase while we wait for this one to sell," he said, scrubbing his fingers through his hair, a wry expression on his face.

"I've got a call in to my brothers."

"To do what?"

"To act as our financial backers."

He hesitated. "You're sure you want to do that? From what you've told me, it doesn't sound as if you're convinced that they've got your best interests at heart. Besides, what if they want to take charge of what we're doing? What if they're convinced that I'm using you to get funding for the inn?"

"They won't. Scott and I have come to an understanding, and he's the one who's getting the other three together for a conference call. I'm ready to exert some pressure on them to fund our purchase of The Mirabel."

"You're serious?"

"Yes. They should be calling me any minute now. I imagine Liam and Gordon are at my parents' house already, and Alex is on his way from Philadelphia. Scott is probably leaving his office." She checked her watch. Why hadn't they called back by now? In all the excitement, she hadn't paid attention to what time she'd talked to Scott, but it had to be an hour ago at least. "Have you seen my cell phone?"

"It's on the sofa," he said, a quizzical expression on his face. "You'd do this for me? You'd go into business with me?"

She scrambled off the floor, grabbed her phone and returned to sit next to him. "Why not? If we're going to be together?"

"But loving someone is not the same as being financially involved with them. We'd be working together, living together…"

She nodded, feeling completely exposed and vulnerable. "I've been accused of never doing anything halfway."

He twined his fingers with hers and pulled her into his arms. "If I could, I'd marry you tomorrow."

"On Christmas Day?" she asked, fighting back laughter.

*There you go again. When someone is being serious, you fall back on humor.*

"On any day you like," he said, as he pressed his forehead gently to hers.

She clung to him, and in that quiet instant she saw her life laid out before her; a life filled with the family she and Luke would have, the friends they'd share and children of their own maybe…. "You mean that," she whispered, her arms going around his neck as she leaned into his embrace. Driven by the groan of need emanating from him, she moved her mouth to his neck and the lovely warm V of his throat, lightly nipping at his skin.

"I do." His powerful hands swept her shoulders, pulling her closer.

"Why didn't you say this earlier? For a while I thought that maybe you weren't really serious, that I'd made a fool of myself before the entire staff."

"Never a fool, my love, never that," he murmured as he stretched out on the floor and pulled her on top of him.

She squirmed in pleasure. "Do you have any idea what I've been up to since I last saw you?"

"Talking to Scott?"

"Yes, and a few other things."

"I've had a few things on my mind, as well," he said, smiling up into her eyes as he pushed his body up into hers, forcing a gasp from her lips.

"If my plan works, you're going to owe me big time when this is all over," she said, reaching to undo his shirt.

## CHAPTER SEVENTEEN

HE CUPPED HER HEAD in his hands, and drew her down into a deep, demanding kiss that had her moaning with delight as she hurried to unbutton his shirt. Desire, hot and insistent, claimed her, drawing the air from her lungs in a long sigh of need. Running her hands down his body, she reached the zipper on his pants.

A buzzing sound came from somewhere near her side, distracting her. "Wouldn't you know?" she groaned, and rolled off him, retrieving the cell phone.

When she answered, the cheery voices of Scott, Liam, Gordon and Alex rang in her ear.

"Would it be asking too much for you guys to work on your timing a little?" she teased.

"Did we catch you in the act?" Liam said, his loud laugh filling the line.

"They heard about Luke. I didn't tell them, I swear," Scott said over the din. "But between you and me, I believe their curiosity over your new boyfriend was what got them on this conference call."

She glanced at Luke who had climbed to a sitting position beside her. "Who is it?" he whispered.

"My brothers," she whispered against his ear.

He smiled and began playing with the hair at the nape of her neck, driving her insane with desire.

"Are you there?" Scott asked.

"Yes, and I'm delighted to call this meeting to order," she said.

"First things first. When are you going to come home? We miss you and want to see you. It won't be Christmas without you, sis," Liam said.

"I second that," Gordon chimed in.

"The sooner the better," Alex offered. "Scott and Mom have filled us in about your man who's keeping you away from us on Christmas. You realize you'll have to deal with us when you finally do return."

"Don't I always?"

"So, what's up? What's so urgent that we have to hold a conference call on Christmas Eve?" Scott asked.

"I have an investment opportunity for you. It's a beautiful inn near Wakesfield in upstate New York. It's presently owned by Advantage Corporation, and they've put it up for sale."

"So what's your connection to it? How did you get involved and how did you do it so quickly?" Gordon queried.

"Luke, the present manager, and I want to buy it, and we want to form a partnership." His intimate gaze moved lazily over her, and the love and pride in his eyes delighted her.

"You're in love after only a couple of days with a man none of us have met, and you want us to help you buy an inn without anyone in the family seeing it first, or doing any sort of appraisal?" Liam asked, incredulously.

"Did I say anything to any of you when you decided you'd found the person you wanted to spend the rest of your life with?" she countered, compressing her lips in annoyance. Why did they always behave this way?

"But Scott says he's a widower. How do you know

he's not just on the rebound?" Gordon asked. "We don't want to see you hurt."

"And what will you do about your plans for the inn if he suddenly develops cold feet? You remember what happened to my best friend, Louie, after his wife passed away. He hooked up with a woman, only to change his mind a few months into the engagement." Liam's words were hurried.

"Yeah, and add that to your track record with men," Alex said, and she could picture him shaking his head, counting himself out. Worse still, his words were met by a long stretch of silence from the rest of them.

Did that mean none of them approved of what she wanted? Had they ganged up on her yet again? She remembered those other moments when her brothers didn't approve, how defeated she'd felt facing their arguments against what she'd wanted.

Would their attitude ever change where she was concerned?

With her gaze locked on Luke, she organized her thoughts. The worst that could happen was that they would refuse her request, and if they did, she'd find money somewhere else. She wasn't going to let her brothers ruin their plans.

"Look, I'm offering you a great chance here to be part of a new business venture of mine. This is a great inn. It's got a solid clientele. Luke is the manager and he's a good manager and he's got years of experience. If we don't buy this inn we'll buy another one. But we would prefer to pool our management experience and make The Mirabel the best inn in the area, even the country," she said in a heated defense of her plans.

"Sounds great, but what's the deal? Do you get half

ownership for putting up half the money? And do you need a contract with this guy?" Gordon asked.

Anger burned her throat. Why couldn't they see what this meant to her? "Okay, here's the deal. I know that you four have seen my life to date as your personal preserve, a place all of you felt you had a right to interfere whenever you wanted, all in the name of giving me advice you believed I needed. But what you seem to have forgotten is that I successfully ran a beauty salon for years, borrowed my own money for the business and sold my share at a good price. All without your involvement."

"We wanted to help you with the salon but you didn't tell us until it was a done deal," Alex complained.

"That's my point exactly. I had to go behind your backs to do what I wanted."

"Sis, we didn't mean it that way," Liam said, to the tune of the other brothers' muted agreement.

"It's not about what you meant, but about how it affected me. Every time I ever went to do something—from buying my first car to choosing who I wanted to date—you guys jumped in with all sorts of unsolicited advice. I realize it all started with my health, but just because I've spent time in and out of hospitals doesn't mean you have to treat me like I'm someone who needs your constant input. I'm thirty-five years old, for heaven's sake!"

She looked to Luke for reassurance. He squeezed her shoulders and smiled encouragingly.

"We didn't intend to make you feel that way," Scott murmured, his tone contrite. "We love you."

"You're our little sister," Liam chimed in.

"Well, I'm not your little sister anymore. I'm a grown woman with plans, and if you guys want to prove you want to change, you can start now."

"What do you say, men? Do we take this opportunity to trust Marnie's good judgment?" Gordon asked.

"Well...I'm still in need of a little convincing," Alex said. "This inn has to be worth a few bucks, my guess is a couple of million. Are we ready to split that among the four of us? If we're going to treat Marnie like any other investment, and not our sister, we'll also need to know what plans they have for the inn."

"Just so you know, Luke and I would be willing to look at other sources of funding to make up any shortfall."

They all began speaking at once, and after the noise died down, Scott said, "We're ready to talk about your plan, and of course we'll have to see the proposal in writing, and the price you settle upon once you've put in the offer. We'll also need to meet Luke. What's his last name?"

"Luke Harrison."

"And what do you know about him, beyond his personal appeal, obviously?" Alex asked.

"You'll have to wait until we come to Boston to find out. Until then I want you four to think seriously about this. I'm fed up with your attitude where I'm concerned. Put your money where your attitude is, no strings attached, or I'll go elsewhere."

Aware of the silence on the other end of the phone, she sought Luke's reassurance. He immediately put his hand in hers, his touch warm and intimate. "I didn't mean to sound so harsh, but I deserve a chance to be happy like you guys, don't I?"

"You do," Scott affirmed.

"Absolutely," the others chorused, much quieter now.

She imagined them texting one another while she waited, and whatever they were saying had to be pretty lengthy, given how long it seemed since they'd spoken to her. She could almost hear the comments that would be made around the dinner table tonight in her absence. "Hello, anybody home?"

"Marnie, tell you what. We'll agree to fund your venture on one condition," Scott said.

Her gaze flew to Luke. He tucked her under his arm, holding her close, and her confidence came flooding back. "What's that?"

"You and Luke have to come to Mom and Dad's the day after Christmas. We need to meet your new family."

"But only to meet him. No trial by the brotherhood, promise? No grilling him about his sports-team likes and dislikes, no arm wrestles."

Luke laughed.

"Is that him we hear in the background?"

"Yes."

"Put him on," Alex said.

"Not until you promise to behave yourselves."

"Marnie, we won't do anything to Luke. We only want to welcome him to the brotherhood," Scott teased to grumbled assents from the other three.

She held the phone out to Luke. "They want to talk to you, but if they give you any trouble—"

"Leave them to me. I've always wanted a few brothers of my own, and this lot will probably do," he said, chuckling as he took the phone.

Marnie listened to Luke's side of the conversation, which seemed to consist mostly of "yes" and "no" and "love to." But if his eyes were an indicator of what her brothers were saying they hadn't managed to offend him. She let out a long sigh of relief and snuggled closer to him, listening contentedly.

"They want to speak to you one more time," he said, looking so handsome and adorable.

She took the phone. "Okay, what is it now?" she asked, trying to maintain her usual snappy dialogue when it came to the fearsome four. Yet she was still a little worried, as they'd never given in like this before.

"We're going to see you in two days' time. We've also arranged to take your man to a hockey game in Boston in January, so you can relax. And now, Mom and Dad are waiting for us to get started on our Christmas Eve dinner, so we'll talk to you tomorrow," Alex said. "And Marnie, merry Christmas."

"Merry Christmas," the others chimed in.

"Merry Christmas, and see you soon—"

A huge lump rose in her throat, tears pricked her eyes. She wouldn't be there to celebrate with them, and suddenly she felt so guilty. She was torn…then she felt Luke's hands massaging her shoulder, his fingers so gentle. She glanced his way to see his eyes focused solely on her.

"I love you," he whispered.

She held the phone against her chest, her heart thudding so hard she was sure her brothers could hear, but they'd understand. She had finally found the man for her, and the life she'd been searching for, and she had no intention of ever letting anything come in the way of her happiness.

"Tell Mom and Dad I'll call later this evening."

"Got it," Scott said. "See you soon, Marnie. And merry Christmas."

"Merry Christmas," she said, and clicked her phone closed.

"We can leave for Boston right now, if you want," he offered.

"But Ethan needs to be here. Santa's coming tonight," she said.

"Santa will be wherever Ethan is, trust me."

As tempting as the idea was, she couldn't do that. As lonesome as she was right now, she would never do anything to ruin Christmas for Ethan or for Luke, or for the staff here at the inn.

She took a deep breath. "No, I want to spend Christmas here with you."

LUKE WAS FASCINATED by Marnie's conversation with her brothers. His few minutes of conversation with them had made it clear how much they cared about her. He also understood what able adversaries they'd be if anyone ever tried to harm their little sister.

All of it left him wishing he had a family like hers, that he had a brother or sister he could call, especially now at Christmas, when he had so much happiness to share, and Ethan needed family. He hadn't heard a word from his parents but they were probably on their way to Australia.

"What now?" she asked, swiping at her damp cheeks, her face turned to the tree. Leave it to Marnie—the woman he loved was too proud to let him see her tears.

"Turn around," he whispered. "Look at me."

She turned her head to meet his gaze. "Defending my right to choose the man in my life is not easy for me. I have a spotty record where men are concerned, and my brothers never miss a chance to remind me."

"Your brothers love you."

"So they got to you, too," she said, doing a passable mobster imitation.

He couldn't help but laugh. "They did. You're one lucky woman to have a family who cares so much." He pulled her close to him, reveling in how good she felt in his arms. "And since I'm about to spend the rest of my life with you, your spotty record is history. I'm going to see to that."

"I'm really looking forward to watching you." She blinked back tears. "And these are tears of joy, I might remind you."

He wanted to make love to her more than anything, but Ethan was bound to come roaring through the door any minute with Mary in tow. He settled for kissing her, feeling her body melt into his. But once he started, he couldn't resist the touch of her hands on his chest, her breath on his lips, the heat of her body pressed to his. He nuzzled her neck, and let his hands roam over her breasts taking pleasure in her sudden gasp. Breathing hard, he stroked her hair, the light from the Christmas tree highlighting the glow in her eyes. "Starting now we are going to have a life together. That means I want you to share your feelings with me, the good and the not so good."

Her fingers played with the gold chain at his neck. "Expressing my feelings has always been a bit difficult for me."

"But I want to know how you feel, how I make you feel. Promise me?"

Her voice thick with emotion, she murmured, "I promise."

He heard the door open, followed by Ethan's animated chatter, and moved back, pulling Marnie to a standing position. "Darn, and we were just getting started."

"The other member of the family has arrived." She eased away and peeked around him, looking for Ethan.

Mary entered the room, a look of surprise on her face.

"You both look so…natural there in front of the tree, but I'm afraid I have to run. One of the guests spilled wine on the carpet in his room, and we're really busy with getting all the guests settled and the Christmas getaway activities going."

"Not a problem, Mary, and thank you so much for babysitting Ethan. Marnie and I'll take it from here. I've got Francine's sister coming to look after Ethan during dinner tonight."

"Oh, that's the other thing I needed to tell you. She called while you were meeting with the people from Advantage to say she's ill. I could come back and stay with him if you like."

"Absolutely not. You're here all the time as it is. Leave it with me. I'm sure there's someone in the village who's available."

"Dad!" Ethan tossed his winter jacket on the floor by the door, and raced over to the tree, his face alight with enthusiasm, his cheeks a bright pink.

Luke picked up his son, his cool cheeks and scent of outdoors filling his nostrils. "You've been outside play-ing, haven't you?" he asked.

Marnie pulled Ethan's hat off his head, smoothing his curls.

Ethan leaned back in his father's embrace. "I made a snowman. He's this big, with a carrot for a nose." Ethan spread his arms wide, bumping Marnie's cheek.

"Hey, easy there, big guy." Luke's eyes met Marnie's.

"No damage to report," she said, grinning as she took Ethan's fingers in hers.

Ethan frowned. "Why you not go outside with me?"

"I was talking with your daddy. I'll go the next time, I promise."

"Now?" Ethan asked, his head coming to rest on his

father's shoulder, filling Luke with an unfathomable ache. How was it that until Ethan's arrival in his life, he'd believed he had experienced all love had to offer? Yet loving Ethan was so different, so intense—an all-encompassing love that never failed to surprise him.

"It's time for dinner and bed, my man," Luke said, holding his son close.

Ethan lifted his head off his father's shoulder, squinting as he pulled at his father cheek. "Can I have mac and cheese?" he asked.

"Don't you eat anything else?" He hitched Ethan farther up into his arms.

"Hot dog?" Ethan asked, pulling at his father's nose.

"I can make either," Marnie said.

"Mac and cheese it is," Luke said, lowering Ethan to the floor.

Luke and Ethan followed Marnie into the kitchen where Ethan promptly climbed into his favorite chair and watched expectantly as Marnie moved about the space.

*Oh, man, how I miss this.*

Emotion clogged Luke's throat. He scrubbed his face to prevent Marnie from seeing the tears threatening to overcome him.

*Who's the one hiding their emotions now?*

Thankfully, Marnie was busy at the stove. He settled into a chair at the table and soaked up the comforting feeling of having her there with him, moving about the kitchen as she fixed Ethan's dinner.

Marnie placed Ethan's plate in front of him and sat down at the table across from Luke.

"What are you going to do about a babysitter for tonight with Francine's sister ill?" she asked as they watched Ethan devour his meal.

Checking his watch, he was appalled to discover that the Christmas Eve dinner would be starting in less than an hour and he didn't have a babysitter. "Oh, no, I forgot! Let's see. I have a list here of possible sitters." He reached behind him to a drawer where he kept the phone book, and began to scan the list.

"Why don't I stay with Ethan?" Marnie asked.

"Don't you want to go to dinner with me?"

"I do, but we'll have lots of dinners together in the future. Besides, It'll give me a chance to get to know the new men in my life a little better." She gave him an impish smile.

He had no intention of leaving her out of his plans tonight. He'd had a hard day and needed her with him. "Not an option. I'm not letting you out of my sight." He searched the phone book, and retrieved two names and numbers, and began dialing. To his dismay, neither babysitter was available. Of course not, it was Christmas Eve. Who'd want to babysit tonight? "I should have done better than this. How could I not have had a backup plan?"

"It's been a busy day, and you've had a lot on your mind."

"But I wanted to take you to dinner," he said.

"I understand, but we can't do anything about it now." She checked the kitchen clock. "And you have to get dressed."

As much as he hated to agree, she was right. "On one condition. You're staying over tonight."

"Are you sure that's what you want?"

"Why wouldn't I want it?"

"We… Our relationship…it's new. It's Christmas Eve—"

He placed his hands on her arms. "Marnie, it's what I

want. I'll get Max to make you a special dinner, and I'll bring a bottle of champagne for our private celebration after I'm finished with my hosting duties."

She brushed her hair off her face, her glance skipping to Ethan. "Okay, but we have a very special mission tonight." She nodded in Ethan's direction. "Getting ready for Santa," she mouthed over the scraping sound of Ethan's spoon over his bowl.

"More!" Ethan held out his spoon and bowl to Marnie.

She scooped out more pasta from the pot on the stove and topped up Ethan's apple juice. "We'll have lots of time to celebrate when you get back."

His heart shifted in his chest as he followed her to the stove and pressed his lips along the nape of her neck, his body responding in a very obvious way. "I'd better get out of here before I do something that will have Ethan talking for weeks."

"Mmm. That feels wonderful," she sighed, leaning back into his arms.

"Don't tempt me," he warned.

"Hurry back," she said, turning in his arms and pulling his face down for one last kiss.

Not wanting to leave, he held her for a few minutes longer. "Oh! Forgot to mention. I'll have another man with me when I return. Henry is probably still in his bed behind the reception desk, but he likes to spend his nights with Ethan."

"Henry likes cookies," Ethan announced triumphantly, and they both laughed.

## CHAPTER EIGHTEEN

MARNIE WAS AWASH IN FEELINGS she couldn't describe as she watched Luke stride out of the kitchen and down the hall toward his bedroom. It was as if she had finally come home, as if being here with Luke and Ethan was the most natural thing in the world.

She waited for Ethan to finish his dinner and then cleaned up the kitchen. Ethan asked a million questions about Santa—when was he coming, would his daddy be back when Santa got here and whether Santa would come into his room. She answered all of his questions, as best she could, only to have him come back to some of the questions again and again.

When she was done cleaning up, Ethan raced into the living room, scooped up his jacket and searched his pockets. "I got the treat for Santa," he said, waving a clear plastic bag containing a half-dozen cookies over his head.

"That's great. What will Santa drink with his cookies?"

"Chocolate milk," Ethan said with conviction as he eyed the bag. "I'll give him just one cookie."

"And who will get the rest?" she asked, knowing the answer.

"Me...and Henry." He looked at her from under furrowed eyebrows.

Luke came down the hall, dressed in a tuxedo, and

looking so handsome it made her gasp. "Wow! Now I wish I was going with you. I'd better dust off my club."

"Your club?"

"All the better for beating off the women trailing after you," she teased.

Luke laughed. "What women? There are no single women here, remember?"

"You're a sitting duck if you believe that married women aren't tempted."

"You could always send Ethan to ward off the women," he joked.

"I'm not sure your guests are ready for rocket man, and besides he's got a previous engagement with me." She tousled Ethan's hair.

"You can read to me," Ethan announced, his head bobbing as he raced off to his room and returned with an armload of books.

Ethan dropped his books on the coffee table and held his arms out to Marnie. She picked him up. "I guess I'm reading."

Once he was settled in Marnie's arms, he leaned toward his father. "Love you, Daddy."

He kissed Ethan's cheek. "I love you, too." He leaned toward Marnie and kissed her on her lips, a lingering kiss that had Ethan squirming in protest.

Luke put his hands on her shoulders, sandwiching Ethan between them. "Don't let him go to bed before I get back, if you can help it."

"I don't think that'll be a problem. We're in the middle of negotiations over whether Santa should have all the cookies, or whether Ethan and Henry should have some of them. I see a sugar high in his future."

Luke chuckled as he made his way to the door. "See you later."

"Bye, Dad," Ethan yelled in his outdoor voice, making Marnie wince.

He wiggled out of her arms and made for the sofa. She read the first two books to him and then insisted that he get his teeth brushed and his pajamas on. He went willingly, the cookies forgotten at least for now.

Max arrived with her dinner, a Cornish hen with stuffing, garlic potatoes, a Waldorf salad and plum pudding in a tiny baking dish. "I wish I could stay and visit, but things are hopping in the kitchen and I need to get back. You're keeping the kid? No babysitter I hear," he said.

"Yep. And we're enjoying ourselves. I've been reading to him, and he reads along with me."

"He's one bright little boy," Max said as he turned to leave.

"Thanks for dinner."

"Anytime." With that, he was out the door, and Marnie took her meal to the kitchen, sitting in a chair where she could keep an eye on Ethan while she ate what turned out to be the best meal she'd had in ages. After she took her last bite of plum pudding, she settled on the sofa and watched a children's Christmas program with Ethan for a while, marveling at how engrossed the child was in the story of the Grinch who stole Christmas.

Taking advantage of the break, she dug her cell phone out of her purse.

Despite her feelings around the call she'd had with her mother earlier, she felt guilty that she wouldn't be there this evening. She glanced over at Ethan, who was sucking his thumb, watching wide-eyed as the Grinch did his worst to ruin Christmas.

Was this her Grinch performance? Deserting her

family at Christmas? She dialed her parents' number, and her dad picked up on the first ring. "Hi, there."

"Hi, Dad," she said, instantly missing everyone, especially her time with her dad making caramel popcorn and chocolate fudge to the blaring accompaniment of Bing Crosby, her father's favorite Christmas crooner.

"How's your Christmas Eve going? I hear there's a new man in your life," her father said, his voice nearly lost in the background confusion of people singing along with the music.

"Yes, Dad, there is—" Tears clogged her throat, and she choked on her words.

"I'm happy for you. I really am, but it's not the same here without you."

"You mean you miss my cooking and bartending," she said, attempting to keep a teasing tone in her voice.

"I miss *you*. So does your mother. Here, I'll put her on before she tears the phone from my hands."

"Hi, Marnie."

"Hi, Mom."

"Wait a minute. I'm going to the bedroom so I can hear you," her mother said. "Are you having a good Christmas Eve?" *Without us* was implied but not spoken.

"I'm having a wonderful evening with Ethan, Luke's son."

"He left you alone on Christmas Eve?"

"Only for a couple of hours while he hosts a dinner for his guests."

"Marnie, I don't understand. What happened to his wife?" her mother asked carefully.

"She died in a car accident three years ago. Ethan was one at the time."

"Oh, how difficult it must have been for Luke…for his little boy."

"Yes, it was, but he…we've been given this chance to be happy. And I love him, and he loves me. He's hosting a dinner tonight, but he'll be back in time to put Ethan to bed, and then we'll put the Santa gifts out for Ethan."

"Marnie, you sound so happy."

"I am, and I want you to be happy for me."

"Marnie, I shouldn't have said some of the things I said to you earlier. I was a little upset at not having you here for Christmas. But it would appear that your life has taken a whole new direction. I can't wait to see you and hear all about it."

"We'll be there the day after tomorrow. Luke wants to meet you and the family and have you meet Ethan. You'll love them both, you really will," she said hopefully.

"If you love him, that's all that matters."

"Luke plays the piano," Marnie said, looking for something to connect her mother to him.

"The piano?" Her mother's voice mellowed. "That's how your father and I met. He was playing in a jazz club to pay his college expenses, and I was giving music lessons to cover my tuition."

"I didn't know that."

"No? I guess the subject never came up before."

"How did I not know about you and Dad meeting that way?"

"There's a lot you don't know about your father and me. And a lot we don't know about you, it would seem."

"Mom, I need you to understand that the minute I met Luke I knew this time it was different. I can't explain it…somehow there was this feeling, this sensation that I'd been waiting for this person."

"That's how I felt about your dad. It was the first time I'd been in a jazz club. I hated jazz, but I loved your father from that moment on. But let's talk about all that later. Is there any chance he and his son could stay here for the week between Christmas and the New Year?"

"I could ask him."

"When will you be home?"

"We'll be there sometime the day after Christmas."

*Please trust me, Mom. Please let me find my new life with Luke. I need you to believe in me.*

"Marnie, I want you to be happy, to have someone in your life who loves only you."

Marnie swallowed and wiped the tears from her eyes. "Mom, I can't wait to get home to you and Dad."

"And we can't wait to see you. Meanwhile, you enjoy your time with Luke and Ethan. I'll miss you this evening and tomorrow, but we'll see each other soon."

"Thank you, Mom. Merry Christmas."

She put down the phone and looked around the room with its Christmas decorations and the little boy lying on the sofa. Her heart swelled with emotion—with love for everyone on this night of all nights.

She settled in to watch *How the Grinch Stole Christmas* with Ethan. He rested his head on her shoulder, and she kissed his curls, thinking that this could easily be the best Christmas ever.

LUKE LOOSENED HIS TIE as he ran down the corridor toward his apartment, with Henry in hot pursuit. He couldn't wait to see Marnie and to get started on their first Christmas together. Suddenly his life was rife with possibilities.

He eased open the door and tiptoed in to find Marnie and Ethan snuggled together on the sofa, the TV turned off. Henry promptly climbed up on the sofa, giving a huge sigh of relief as he flopped down. Next to the tree,

Ethan had set out a glass of milk and three cookies, which meant that Marnie must have negotiated pretty hard with Ethan. They both appeared to be asleep.

He touched the back of the sofa, and Marnie woke suddenly, glancing around before her eyes came to rest on Luke. The smile she gave him flooded his heart. "Sorry, didn't mean to startle you," he whispered.

"What time is it?" she asked, yawning as she sat up.

"Nearly nine. I'll put Ethan to bed, and then we can get back to us." He came around and gathered his son in his arms, the faint smell of cookies filling his nostrils as he lifted him up against his shoulder. Ethan squirmed, opening his eyes for a few seconds before falling back to sleep.

Marnie stood up and stretched. "He cuddled right into my arms tonight and fell asleep," she murmured wistfully.

He smiled at her. "The two of you looked like you belonged together."

"We do. I love him." She smoothed Ethan's curls off his forehead and placed a light kiss there.

"What about me?"

"Your turn is coming," she teased.

"I'm counting on it," he said before heading down the hallway to Ethan's room. Henry jumped off the sofa and followed him.

He put his son in bed, pulling his Spider-Man sheets over his sleeping form before kissing him gently on the forehead, a ritual that had been part of his life since the day Ethan had been born. "Merry Christmas, Ethan," he whispered.

Henry curled up on the rug next to Ethan's bed, and heaved a huge sigh of contentment. Luke crossed the hall to his room and changed out of his tuxedo and into a T-shirt and jeans.

Back in the living room, Marnie met him with a glass of red wine. "By the way, my dinner was fantastic. You have a great chef."

"Don't you mean 'we have a great chef'?" he asked, taking the wine and raising his glass in a toast. "To us and our new venture. In business and in life."

"To us," she said, clinking her glass with his, her face radiating happiness.

"And to our first Christmas," he said, kissing her, welcoming the way she moved her body against his. "Keep that up and there will be consequences," he said.

"Why shouldn't I?" she asked, putting their glasses on the coffee table and sliding her arms around his neck. "We're alone, finally. We love each other."

"And we still have some work ahead of us. Remember who's coming tonight?"

"Will Santa be the only one?" she asked, her expression sexy and playful.

"Definitely not, but first I have Santa duties to perform."

"Hmm. I have a few performances in mind, as well."

"Ooh. Can't wait," he said, kissing her before practically galloping to the hall closet where he reached up to the top shelf, behind the box of Ethan's shoes and boots.

"I got him the train set he wanted, and another set of Lego. The rest of his gifts are in the closet in my bedroom."

They knelt down together, and Luke began assembling the train.

"You don't wrap the Santa gifts?" she asked.

"No. When I was little, the floor in front of the tree

was always covered in unwrapped gifts from Santa, and of course, the milk and cookies were gone."

"Ours were never wrapped, either. I was always the first one up because I couldn't wait to see what Santa had brought me."

Luke finished up what he was doing, and then turned to her. "I've waited so long to feel…to love again."

She took his hand. "Me, too."

He went out to the kitchen, and brought back two glasses, and then popped the cork on the champagne. They toasted again and sipped the bubbly liquid. As they sat together, with the light of the tree on her face, he knew he was the luckiest man alive. "I have something for you," he said.

"Oh, no! You didn't buy me something, did you? I didn't get anything for you or for Ethan, either. How could I have been so thoughtless?"

He took her hand. "What matters is that you're here with me." Dropping her hand, he went into his bedroom and came back with a small parcel. "Open it," he said, his voice suddenly tight with emotion.

She took the jeweler's box and slowly untied the ribbon, her gaze questioning. "What is this?"

"Something I saw when I was in the village after they finally cleared the snow. It seemed like the perfect gift for you."

She opened the box, and there, nestled in velvet, was a charm bracelet with a silver disc dangling from it. She turned the disc over in her fingers. *Marnie and Luke.*

"It's beautiful," she whispered, "but I feel so bad—"

He stopped her with a kiss. "I have the right to buy you something special without you feeling you have to do something in return."

She nodded, her eyes shining with joy.

They settled on the sofa, their arms wrapped around each other. Glancing up at the glowing tree, Luke let the moment wash over him, the love, the happiness and how good she felt next to him.

"If I'm staying the night—"

"There's no 'if.' You're staying."

"What will Ethan say?"

"Do you think he'll have eyes for anything but Santa's gifts when he wakes up?" He kissed her lips, and ran his fingers through her hair, seeing the way her eyes widened in pleasure. "I'll bet you could run naked through the living room tomorrow morning and Ethan wouldn't even notice."

"Should we test your theory?"

"I'm game if you are," he said, pouring more champagne.

"I'll have to get a few things from my room."

"Like what?"

"Toothbrush. Nightie."

"I've got spare toothbrushes and you won't need the nightie. You're not leaving me tonight no matter what."

"That's easily the best offer I've ever had."

"I couldn't agree more," he whispered against her cheek as he took her champagne flute from her hand. "We have a long night ahead of us," he warned as he began to undress her.

# *EPILOGUE*

*Two days before Christmas*
*One year later*

LUKE HIT REDIAL ON HIS cell phone. Where was Marnie? She'd gone into Wakesfield hours ago, and should've been back by now. He glanced at his watch as the numbers he dialed sounded over the line. She didn't pick up.

He put the phone down on his desk and tried to concentrate on the printout in front of him. He and Marnie had bought the inn together almost a year ago, beating out another potential buyer with a little help from Marnie's brothers—men who Luke now considered his friends. He'd consulted with them after a Boston Celtic's game about his intention to marry Marnie, and they'd given him their full support on the condition that they could throw the bachelor party.

In return he'd sworn them to secrecy, emphasizing that he wanted this to be a surprise for Marnie, and if she got wind that they knew about it before she did, it would add fuel to her argument that her brothers were still trying to meddle in her life.

They'd wholeheartedly agreed, which meant he would be facing a bachelor party put on by four guys who loved nothing more than a good party. He was a little concerned, in light of some of the stories Marnie had told him about her brothers and their escapades.

But he'd do just about anything to tie the knot with the woman. God only knew how complicated planning a wedding might be with Marnie's family wanting to be so involved in everything. But he was up to the challenge. He'd never been happier in his life. Since they'd bought the property and Marnie had become a partner in the business, their relationship had thrived. He was thrilled to discover how easily they worked together, and they had all kinds of ideas for making The Mirabel Inn one of the top vacation destinations in the region.

It all seemed almost too perfect. And that made him a little uneasy—and reminded him of another night during the Christmas season.

*Don't go there.*

Ethan was with Marnie, as she'd taken him to his last dress rehearsal before the local theater production of the Christmas pageant. Ethan was one of the sheep in the nativity scene. They were coming home long enough to get Ethan his dinner, and then going back for the performance, after which Luke planned to propose to Marnie in front of their Christmas tree with Ethan tucked quietly away in his bed.

He reached into his desk drawer and took out the navy blue velvet box containing a diamond ring he'd bought for her a few weeks ago in Boston. His excuse to Marnie for making the trip was that he needed to talk to Scott about promotion possibilities for the inn. Luke had managed to get through the meeting while keeping the ring a secret from Scott. Marnie would be the first to know…if she ever got home.

His concern rising, he hit Redial again, and again the call went to voice mail. He glanced at his watch. Had she turned her phone off? He supposed she might during the rehearsal, but the rehearsal was over at five. He tapped the desk in thought.

Marnie had been a little preoccupied the past few weeks. He'd found her a couple of times sitting in the library staring out the window, and she'd been slower than usual to get out of bed in the morning. He'd teased her about it, but she didn't seem to care.

Things had been pretty frantic around the inn, while they'd organized this year's Christmas Getaway event, but it had sold out early, much to their delight. Maybe all the anxiety around getting things ready was the reason for her change in behavior. She probably needed a break from the pressure of running an inn.

Luke had insisted that they celebrate their success this evening with an intimate dinner—his cover for the surprise proposal he had planned.

Now all he needed was Marnie and Ethan to come through the door. Unable to sit at his desk any longer, he got up and went out into the main lobby, past the reception desk to the front door. From the dining room he could hear one of the guests playing "Silent Night" while others sang along.

As he peered out through the glass panels, watching for the lights of Marnie's SUV, he was reminded of the night he'd paced in front of this same door, waiting for her to come back to the inn so he could tell her how much he loved her. He'd failed miserably in his plan that night, but tonight would be different. He was proposing to Marnie tonight.

MARNIE HELD ETHAN'S HAND in hers as they exited the theater with his sheep costume tucked away in a bag, serenaded by Ethan's version of "Away in a Manager." Any other time she would have sung along, but her visit to Dr. Spencer had left her at a loss for words. She'd left Ethan with Francine earlier in the afternoon while she kept her appointment with the doctor, believing that she was simply overtired and needed a vacation.

Instead, she and Luke were expecting a baby.

A baby she'd never believed she'd have. The surgeon who had performed the surgery on her pelvis and hip after the accident had warned her that she might have difficulty getting pregnant, and because of that, she had always been cautiously realistic when it came to the prospect of having children.

She told herself she was managing her family and Luke's expectations. The truth was somewhat different. She had been afraid that she might never conceive and if she did, she would be unable to carry the child to term. Now it seemed fate had intervened and made the decision for her. In roughly seven months she and Luke would have a baby.

"Marnie, listen to me." Ethan pulled on her hand.

Startled, she glanced down at the boy she had come to love so much. "I'm listening."

"No, you're not." He let go of her hand and raced ahead to Marnie's SUV parked on the side of the street.

"Be careful, Ethan," she called, moving quickly to catch up with him.

He reached the back door of the vehicle and grasped the handle. "Will you sing with me on the way home?"

"Of course, honey," she said as she helped him into his car seat.

She checked the trunk of the SUV to make sure the antique office chair she'd purchased to match Luke's antique desk was packed in tight before getting in the front and starting the engine. She'd found the chair at an antiques auction in October, and couldn't resist buying it for Luke for Christmas. Concerned that he might discover her gift and ruin the surprise, she'd asked Francine to keep it at her house until today.

She pulled away from the curb, her mind on the idea that next year at this time she could have a baby car seat in the back next to Ethan. Her heart warmed at the idea that Ethan would have a baby brother or sister.

Suddenly a horn blared. She glanced sideways to see another car pass them, the driver glaring at her.

"You almost had an accident," Ethan announced.

"I'm sorry. It won't happen again." *Pay attention!* "We're fine. Not to worry."

"Marnie! You be careful!" He kicked the back of the front passenger seat for emphasis. "Miss Brown says we should all practice safety first."

Miss Brown was Ethan's kindergarten teacher, a woman whose opinions were offered up by Ethan on a regular basis. "I promise to be more careful," Marnie said as she drove slowly along the main street in Wakesfield, the windshield pushing the wet snowflakes out of the way. Thankfully Luke would be driving when they returned for the Christmas pageant.

She was so excited to share her news with Luke, but worried at the same time. Dr. Spencer had reviewed the gynecologist's report written a year after she'd had her accident, and he was well aware of her concerns.

Would telling Luke now be the best decision? Given her medical issues, should she wait for another month, until the end of her first trimester? And would that be fair to Luke?

As she headed back out onto the highway, she was reminded of the beauty of the landscape around her. She hadn't regretted moving here for a single minute, and her life was about as perfect as it could be. And *that* was her major problem when it came to telling Luke. Sure, they'd talked about having a family, but only in the most general terms because of her fear that she might not be able to carry the child to term. How could she tell him about the baby if they might lose it?

They were so happy, and so busy with things as they were—she'd turned The Mirabel's spa into the best facility anywhere in northern New York State, and it was fully booked most days either by hotel guests or daytrippers from the surrounding communities.

As the inn came into view, Marnie smiled in pleasure.

She pulled into the long driveway and navigated the narrow turns leading to the entrance. Glancing at the clock on the dashboard, she saw it was after five, which meant Luke was probably beginning to worry.

Sure enough, Luke came out the door before she'd even put the SUV in Park.

"I was about to send out a search team," he said, opening the front passenger door.

"Sorry I'm so slow, but Ethan sang us home," she said, smiling across at Luke.

"I imagine he did," Luke said. He leaned across the console and kissed her. "I missed you."

How could she ever keep anything from this man? They were in this together. "I missed you, too."

"Dad, I'm singing tonight! So are the shepherds." A pout appeared on Ethan's. "Emily got to be a shepherd and she's a girl!"

"Got something against girl shepherds, do you?" Luke asked, his eyes on Marnie, his smile tugging at her heart.

Ethan wasted no time in getting out of his seat and opening the door before running around and throwing himself into his father's arms. "I don't want to be late for the play."

"We won't be. We're going to get there on time, buddy, but first you need to have dinner," he said, giving Ethan a hug.

As Marnie watched Luke with his son, there was one other small matter that had been niggling away at the back of her mind. When she first suspected she might be pregnant, she thought right away that she wanted to be married. Sure it was probably an old-fashioned idea for some people, but not for her.

She wasn't sure if being married was all that important to Luke. Although he'd been happily married before, he seldom talked about marriage with her, and she'd taken her cue from him, believing there was no pressing reason to consider a change.

But now there was. Being married to the father of her child was very important to her. She wanted both her children to grow up with a mom and dad who were married.

LUKE AND MARNIE PREPARED Ethan's dinner to the sound of Ethan singing "Away in a Manager" off-key. They were about to leave for the pageant when Julie called to say she and Shane had a party planned for Luke and Marnie when they got to Boston the day after Christmas. Julie sounded happier than she had for years, and Shane, as well. Gina had left Shane last February, but he didn't seem to mind. He and Julie were now partners in Total Elegance, and loving it.

Luke and Marnie, along with Ethan in his sheep costume, made it to the play just in time. They sat as close to the front as possible, eager to watch Ethan perform.

He didn't disappoint as his slightly off-key voice rang out over the other children's voices.

Back in the apartment, they listened to Ethan's chatter while they bathed him and got him into bed. When he had finally fallen asleep, they stretched out in front of the tree with the sofa against their backs and gazed up into the brightly decorated branches.

"Happy?" he asked, enjoying having Marnie to himself.

She linked her fingers with his, and smiled up into his eyes. "Never more so," she answered.

Now was the moment he'd been waiting for, and yet he found himself searching for the right words. It wasn't as if he hadn't done this before, but that had been another time and place, and he'd been so much more confident back then. He reached into his pants pocket, checking to make sure the velvet box was still there.

"What are you thinking?" she asked, studying him.

"That this is the perfect Christmas," he said, marshaling his thoughts.

*Do it now, before you lose your nerve!*

"I couldn't agree more." She squeezed his hand. "Luke, I have something I need to tell you, and I'm a little nervous about saying it."

"I know that feeling," he mused, suddenly aware that her voice was trembling.

Marnie nestled closer to him. "I went to the doctor today."

Fear constricted his throat. "Why?"

She toyed with his fingers. "I haven't been feeling all that great lately, and so I made an appointment with Dr. Spencer a few weeks ago."

"Marnie, whatever it is, we're in this together," he said, his heart pounding in his chest.

"Yes, that would be true… You could say that, especially under the circumstances."

He looked at her dumbfounded. "What? What would be true?"

"That we're in this together. You're as guilty as I am." *She wasn't making any sense.*

"Of what? What are you talking about?"

She climbed into his lap, cupping his cheeks in her hands the way Ethan so often did. "Look at me," she ordered.

He looked at her, at the smug expression on her face, the way her upper lip formed a perfect bow. "I'm the luckiest man alive."

"No, silly, not that. Thanks, but that's not what I'm talking about at all."

"Feel free to tell me, sooner rather than later if possible." He couldn't resist kissing her lips. "We still have our Santa duties to perform, and after that I've got a celebration dinner planned for us."

"Celebration?"

"We've been together one full year."

Her eyes widened in surprise. "Oh, yeah…"

"You don't want to celebrate?"

"Absolutely. And we have something else to celebrate." Her lips lingered on his before releasing him. She pushed her hair off her face, looked up at the ceiling and back into his eyes. "We're going to have a baby."

"We're going to have a what? A baby?" He stared at her.

"You're not happy," she said.

"I am. I'm really happy…. Are you sure?" he asked, his words cautious.

"Of course!" She scowled and climbed off his lap. Damn! "I fumbled this pretty badly. Can I start over?"

She crossed her arms over her chest as she settled back beside him. "Be my guest."

"Probably the smartest thing for me to do right now would be—" he reached into his pocket and brought out the velvet box "—to give you this. I planned to tell you the minute we sat down here, but you beat me to it. I've been waiting months to do this."

She gasped as he snapped the lid open. Her eyes widened. "Oh, my goodness…"

"Hold it. I want to get this part right." He took the ring from its velvet setting. "Marnie McLaughlan, will you marry me…be the mother of our children?" he asked as he slid the ring onto her finger.

She stared at it, a gleam in her eyes as she held up her hand to inspect it more closely. "Luke Harrison, I love you. And I accept your proposal, provided you promise to love, honor and share in the diaper changing."

He grinned and kissed her. "I do."

She kissed him back and climbed back into his lap. "And you made the right move at the right time."

"How so?" he asked, overwhelmed by his love for this woman who made his heart sing.

"If I had had to go home tomorrow after we opened our gifts, and tell my brothers that I was pregnant and you hadn't proposed…yet. Well, I couldn't have been held responsible for the consequences."

"Your family has nothing to worry about."

"I'll be sure to tell them," she murmured, working the buttons on his shirt free as she kissed him again, her lips more demanding than before.

"Go ahead. Have your way with me," he growled, shifting her body on top of his as he stretched out on the floor in front of the tree.

"I plan to," she murmured against his lips. "Just as

soon as you feed me. By the way, where's the dinner you promised?"

"Max is waiting for my call."

"Then, call him. I'm famished," she said.

He laughed and hugged her close. They were going to have a baby, their baby, their life…together. "Merry Christmas, darling."

"Merry Christmas."

\* \* \* \* \*

**COMING NEXT MONTH**
**from Harlequin® SuperRomance®**

AVAILABLE NOVEMBER 27, 2012

### #1818 THE SPIRIT OF CHRISTMAS
**Liz Talley**

When Mary Paige Gentry helps a homeless man, she never imagines the gesture would give her the windfall of a lifetime! The catch? Having to deal with the miserly—but gorgeous—Brennan Henry, who clearly doesn't know the meaning of the season.

### #1819 THE TIME OF HER LIFE
**Jeanie London**

New job, new town...new man? Now that Susanna Adams's kids are out of the house, she's ready for a little *me* time. But is she ready to fall for Jay Canady, her irresistible—and younger—coworker? The attraction could be too strong to ignore!

### #1820 THE LONG WAY HOME
**Cathryn Parry**

Bruce Cole has made avoidance a way of life. But when he goes home for the first time in ten years, he has to face the past he's been running from. And Natalie Kimball, the only person who knows his secret....

### #1821 CROSSING NEVADA
**Jeannie Watt**

All Tess O'Neil wants is to be alone. After a brutal attack ends her modeling career, she retreats to a Nevada ranch to find solitude. Which isn't easy with a neighbor like Zach Nolan. The single father and his kids manage to get past her defenses when she least expects it.

### #1822 WISH UPON A CHRISTMAS STAR
**Darlene Gardner**

Her brother might still be alive? Private investigator Maria DiMarco has to track down this lead, even if it's a long shot. Little does she imagine her search will reunite her with her old flame Logan Collier. It could be that miracles do happen!

### #1823 ESPRESSO IN THE MORNING
**Dorie Graham**

Lucas Williams recognizes the signs. When single mom Claire Murphy starts coming into his coffee shop, he sees a troubled soul he's sure he can help—if she'll let him. First, he'll have to fight his attraction to be the friend she needs.

You can find more information on upcoming Harlequin® titles, free excerpts and more at www.Harlequin.com.

HSRCNM1112

# REQUEST YOUR FREE BOOKS!
## 2 FREE NOVELS PLUS 2 FREE GIFTS!

*Exciting, emotional, unexpected!*

**YES!** Please send me 2 FREE Harlequin® Superromance® novels and my 2 FREE gifts (gifts are worth about $10). After receiving them, if I don't wish to receive any more books, I can return the shipping statement marked "cancel." If I don't cancel, I will receive 6 brand-new novels every month and be billed just $4.69 per book in the U.S. or $5.24 per book in Canada. That's a saving of at least 15% off the cover price! It's quite a bargain! Shipping and handling is just 50¢ per book in the U.S. and 75¢ per book in Canada.* I understand that accepting the 2 free books and gifts places me under no obligation to buy anything. I can always return a shipment and cancel at any time. Even if I never buy another book, the two free books and gifts are mine to keep forever.

135/336 HDN FC6T

| | |
|---|---|
| Name | (PLEASE PRINT) |
| Address | Apt. # |
| City | State/Prov. | Zip/Postal Code |

Signature (if under 18, a parent or guardian must sign)

Mail to the **Reader Service:**
**IN U.S.A.:** P.O. Box 1867, Buffalo, NY 14240-1867
**IN CANADA:** P.O. Box 609, Fort Erie, Ontario L2A 5X3

Not valid for current subscribers to Harlequin Superromance books.
**Are you a current subscriber to Harlequin Superromance books
and want to receive the larger-print edition?
Call 1-800-873-8635 or visit www.ReaderService.com.**

* Terms and prices subject to change without notice. Prices do not include applicable taxes. Sales tax applicable in N.Y. Canadian residents will be charged applicable taxes. Offer not valid in Quebec. This offer is limited to one order per household. All orders subject to credit approval. Credit or debit balances in a customer's account(s) may be offset by any other outstanding balance owed by or to the customer. Please allow 4 to 6 weeks for delivery. Offer available while quantities last.

**Your Privacy**—The Reader Service is committed to protecting your privacy. Our Privacy Policy is available online at www.ReaderService.com or upon request from the Reader Service.

We make a portion of our mailing list available to reputable third parties that offer products we believe may interest you. If you prefer that we not exchange your name with third parties, or if you wish to clarify or modify your communication preferences, please visit us at www.ReaderService.com/consumerchoice or write to us at Reader Service Preference Service, P.O. Box 9062, Buffalo, NY 14269. Include your complete name and address.

*Turn the page for a preview of*

# THE OTHER SIDE OF US

*by*

## Sarah Mayberry,

*coming January 2013*
*from Harlequin® Superromance®.*

*PLUS, exciting changes are in the works!*
*Enjoy the same great stories in a longer format*
*and new look—beginning January 2013!*

**Coming January 2013**

THE OTHER SIDE OF US
*A brand-new novel
from Harlequin® Superromance® author
Sarah Mayberry*

*Oliver Garrett was only trying to introduce himself to his new—and very attractive—neighbor, Mackenzie Williams. Nothing wrong with being friendly, right? But then she shut the door in his face! Read on for an exciting excerpt from THE OTHER SIDE OF US by Sarah Mayberry.*

OLIVER STARED AT THE DOOR in shock. He was pretty sure no one had ever slammed a door in his face before. Not once.

He walked to his place.

Clearly, Mackenzie Williams was not interested in being friendly. From the second she'd laid eyes on him she'd been willing him gone. Well. He wouldn't make the mistake of doing the right thing again. She could take her rude self and—

He paused, aware of the hostility in his thoughts. Perhaps too high a level given his brief acquaintance with Mackenzie. They'd been talking, what? For a handful of minutes?

Six months ago this incident would have made him laugh and worry about her blood pressure. Today he had the urge to do something childish to let her know that he wasn't interested in her anyway.

But that wasn't entirely true.

Because he *was* interested. When he'd gotten that first glimpse of her, had seen her gorgeous toned body, he'd lost track of his thoughts. And it had taken a second or two to remember what he'd intended to say.

So, yeah. He did want to know his new neighbor. He wanted to think there was a good explanation for her rudeness, that it wasn't a reaction to the sight of him.

*Guess that means another trip next door.*

Next time, however, he'd be prepared. Next time he would give her a strong reason *not* to close the door.

*What will Oliver's plan to win over Mackenzie be?*
*Stay tuned next month for a continuing excerpt from*
*THE OTHER SIDE OF US by Sarah Mayberry,*
*available January 2013 from Harlequin® Superromance®.*

ROMANTIC
SUSPENSE

**Get your heart racing this holiday season with double the pulse-pounding action.**

# Christmas Confidential

### Featuring

### *Holiday Protector* by **Marilyn Pappano**

Miri Duncan doesn't care that it's almost Christmas. She's got bigger worries on her mind. But surviving the trip to Georgia from Texas is going to be her biggest challenge. Days in a car with the man who broke her heart and helped send her to prison—private investigator Dean Montgomery.

### *A Chance Reunion* by **Linda Conrad**

When the husband Elana Novak left behind five years ago shows up in her new California home she knows danger is coming her way. To protect the man she is quickly falling for Elana must convince private investigator Gage Chance that she is a different person. But Gage isn't about to let her walk away…even with the bad guys right on their heels.

**Available December 2012 wherever books are sold!**